A BIRTHRIGHT OF BLOOD

A BIRTHRIGHT OF BLOOD

THE DRAGON WAR, BOOK TWO

DANIEL ARENSON

ISBN: 978-1-927601-08-2

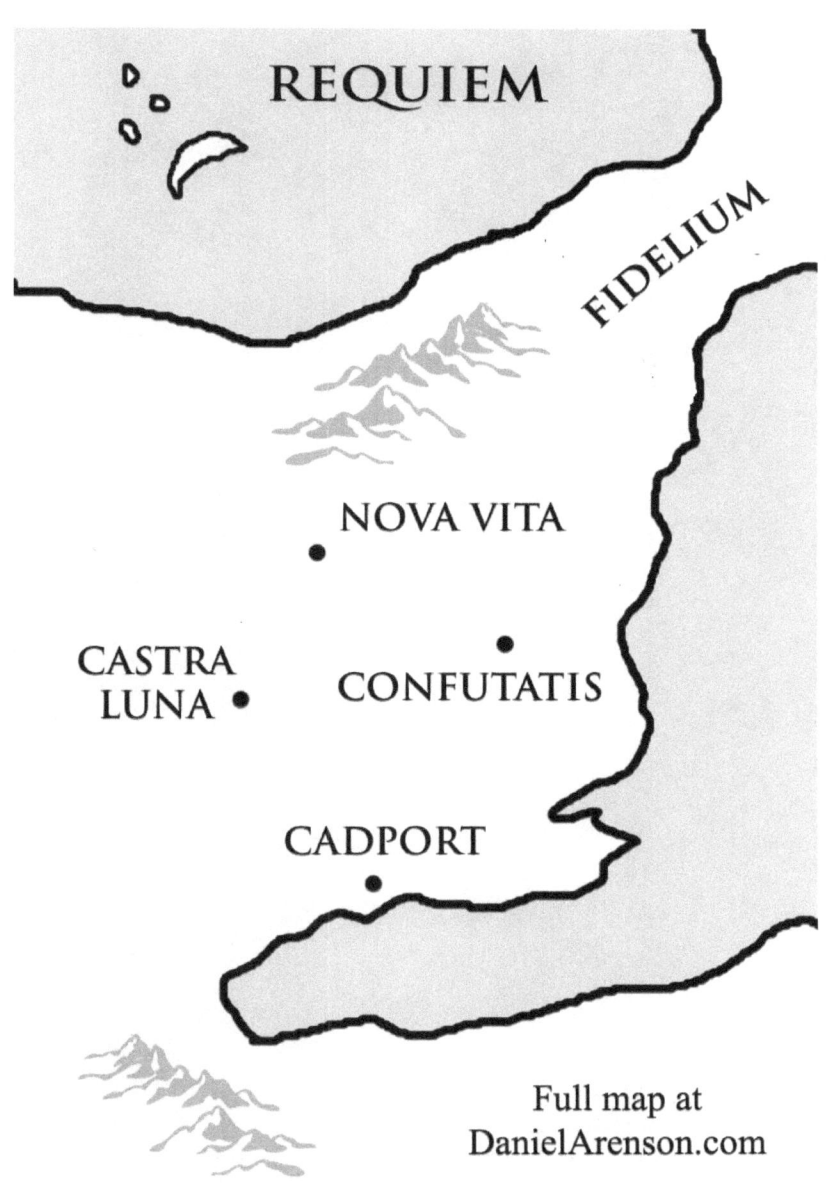

REQUIEM

FIDELIUM

NOVA VITA

CASTRA
LUNA

CONFUTATIS

CADPORT

Full map at
DanielArenson.com

KAELYN

They stood in the heart of evil, a woman and a man, two souls
alone in a sea of steel, bloodlust, and fire.

All around them, line by line, stretched the ranks of a dark
empire. Five hundred thousand strong they stood, the soldiers of
the Legions, automatons of steel coated in plate and helm. Half a
million demons. Half a million blades. Half a million souls
screaming for blood and glory.

Youths broken and molded into beasts, Kaelyn thought, standing
among them. Hidden within her helm, her eyes stung with tears.
The Legions crushed their hearts; only fire burns within these breasts.

The soldiers covered the great Square of Cadigus, a cobbled
expanse wider than entire towns. Not a boot strayed out of line.
Fifty brigades mustered here, and within each, smaller units stood
in perfect formation--milanxes divided into phalanxes divided into
flights--paths running between them. Soldiers stood with drawn
blades. Officers held the standards of Cadigus; each pole rose
twice a man's height, topped with iron dragons perched upon red
spirals. Flying above, a true dragon would see a great machine of
metal, every soldier a single cog perfectly aligned, an imperial
clockwork built to kill.

Kaelyn turned her head only slightly, for only a second, and
glanced at the soldier who stood beside her. To the world, he was
another legionary. Black steel coated him, the breastplate
engraved with a spiral. His helm hid his face. He bore a dark
shield and a longsword. He was one in myriads, a gear of metal
and fire, identical to her and to half a million more.

He was, Kaelyn knew, the most important man in the world.

Be strong, Rune, she thought, wanting to whisper to him, hold his hand, and comfort him, but daring not. *We are in the lion's den. Be strong. I'm with you. Be strong and we will live.*

She looked back ahead. She vowed to not look aside again. One wrong glance, one tilt of the head, could mean bones broken upon the wheel.

Across the square, the palace loomed above the Legions. Obsidian tiles covered its bricks, the black stones so polished they shone white in the sun. Battlements lined the great hall, cannons peering between merlons like iron eyes. The banners of House Cadigus hung from the crenellations, each one sporting a red spiral against a black field.

Above this hall, stretching like a blade from a hilt, rose the tower of Tarath Imperium, the great steeple of the empire. A thousand feet it rose, piercing the clouds, the tallest structure the world had seen. Black were its bricks, and arrowslits squinted upon its walls. Its crest flared out into a crown of black spikes, watching Requiem in eternal vigil.

Before she had fled her father's rule, Kaelyn had once stood upon that black crown, a thousand feet above the empire. The city of Nova Vita, a million people strong, had rolled around her. Beyond the city walls, she had seen distant forests and mountains, Requiem sprawling into the horizons.

Today her father perched upon that crown. The Legions in the square below stood in human forms, soldiers clad in steel, but Emperor Frey Cadigus roared as a dragon. His golden wings spread wide. Fire shot from his jaws, a flaming pillar rising into the sky. His howl rang across the city; even standing below, Kaelyn winced at its depth and rage.

"Hail the red spiral!" cried the emperor.

Across the square, the Legions roared.

Half a million soldiers shouted together. Their fists rose, then slammed against chests. The sound exploded like thunder.

"Hail the red spiral!" the Legions shouted, and Kaelyn shouted among them.

The emperor's wings stretched like curtains of night, as if he could engulf the world. Smoke and flame rose from him. His eyes burned red. He perched upon the tower top like a gargoyle of molten fire, like a demon risen from the Abyss. He was scale, flame, and steel. He was the wrath and might of an empire.

He is my father, Kaelyn thought and her eyes burned. *He is the man I must someday slay.*

"An evil has risen in the south!" roared Emperor Cadigus. "A rot spreads. The Resistance raises its head in mockery."

The Legions howled, fists raised and voices torn in rage. The cries shook the square. The sound thudded in Kaelyn's chest and slammed against her ears. She shouted with them. She raised her fist and cried in fury. Yet she did not share the bloodlust of the thousands around her. She thought of how her father would beat her, how his hot irons would sear her flesh, and how his rod of lightning would thrust against her. The fires of old pain flared inside her, and Kaelyn screamed with the rest of them, letting her memories burn.

At her side, Rune shouted too, his voice hoarse, his fist raised. Kaelyn did not know where he found his rage, but she could guess. The Cadigus Regime had burned his home and slain his father. There would be rage enough in him to fuel a forge.

Emperor Frey blew fire, then shouted again.

"We have defeated the old enemies of Requiem!" His wings beat, churning flame around him. "We've slain the griffins, the salvanae of the west, and the weak men of the east. We've burned the desert barbarians south of our sea. The world is cleansed of their evil! Yet still darkness writhes among us."

The Legions roared in the square. They chanted for Requiem. They banged fists against breastplates. They were a smelter ready to spill over.

And they will cover the world, Kaelyn thought, standing among them in her disguise. *They will drown all lands in their shadow, unless our small light can hold back the tide.*

"We will slay the evil that has risen!" Frey howled upon the tower. "We will stamp out those who betray the empire. We will crush any weakness within us. Requiem must be united in its honor, pride, and strength." He roared fire. "We seek *purification!*"

The crowds below chanted, banging their fists.

"Purification! Purification!" Their cries rang across the city. "Hail the red spiral!"

Flames spewed from the emperor's maw and wrapped around him. He bellowed to the skies, wings roiling smoke and ash.

"All weakness must be eradicated!" he cried. "The sick must die. The old must perish. The traitors must be broken. Requiem will be pure in its strength and glory."

The crowds roared. "Purification! Purification!"

Kaelyn shouted among them. Rune did too. Her eyes burned.

So the stories are true, she thought. Whispers had reached their southern camp, speaking of the Axehand Order--the elite thugs of the emperor--slaying the sick and weak. Refugees spoke of axehands storming infirmaries and homes, snatching all those deemed impure. The ill, the handicapped, the wounded, the frail and old--all taken at night, never seen again.

"Purification!" chanted the crowds, banging fists against steel. "Purification!"

Above them all, the great golden dragon howled. "Requiem will be pure! Weakness will be crushed. The southern rebels will be broken. *Purification!* Axehands—reveal the prisoners!"

Men of the Axehand Order stood upon the great hall's battlements. Their black robes swayed. Their hoods hid their faces. Their left arms ended with axe blades strapped to stumps; with their right hands, they grabbed and twisted cranks. The banners of Cadigus, sweeping black fields emblazoned with red spirals, began to rise from the walls like curtains.

Kaelyn winced. Tears budded in her eyes. She couldn't help it; a wail fled her lips.

It was a mistake--wailing here could cost her life--but none heard her. All around, the other soldiers roared with renewed rage. Their shouts rang, battle cries of unending hatred, shrieks of primordial fire.

"Oh stars," Rune said beside her, voice shaking; Kaelyn doubted any of the screaming soldiers heard him either.

As the banners rose, Kaelyn stared at the unveiled, bloody walls of the palace. Tears streamed down her cheeks.

"I'm sorry," she whispered. "I'm so sorry."

Upon the castle walls they hung from chains, twenty wagon wheels. Each wheel held a broken man, woman, or child, their shattered limbs slung through the spokes. They were still alive. They twisted and bled, too weak to scream.

"Behold the rot among us!" Frey called from his tower, a beast of flame and tooth. "Behold the so-called resistors caught lurking in our pure city. See their might now! See their wives and children broken upon the wheels. See the impure and cowardly crushed!"

Kaelyn wanted to look away. She knew these men. She knew their wives. She had played with their children. Tears blurred her vision, her throat tightened, and her fists trembled, yet she could not look away. She stared at them, her brothers in arms, now shreds of humanity.

They were naked, their flesh whipped and burned. Their bones had been shattered with hammers. Their spines had been cracked. They coiled through the spokes like ropes of flesh, and they bled, and they whimpered. A few were children barely older than toddlers.

Kaelyn wanted to fly to them. She wanted to shift into a dragon, to burn them dead, to end their pain, then flee this city. Yet she could not. If she shifted now into a dragon, the Legions would swarm, and she too would be broken. She too would hang among her comrades.

She clenched her fists, trembled, and bit her lip so hard she tasted blood.

They served me. Her throat was so tight she could barely breathe, and she tasted tears on her lips. *They served my rebellion. I doomed them to this fate. I'm sorry, my friends.*

"So will happen to all who stain our purity!" Frey said from the tower top, voice ringing across the square. "Axehand Order—remove these wretches from the wheels. Send them to infirmaries. Heal their bones. Heal their spirits." His voice rose to a shriek, a sound like steam fleeing a kettle. "We will break them anew every year! They will hang here every summer, spines and limbs shattered, and we will heal them again, and break them again, and they will scream for decades, and we will never let them die. They will suffer! The enemies of Requiem will suffer! *Purification!*"

The Legions roared. "Purification!"

"Hail the red spiral!" cried the emperor.

"Hail the red spiral!" answered the crowds.

"Requiem is strong! Hail the red spiral!"

Kaelyn looked around her, feeling like a woman drowning in a sea of steel and hatred.

How? she wanted to shout. How could so many people worship blood? How could so many people cheer the torture of children? These were her people! They were fellow Vir Requis, children of starlight! They were born to an ancient race that, for thousands of years, had worshiped the stars and fought for justice. How could they now scream for blood?

Eyes burning, Kaelyn looked around at the howling soldiers. Though the slits of their visors, she saw young eyes. The eyes of boys. Of young women. Many were no older than her own nineteen years. And Kaelyn understood.

They were just babes when my father took the throne, she thought. *And he molded them. He forged their souls into his blades of darkness. He turned a generation into a machine of murder.*

Kaelyn looked up at her father. The golden dragon cackled atop his tower, wings drawing in smoke and flame, jaws spraying fire. Kaelyn snarled.

I will kill you, Father, she vowed silently. *You will fall. I will restore Requiem to starlight.*

The men upon the battlements twisted winches, and the wheels began to rise on their chains, leaving trails of blood along the walls.

Now Kaelyn could finally close her eyes. She wanted to reach out and clutch Rune's hand, but dared not. She prayed silently to the stars of Requiem, the old and forbidden gods.

Give them strength, stars of my fathers. Or show them mercy and let them die. Please, stars, let them die. Pity the children at least.

Yet could the stars even hear her? The ash and fire of Cadigus covered the sky. Darkness cloaked Requiem. The noble kingdom had fallen; the bloodstained empire rose.

The rally ended at sundown.

The troops marched back to their barracks. Their officers flew as dragons, blowing flames over the city roofs. The sun sank behind the walls and towers of Nova Vita, and Kaelyn's work began.

I will not fail, she swore in the shadows. *I will keep fighting. For the memory of those fallen. For the sacrifice of those suffering. I will do my task. The tyrant must die.*

In the night, she and Rune marched with the troops. Thousands of boots thudded along the cobbled streets. Thousands of faces stared forward through slits in dark visors. They moved through the city like a coiling snake of steel, each soldier a single scale. At their lead, their standard-bearers marched with their banners. At their sides, the city rose: rows of homes four stories tall, barracks of troops, smithies where hammers rang against anvils, the amphitheater where Frey executed his enemies, and everywhere statues of the emperor, fist to heart, eyes watching the city.

No civilians could be seen. The sun had fallen; the curfew reigned. Years ago, they said, light and laughter had filled these streets at night. Jugglers and singers would perform, merchants would hawk wine and pastries, and the people of Nova Vita would walk under ever-burning oil lamps. Since Cadigus had taken the throne, only steel filled these streets after dark. The singers, the jugglers, the merchants--they hid in their homes, languished in dungeons, or lay buried.

Kaelyn sneaked a look at Rune. He marched at her side, staring ahead, body stiff. He did not glance her way. He looked every inch a soldier, boots thudding and fist clutching his sword, but she saw the fear in him. She *felt* it.

Be strong, Rune, she thought, as if she could transfer those thoughts into him. *Be strong and we will survive.*

They marched with the Flaming Eye Brigade, a host of ten thousand warriors stationed here in the capital, tasked with defending Nova Vita. Rune and Kaelyn's armor, taken from the bodies of slain soldiers, fit snugly. Their armbands sported two stars each--the rank of *corelis*, low enough for officers to ignore, high enough to wield some respect among fellow soldiers.

Everything is perfect, Kaelyn told herself as she marched down the streets. *Our armor fits. Nobody can see our faces behind these helms.*

Nobody knows of the two legionaries we killed. We are nothing but two more cogs with perfect hatred.

And yet fear pulsed through her, and every officer she passed sent her heart thrashing. What if something wasn't perfect? What if somebody found the corpses of the soldiers she and Rune were mimicking? What if they stood too tall or short? What if somebody saw their eyes through their visors and spotted the ruse?

What if we're caught?

Kaelyn swallowed a lump in her throat, knowing the answer.

If they catch us, they won't kill us. They will break us. They will hang us in the square every year, then heal us, then break us again, an endless cycle until our minds break too.

She tightened her lips and gripped her sword. She kept marching with the thousands, passing from street to street.

Then we must not be caught, she told herself. *We must not fail. We will do our task. We will live. And then we will flee far away from this place, back south to safety... and to Valien.*

They marched, passing from snaking streets to a wide boulevard. Ahead rose a fortress all in black, its walls tiled in obsidian, its battlements topped with cannons and armor-clad dragons. Torches blazed upon these walls, their shadows dancing like dead spirits rising from graves. Four towers rose here, capped with merlons like the teeth of stone giants. The banners of Cadigus thudded upon each tower, hiding and revealing red spirals.

"Castra Draco," Kaelyn whispered. "The heart of the Legions."

Its towers dwarfed the buildings around it. Its halls held three brigades, thirty thousand troops in all. The generals of the Legions ruled from this place. If Tarath Imperium was the heart of the empire, here was its iron fist.

Castra Draco. Center of Requiem's military might. She winced.
The place the two soldiers we mimic served.

She glanced around. Thousands of troops marched,
clockwork demons of fire and steel. Boots thudded in unison.
Eyes stared ahead, never moving, never straying. The fortress
loomed above, and Kaelyn swallowed. She could not enter those
dark halls, the place where bones were broken, where souls were
forged, where the wrath of Requiem simmered. In there she and
Rune would have to remove their helms, unveiling their
deception. If she entered that darkness, they would not emerge.

"Come on," she whispered under her breath. "Where are
you, Lana?"

She looked up at the rooftops along the streets, seeking
movement. She kept marching with the troops. The fortress
grew closer, rising like a tombstone for a god. Soon they were
only a hundred yards away. Kaelyn bit her lip and cursed under
her breath. She sneaked another few glances to the roofs of
surrounding homes and shops.

Hurry up, Lana, she thought, chewing her lip. At her side,
she saw Rune too searching the rooftops, his fists clenching and
unclenching at his sides.

What if soldiers had found the woman, friend to the
Resistance? What if Lana now languished in a prison or lay dead?

Kaelyn stared ahead. The gates of Castra Draco rose only
yards away.

We'll have to escape on our own, Kaelyn decided and sucked in
her breath. Yet how could she? She marched among thousands.
She and Rune moved in flawless formation, their boots thumping
with the others in a perfect beat. If they fled now, they would be
seen. They would be caught. They--

There!

A shadow appeared upon a roof.

Kaelyn sucked in her breath, and hope sprang in her chest.

The silhouette of a woman stood above, clad in leggings, tall boots, and a fluttering cloak. In one hand, she held a banner; her other hand rested on the pommel of a saber. The clouds parted, and moonlight caught her standard, illuminating a two-headed dragon, sigil of House Aeternum. The pale light shone upon the woman too, revealing mocking lips, a mask with only one eye-hole, and long black hair with a single white streak.

Lady Lana Cain, Kaelyn thought. *My dearest friend.*

"Soldiers of Cadigus!" the lady shouted from the roof and raised her banner high. "King Relesar Aeternum returns! See his banner. Hear his call. Requiem--may our wings forever find your sky!"

Chaos erupted.

The troops below spun toward the roof. Officers shouted orders. Soldiers shifted into dragons, armor morphing into scales, swords into claws.

"Death to the tyrant!" Lady Lana cried above, laughing and waving her flag. "Death to Cadigus!"

With that, the masked woman shifted and soared. A black dragon with a white stripe across her back, she vanished into shadows.

All around Kaelyn, officers shouted and pointed at the roofs. Dragons took flight. Fire spewed from maws, lighting the night. Cries and roars rang.

Rune stood staring, frozen in place. Kaelyn grabbed his arm and tugged him.

"Come on, you woolhead!" she said.

She pulled him away from the chaos and into shadows, praying no eyes were watching. But it seemed everyone was busy shouting, flying after Lana in dragon form, or watching the commotion--including Rune, who was still sneaking glances toward the rooftops.

"Come *on!*" Kaelyn said, tugging him.

They slunk into an alley, leaving the brigade and disappearing into shadows. Kaelyn began to scurry deeper into the darkness, her boots now silent upon the cobblestones. She pulled Rune with her. The sounds of the boulevard faded into a muffled storm.

A hundred yards into the alley, Kaelyn found a moldy barrel. She drew her dagger, loosened the barrel's lid with her blade, and pulled it free. She stood on tiptoes and gazed inside. Rotten turnips festered there, rustling with bugs.

"Bloody stars," Rune muttered and lifted his helm's visor. "Did she have to use rotten turnips? Why not a barrel of strong ale, or-- Ow!"

Kaelyn kicked his leg hard. "Quiet, Rune, and help me dig."

Standing on her toes, she reached into the barrel and rummaged through the rotten tubers. Bugs scurried around her fingers, and she thanked the stars that legionaries wore thick leather gloves. Rune rooted around beside her, grimacing.

"Disgusting," he said. "I think I felt a rat in there. Or maybe a turnip that's gone fuzzy."

"Quiet!" Kaelyn whispered and reached elbow deep. She rifled around, then smiled. "There! I feel it."

She gripped her catch and pulled, fishing out a bundle of leather. She brushed it clean, placed the bundle on the ground, and unwrapped it.

She revealed parchment placards, each about a foot long. Her eyes dampened.

Each poster displayed the sigil of House Aeternum--a two-headed dragon wreathed in leaves of birch, the holy tree of Requiem. Above the dragon's heads, inked in silver, appeared the constellation Draco--the stars of Requiem. Letters too were drawn upon each scroll:

"Relesar Aeternum, true king of Requiem, reigns in the south. Join the true king! Death to Cadigus!"

Beneath this, in smaller script, appeared the Old Words of Requiem, the forbidden prayer that priests had sung for thousands of years.

"Requiem! May our wings forever find your sky."

Rune stared at the posters and tapped his chin.

"Not bad," he said. "Lana did a decent job, though she could have added something about how I'm also breathtakingly handsome."

Kaelyn sighed. "We're here to spread the truth to the empire, Rune, not inundate the people with more lies." She grabbed a sheaf of posters. "Now lift half of them! It'll be a long night."

"I don't understand," Rune said as he stuffed placards into his pack. "Why wouldn't we just sneak into this city at night? Why bother seeing your father speak and marching down the streets? We could have just come to this alley in the first place." He shuddered. "Oh stars, Kaelyn, the rally... the men he breaks... And we just stood there and watched."

Kaelyn sighed, rolling up posters and shoving them into her own pack.

"We needed to be there," she said softly. "We need to see, hear, and shout his evil. We need to know the full rot of his soul." She lowered her head, still seeing those broken bodies upon the wall, and when she looked up at Rune, she saw them haunting his eyes too. "One must grasp the depth of evil before one can fight it."

When they'd packed all the posters, they crept back to the alley's mouth. Kaelyn heard nothing. The boulevard seemed barren. All the soldiers had either entered Castra Draco or flown in pursuit of Lana.

"Fly high, Lana," Kaelyn whispered and looked up at the sky, as if she could see her friend flying there. "Fly far. Thank you."

Her eyes stung. She knuckled them, tightened her lips, and stuck her head outside the alley. She peered from side to side. Seeing no one, she grabbed Rune and pulled him out into the street.

"Now come on," she whispered to him. "We're just two soldiers on patrol, part of the Flaming Eye Brigade. Curfew is on, the rally is over, so these streets should be quiet. If anyone stops us, we're just doing our rounds, and Castra Draco has our names to prove it."

They began to walk, moving away from the fortress. Kaelyn had grown up in this city; she'd spent sixteen years here before fleeing her father's rod and wrath. She knew these streets like the scars her father had given her. After walking several blocks, they reached a wide brick building. Smoke plumed from its four chimneys, and the scents of wine, ale, and roasted meats wafted. Behind the stained-glass windows, she saw the shadows of men moving, and she heard them singing hoarse drinking songs.

"The Green Duck," she said. "A favorite alehouse among the soldiers."

Rune raised an eyebrow. "The Green Duck? This is Nova Vita, heart of the Cadigus Regime. I figured alehouses here would have names like The Tavern of Steel, The Goblet of Glory, or Frey's Firkin. Something more... imperial."

Kaelyn allowed herself a wan smile. "This tavern predates my father's regime. He did rename Lynport after himself--and about half the other towns in the kingdom--but soldiers have been drinking in the Green Duck for two hundred years. If he changed *this* name, he'd truly have a rebellion on his hands." She patted Rune's cheek. "You owned a tavern; you know how soldiers are with their drink. Now quickly--help me with a poster!"

She looked around furtively. The street was empty. The soldiers inside the tavern were singing raucously. Kaelyn unrolled a poster, and Rune opened a bottle of glue. Within an instant, the poster bedecked the tavern's outer wall; it would greet anyone come to drink.

"Relesar Aeternum, true king of Requiem, reigns in the south. Death to Cadigus!"

Kaelyn grabbed Rune's arm and tugged him.

"Now come on! We have many more posters to hang, and the night won't last forever."

He walked after her, wincing. "Kaelyn, your fingers have bruised my arm by now--and that's with me wearing armor!"

She glared at him. "If we're caught, you'll have more than bruises. Hurry. And be quiet."

They walked down the silent street. Torches stood in palisades, lighting the night. Dragons flew in patrols above, blasting streams of fire that crisscrossed the night. Every few blocks, they encountered more soldiers. Most were other pairs on patrol, their rank low and their faces hidden behind helms; they did not spare Kaelyn and Rune a glance. On one street, they passed an officer; he bore two red spirals upon each shoulder, denoting him a *dialanse*, a young officer two or three years out of the academy.

"Hail the red spiral!" Kaelyn and Rune said, standing at attention and saluting.

The officer regarded them, gave a lazy salute, and kept walking down the street. His legs wobbled. This one was drunk.

If my father caught an officer wandering the streets in his cups, he'd have the man flayed, Kaelyn thought. But for now, she had more pressing concerns than the fate of a young commander. She kept marching down the streets until she and Rune neared the amphitheater.

It loomed before them, a great ring of stone, large enough to seat fifty thousand souls. Her father used to force Kaelyn to come here, sit in the upper tiers, and watch prisoners fed to lions and wolves. Frey rarely hanged or beheaded his enemies; to him, death was a show, a horror to celebrate. Frey was not a man for the noose or the axe, killings too quick for his liking. He lusted for disemboweling, for quartering, for flaying, for feeding flesh to wild beasts. And he delighted in sharing his love with his children.

Shari always loved the executions, Kaelyn remembered. Her sister herself had once broken a man upon the wheel, grinning as she swung the hammer.

Her knees began to shake, and sweat ran down Kaelyn's back. For a moment, the past pulsed too powerfully, memories of her family torturing its enemies... and torturing her. She too had felt their lust for blood. Her flesh still bore the scars of Shari's blades, of Frey's punisher, of the joy they took in beating her.

Only Leresy never hurt me, she remembered. *He always cried when Father and Shari beat me. He always comforted me afterward.*

But of course, her twin brother too enjoyed his bloodshed. Leresy would watch in fascination as beasts tore into flesh. He would stay up all night, reading books of old battles. He would collect torture instruments in his chambers like some men collected statues.

But he never hurt me, Kaelyn remembered. *I'm his twin. He sees me as part of himself. And he loves himself more than anything.*

"Kaelyn?" Rune whispered. "Are you all right?"

She looked at him. He was watching her in concern.

"No," she whispered. "None of this is all right. But we will make it right. Grab a poster."

Kaelyn kept guard, glancing around with her hand on her sword, while Rune glued a poster to the amphitheater's wall. They moved onward, two soldiers on patrol.

We don't have much time, Kaelyn thought. *When the first posters are seen, dragons will swarm. This city will burn.*

"Hurry," she said to Rune.

They kept moving. Kaelyn no longer sought buildings of importance; that was taking too long. Every shadowy wall she passed, she pasted another placard. They moved from street to street. Their bundles of posters dwindled. Soon they were down to twenty or fewer.

They left the wide, clean streets of northern Nova Vita behind, heading south into the slums. Here the houses rotted. Here beggars huddled in alleys, peering with frightened eyes, then scurrying into hiding as they saw Kaelyn and Rune. Stray cats stretched on roofs and rats scuttled in gutters.

"You want to raise this place in rebellion too?" Rune asked, looking around dubiously. "I thought you wanted to target lords and soldiers to rise up against Cadigus, not the poor."

Kaelyn smiled softly. "Great rebellions rarely begin with soldiers or lords; they rise from among the poor and hungry."

They walked between crowded, dilapidated buildings. Shop awnings touched above their heads, turning alleyways into corridors. The houses here had no glass windows like the abodes of the wealthy, only wooden shutters. Nightsoil flowed in gutters, and bugs scurried along the cobbled streets.

"Here," Kaelyn said and pointed at a wide, brick building. "This place. Let's hang one here."

It was the largest house in the neighborhood, but it nestled into shadows, hiding from the city. Laughter rose from within, and candlelight burned behind the curtains. A sign hung above the door; it read "The Bad Cats" and featured two cats licking their paws.

Rune squinted at the building. "What is this place?"

A door burst open, and a woman stumbled into the alleyway, squealing and laughing. She clutched scarves of silk to her naked body, and her hair hung wild across her shoulders.

"Come back here!" rose a man's voice from within, thick with ale and lust. "I paid good coin for you. Back in!"

The woman laughed, saw Rune and Kaelyn, and forced her mouth shut. She winked, held a finger to her lips, and rushed back inside.

"Oh," Rune said. "We had one of these places in Lynport."

He thought back to Lynport's brothel along the boardwalk. The Cadigus family had burned it down years ago, killing all those inside. Only one person had fled the inferno: a young girl with short brown hair and blazing eyes. Her name was Erry Docker; she had spent the following years living on the beach, eating crabs and whatever she could steal.

Kaelyn nodded. "My father does not approve of brothels; he calls the men who visit them weak. Yet he accepts some sins if they remain unseen. He allows this place to linger in the shadows to please his generals."

Rune raised an eyebrow. "You mean... the generals of the Legions visit a brothel in a slum?" He gestured around him at the rats and gutters. "They visit *this* place?"

Kaelyn smiled wanly. "As often as they can. I sometimes think this is the heart of the Legions, not Castra Draco. Here they are not generals; they are men thirsty for ale and hungry for women. Let these men see our posters. Let them know that you've returned. We'll hang one right on the door."

Kaelyn pulled a poster from her pack, walked into the alley, and faced the brothel's door. Candlelight glowed through the windows, and laughter and squeals rose. From the upper floor, she heard huffing and a cry of pleasure.

These patrons love freedom, laughter, and good cheer, she thought. *They might join our cause.*

She unrolled the poster, smeared glue across it, and raised it to the door.

Before she could hang the parchment, the door swung open.

Kaelyn gasped.

The young man at the doorway rubbed his bleary eyes. His cheeks were flushed with wine, and he wore fine fabrics of crimson and gold. His fingers, heavy with rings, struggled to unlace his pants. Laughter rose behind him, and women called him to return to their bed.

"Hang on!" the young man called over his shoulder. "I got to piss, damn you. Don't put your clothes on, hang on!" He turned back toward the alleyway and took a step outside, nearly bumping into Kaelyn, then squinted at her. "Hello... do I know..."

He gasped and his hands fell to his sides.

"Leresy," Kaelyn whispered.

My twin brother. Prince of Requiem.

He stared at her, frozen.

"Kaelyn?" he asked, voice rising incredulously.

With a snarl, Kaelyn drew her dagger and thrust it forward.

Leresy screamed. He stumbled backward. Kaelyn was aiming for his neck, but sliced his cheek instead. His blood spilled and he squealed. He drew his sword and barreled forward.

"The Resistance!" he shouted. "Enemy in the alley! Men! Guards! Guards!"

Kaelyn cursed. She tried to stab him again, but he was waving his sword wildly. Soldiers came rushing to the door from within, drawing their own swords.

Rune grabbed her arm and tugged.

"Run, Kaelyn!" Rune shouted. "Fly!"

They turned. They ran. They shifted into dragons and flew.

They soared into the night, moving faster than falcons. The air roared around them, and the city dwindled below, its lights spinning and its streets spreading out like cobwebs. Kaelyn laughed and roared fire and her heart thudded.

"Death to Cadigus!" she shouted, letting her cry ring across the city. "Aeternum rises and Requiem will be freed. The tyrant must die!"

Her heart thrashed and her wings beat mightily. Rune soared at her side. Pillars of flame pierced the night, shooting between them, blazing and crackling and nearly burning her. When Kaelyn looked behind her, she saw a hundred dragons rising in pursuit.

Leresy flew among them, a red dragon shrieking and blowing fire.

"The Resistance attacks!" he screamed. "Awake, dragons of Requiem! Awake, Legions! Fly!"

Kaelyn turned and blasted fire his way.

Her jet blazed through the night and crashed into her brother.

"Kaelyn, fly!" Rune shouted and slapped her with his tail. "Don't fight them, just fly!"

She kept beating her wings. They streamed south. They soared into the clouds, and more flames filled the sky. Dragons swooped from above; Kaelyn and Rune darted between them, swiping their claws. More dragons rose from below. Thousands of flaming jets filled the air.

Kaelyn darted between the flames. Rune flew at her side. They rose higher and clouds enveloped them. Kaelyn could see nothing but Rune at her side, a black dragon nearly invisible in the night.

As they flew south, Kaelyn bared her fangs. She felt light fill her and the fire of battle burn her fear. Thousands of dragons chased them. An entire army roared behind, and fires lit the sky, yet Kaelyn grinned as she flew, and she had never felt more alive.

We struck in the heart of the capital. Now the empire knows Rune is our king.

The Legions roared behind, washing the world in fire, thousands of beasts with blazing eyes. Kaelyn and Rune flew through the night, leaving the city behind, until forests swayed below and the stars of Requiem shone above, the old gods guiding her home.

LERESY

He lay in the brothel bed, his face blazing and his head swimming.

"More wine!" he shouted and waved around his empty mug. "Damn it, more wine!"

Wine would dull his performance in this bed. He knew that. But he didn't care. He didn't have to prove anything to anyone anymore. Not to the whores of the Bad Cats, this rundown cesspool. Not to his men. Not to his father.

"Wine!"

What he did need was to forget. To forget the blazing wound on his face. To forget his lost fortress.

To forget Nairi.

"Bloody whore arses, I said wine!" he shouted, pushing himself up in bed. He blinked, shook his head, and tried to bring the room into focus.

The Bad Cats was a gaudy, stinking mess. Pastel curtains hid the windows, cheap wool woven to look like silk. Murals covered the walls and ceilings, depicting amorous acts and their cost. Each wall showed the woman and man in different positions, the price scribbled below the painted figures. Upon the ceiling, two women--painted in peachy pastels--were pleasing their client together. Leresy had chosen the ceiling's offering; it was the most expensive, but his pockets were deep, and his pain was deeper.

"My lord!" said Dawn, the golden-haired woman to his right. She kissed his ear. "Give your attention to me, not your cups."

At his left, Dusk--an olive-skinned beauty of the east--
stroked his hair. "Give me your love, my lord, not her."

Leresy did not know their true names. He did not care.
They were nothing but cheap flesh. They were nothing but filthy,
base, false mockery. Yet he snarled, tossed his mug aside, and
took them again. He closed his eyes while he used them. He did
not want to see their flushed faces, their eyes fluttering with the
mock pleasure he paid them to feign. He did not want to see
these murals around him, their colors so bright they hurt his eyes.
He moved in the bed, and Dawn and Dusk moved with him, and
behind his closed eyelids, Leresy saw her again.

Nairi.

"She killed her," he whispered and his eyes stung. "My twin
did it. Kaelyn. She killed her. And now I'm dying too."

Dawn and Dusk were moaning so loudly--stars, they
sounded like hogs in heat!--they did not hear. Leresy let them
keep doing their work. He no longer knew where he lay. In the
fog of wine, he was back in Castra Luna. He flew upon the wind,
a red dragon roaring fire, and she flew at his side, an iron dragon
with mocking green eyes. Below them spread his dominion--his
first fort, a mighty outpost, a beacon of civilization in the
wilderness.

"And they took it," he whispered and clenched his fists. His
eyes stung. "The boy Rune and my sister Kaelyn. They took
everything from me."

His fists trembled. He saw it again--the horde of the
Resistance howling his way, and the bodies of legionaries raining
around him, torn to pieces, entrails dangling and limbs severed.

Nairi was gone. His fort was gone. His hope for
inheritance was gone. All that remained was wine and cheap
whores.

"Enough!" he shouted and opened his eyes.

He rose from the bed, shoving Dawn and Dusk off. They fell to the floor, naked, and gazed up at him. Fear filled their eyes.

"My lord?" Dusk asked, her raven hair spilling across her shoulders.

"I said wine, damn it!" he shouted, stepped toward her, and slapped her. "I demanded wine, and you ignored me. Is there no more wine in this whorehouse?"

Dusk recoiled, clutching her struck cheek. Dawn rushed to her and embraced her.

Disgusting harlots, Leresy thought and spat. He grabbed his clothes from the chair, dressed himself, and fished through his pocket for coins. He tossed them a silver each.

"You're not even worth copper," he said and left the room, slamming the door behind him.

Before him, the hallway swayed. Leresy had to hold the wall to walk. Everything spun around him. Other patrons moved from room to room, and women ran naked and giggling, but they were only streaks of color to Leresy, only ghosts of sound. He had to get out of here. This whole house was a nest of disease and filth. The walls were spinning and closing in around him; soon they would crush him.

I have to get out!

He staggered downstairs, falling the last three steps and banging his hip hard. A girl tried to help him up. He struck her, sending her sprawling, and pulled himself to his feet. Holding the wall, he made his way to the front doors and stumbled outside into the night.

The cold autumn air washed over him. His wound, an ugly stitched gash across his face, blazed with new agony. It was here, at this very doorstep, that his twin had slashed him. Whenever he stood here, the wound flared.

"I will cut you too, Kaelyn," he hissed into the shadows. "And I will cut you, Rune, and I will cut you, Shari, and I will cut this whole damn world until we all drown in blood."

Tears filled his eyes.

She scarred me and she killed you, Nairi, he thought, and a lump filled his throat. *She burned your corpse and buried you in a mass grave, and now you're gone. Now I'm nothing.*

He tried to remember every detail of Nairi--her short yellow hair that fell across her brow, her green eyes that were always so haughty and teasing, her pink lips and their crooked smile, her body clad in leather and steel, and mostly... mostly her power.

With his wife fallen, her father was beyond his reach. Lord Herin Blackrose, lord of the Axehand Order, would no longer serve him.

His love. His fort. His power. His face.

"You took them all from me, twin sister," he whispered and tasted his tears. "You will hurt so much when I find you. You will scream so loudly."

He stumbled through the city streets, holding alley walls for support. The smell of frying onions rose from one brick house, invading his nostrils like poison. Leresy fell to his knees, crawled toward a ditch, and retched. He had eaten only scraps all day; he now lost them.

He righted himself, wiped his lips on his sleeve, and kept walking. His father would be furious to see him, a prince of the realm, stumbling alone through the darkness. Princes should march ahead of brigades, soldiers and might surrounding them. Leresy smirked and tightened his cloak around him.

Anything that upsets you, old man, is good.

Finally he saw his new fortress in the distance, a shard of black rising from a dark square. A thousand legionaries served in Castellum Tal, a milanx of battle-hardened men. Leresy snorted.

Men! Who wanted to serve with a thousand sweaty, hairy, disgusting men? Back at Castra Luna in the south, Leresy had commanded thousands of youths, half of them soft females only eighteen years old and frightened. So many beauties had served him--Tilla Roper with her pale cheeks, that scrawny friend of hers with the short brown hair, and so many others to conquer.

Leresy stood in the night, staring up at his new home, at this pathetic little tower with its wretched milanx hidden inside. This was no place for him. This was no fortress for a prince. Yet his father, the bastard, had insisted.

"I demand another training fort!" Leresy had shouted at court, his eyes stinging. "I will break in recruits. I--"

The emperor had only snorted, glaring down from his throne.

"I'll not have my son whoring his way through the Legions," Frey Cadigus had said. "Do you want to train female youths or bed them?"

"Father!" Leresy had cried. "I will train them. I trained the last recruits and--"

"And we saw how that ended," Frey spat. "You commanded a fort for only three moons, and it crumbled. You had a chance to mold youths into soldiers, and you proved yourself weakest among them." He snorted. "My Legions are not your brothel, boy. You will no longer serve among women; they have softened you. You will serve among men now, hardened warriors who've slain enemies in battle. Maybe they'll teach you to be a man too."

Leresy walked across the courtyard, reeling from side to side. When he reached the tower, he banged upon the doors.

"Let me in, bastards!" he howled, pounding. "This is your prince. Let me in, sons of whores!"

The sound of laughter, howls, and song wafted from behind the doors. Leresy pounded with more vigor.

"Open these doors," he shouted, voice hoarse and slurred, "or I'll flay you all and make cloaks from your skin!"

Finally the guards pulled the doors open, and Leresy stumbled into his new tower.

The grand hall swam before him, a cavern of light and sound. Soldiers banged mugs upon tabletops, singing hoarsely. A few were so deep in their cups, they were dancing upon the tables, kicking off plates and mugs. Roasted boars and jugs of wine lay everywhere. Two stray dogs ran between legs, and three whores squealed, clutching silks to their naked bodies and fleeing pursuing men.

"Bring me wine!" Leresy demanded, marching deeper into the hall. His boots stumbled over discarded turkey bones, smashed mugs, and a drunken soldier who lay gurgling. "Wine, sons of dogs, and lots of it!"

When he had taken command of this fortress, it had been a dull, dreary place, its men automatons who knew only to march, drill, and shout "Yes, Commander!" like trained birds. Leresy would have gone mad.

A woman ran naked toward him, holding a jug of wine. He grabbed the jug, drank deeply, and slapped the woman's backside to send her scurrying off.

This, he thought, *is more like a fort for a prince.*

Soon he was lying across a tabletop, pouring wine from a jug, aiming for his mouth but mostly splattering his face. His scar blazed--it was only days old--but Leresy didn't care. Pain was good. Pain made him forget.

Wine poured. Men sang. Memory faded into numbness. Leresy's eyelids fluttered and he smiled.

A shriek tore across the hall.

"What is the meaning of this!"

The singing died at once. Silence fell across the fort.

Lying upon the tabletop, Leresy pushed himself up onto his elbows. He squinted toward the hall doors. A figure stood there, blurred and shadowed. Leresy shook his head and blinked, struggling to bring it into focus.

"Shari?" he asked, squinting.

She came marching down the hall toward him, clutching her sword. Leresy rubbed his eyes, and finally she came into focus.

Shari was ten years older than him, and as a child, Leresy had always feared her. A sadistic youth, Shari had delighted in torturing him--cutting his flesh with her knives, burning his hands upon coals, and once even locking him in a coffin for a day. Today Leresy was a grown man, but Shari still frightened him. She was a tall woman, the tallest he'd ever known, and her body was as strong as any man's; Leresy could see that even through her black armor.

And today she was furious. Her dark, curly hair bounced, her eyes flashed, and her lips peeled back, revealing sharp teeth that had bitten him many times.

"Leresy!" she shouted. "What have you done to this place?"

Leresy shook his head to clear it. Still lying upon the tabletop, he managed a grin.

"Hello, sister!" he said and raised a random mug in salute. "Would you care for some wine, some food, or perhaps a lady of the night?"

She marched toward him. Her gloved hand reached out, grabbed his hair, and tugged. Leresy yowled. Snarling, Shari dragged him across the tabletop by the hair, then slammed him down onto the floor. His hip blazed with pain.

"Ow!" he said and struggled to rise. "Stars bloody dammit, Shari, you--"

She backhanded him. White light blazed. Pain flared across his cheek.

"You will not mention the old gods," Shari hissed and clutched his throat. "You are a son of Cadigus. You serve the red spiral. You--"

"Shari, why are you here?" He shook himself free. He leaned against the tabletop, feigning nonchalance; in truth he was hiding his wobbling knees. "Don't you have any prisoners to torture, puppies to eat, or Father's arse to kiss?"

She grabbed his collar, twisted it, and began dragging him across the hall.

"It's you who'll be begging to kiss it tonight," Shari said. "He demands to speak with you. I would be less comical, Leresy, and more afraid. Very afraid."

He stumbled behind her, his wobbly legs struggling to keep up. Mugs and bones clattered around his feet. She kept dragging him, marching toward the doors.

"Shari!" he said. "Let go, damn it."

He reached for his sword but found it missing. Stars damn it! He must have left it at the brothel again. He wanted to go back and fetch it. He wanted to lie in the bed upstairs again, to make love to Dawn and Dusk, to sleep, to drink, to forget. To do anything but see his sister and father.

I want to see you again, Nairi, he thought, and tears stung his eyes. *I want to die and fly with you through the halls of afterlife.*

But Shari would not release him. She dragged him outside into the night.

"Shari, let me go--"

"Be silent or I'll cut out your tongue, then feed it to you."

She tossed him back, growled, and shifted into a dragon.

Blue scales clattered across her. Her body ballooned, her claws scratched the cobblestones, and her tail flailed. Flames churned behind her fangs like a smelter, and her eyes blazed like molten steel. Her wings spread out in the night--one blue and veined, the other a contraption of leather stretched over wood.

"Twisted freak," Leresy said, staring at her.

The pup Relesar, a soft boy, had ripped off her left wing. Shari had built herself this prosthetic, this mockery of true dragon glory. The wood-and-leather apparatus creaked like a sail.

"You look like a fisherman's barge, Shari!" he screamed at her, voice hoarse, and laughed. "Look at you! A freak. A joke."

She flapped her wings and rose several feet in the air. Her claws reached out. Before Leresy could even stumble back, let alone become a dragon himself, she grabbed him like an owl grabs a mouse.

"Shari!" he screamed and struggled in her grip, but couldn't free himself. He tried to shift now, but her claws constricted him, keeping him in human form.

"Silence, brother," she said. "I'm taking you to him."

She flew. Her wings beat in unison, her true wing and her mechanical monstrosity. Leresy squirmed in her grip, screaming and cursing and spitting. The city rolled beneath him, a whirlpool of black buildings, streaming lights, and streets like veins in a rotted heart. Leresy gagged again, spewing wine into the sky. His head tilted back, he moaned, and he saw it there.

The ground lay above him, the sky below. The palace of Tarath Imperium hung like a stalactite, a thousand feet tall. It ended with a claw of black, jagged battlements. Torches flickered across it, and dragons circled the tower like flies around the hand of a corpse.

Tarath Imperium. The greatest tower in the empire. The home of his father.

It was the very last place Leresy wanted to go.

"We would have ruled this place together, Nairi," he whispered, head dangling. "It could have been ours. It should have been ours. But she betrayed us." He growled and wept. "Kaelyn betrayed us. We will kill her, Nairi! We will kill her."

His eyes fluttered shut. He barely noticed Shari shrieking, descending, and carrying him to the palace doors. Next thing he knew, he was stumbling on his feet again, wobbling so madly he almost fell. Only Shari, who marched while gripping his collar, held him up. He blinked, trying to bring the world into focus, and saw his sister dragging him into the palace throne room.

He blinked madly. Shari was in human form again; he hadn't even noticed her shifting back. He shoved her off.

"Let go!" he said. "Unhand me. I'm not one of your dogs."

He reached for his sword, then cursed when--yet again--he realized it was gone.

Shari laughed, released his collar, and shoved him so powerfully he stumbled several paces back. He hit a column, managed to remain standing, and glared.

The throne room of Requiem was, quite handily, the largest chamber Leresy had ever seen. Dragons could fly here and find it roomy. A hundred columns stood in two palisades, rising taller than the greatest pines. The vaulted ceiling sported paintings of dragons flying among clouds. More dragons, these ones battling phoenixes, coiled across the floor in a mosaic. That floor stretched between the columns, leading to the distant throne of the emperor.

Leresy hissed at that throne. His father sat there, the man Leresy hated most.

"Father!" he cried, voice echoing in the hall. "You wanted to see me, Father. I am here! Your son is here."

He lurched down the hall, swaying from column to column for support. He cackled as he walked, spraying saliva. Finally--it seemed like he walked for hours--he stood before Frey Cadigus, Emperor of Requiem.

The old bastard sat in that ivory throne of his, looking like some stuffed vulture. Leresy imagined him roosting on eggs and barked a laugh. Grooves framed the emperor's thin, frowning lips. His dark hair was slicked back. His shoulders were wider than Leresy's, and his pauldrons made them seem even wider. But his eyes, Leresy thought... his eyes were the hardest thing about him. Those eyes were black, narrow, and cruel. They could see better than eagles, he thought. They could see through him-- through his stained tunic, through his skin, and into his very soul. Staring into them, Leresy found all his mirth dissipating. A chill ran through him, and he couldn't help but shiver.

"Father," he said, and suddenly his legs shook so badly that he fell to his knees. He knelt before the emperor, and tears burned in his eyes.

Frey stared down at him, looking like a man staring at a maggoty corpse. He placed a handkerchief to his nose.

"You stink of booze, vomit, and cheap whores," Frey said. "Stand up."

Leresy rose to his feet and swayed.

"You summoned me, Father," he said to the old vulture. Rage crackled inside him. Why was the old man just sitting there? "Why, Father? Tell me! Speak, damn it."

Frey rose to his feet and his face twisted, red with anger. His lips peeled back, revealing sharp teeth. When he stepped toward Leresy, fists clenched, he seemed more like a swooping vulture than ever. Leresy let out a yelp, stumbled a few paces backward, and fell down hard onto his backside.

"Father!" he cried, holding out his hands. "Father, please, don't strike me."

Shari laughed in the distance. Sweat drenched Leresy and fear churned his gut. Across his flesh, the old scars blazed--the scars Frey had given him throughout his childhood, beating him with belt, whip, and rod.

He's going to beat me again, Leresy realized and mewled. He scampered backward on his bottom.

"Please, Father!"

Frey leaned down, grabbed Leresy's collar, and yanked him to his feet.

"I said stand!" the emperor thundered. "Are you a prince or a dog to lick my heels? Stand!"

Leresy stood, trembling. Frey towered above him, so much taller, so much stronger.

"What do you want?" Leresy demanded, spraying spit. His voice cracked. "Why do you do this? Let me drink! Let me whore. Let me forget. Why do you bring me here? I don't want to be at court. I don't care about this place. Tell me what you want, and let me go sleep."

Frey's voice dripped disgust. "Oh, you can go sleep soon, Leresy. You won't be here long. You might not be here ever again. You are a disgrace of a son. I gave you a fort in the south, and you reduced it to rubble. I gave you a smaller fortress in the city, thinking Castra Luna was too big for you. You turned even this garrison into a hive of drink and debauchery." He snorted. "You don't care about this place, it is true. You don't care about anything, Leresy, that you can't bed or drink. But I wanted you here for this night. I wanted you to hear this in person. I want you to leave here tonight in shame, knowing what you've done."

Leresy barked a laugh. Tears streamed down his cheeks.

"I reduced Castra Luna to ruin?" he shouted and cackled. "It's your daughter Kaelyn who did that! She's the one who flew in with the Resistance. She's the one who slaughtered our men there, who toppled our walls. I defended that fort! I stood in its grand hall, a sword in my hand, and--"

"You cowered behind women, then fled through the window, leaving Shari to die," Frey said, voice twisted in disgust. "You fought? Did you even draw your sword that night? Have you ever slain an enemy, Leresy, or only run from one? You blame Kaelyn?" The emperor snorted again. "Kaelyn betrayed me, that is true, but she fought well that day. She did not flee from battle. She is a traitor, yes, but strong. She has more of my respect than you do, boy."

"Kaelyn is a whore!" Leresy screamed hoarsely, face burning. "She gave me this scar on my face! She is a dirty, cowardly dog, and I will kill her--"

"You will do nothing," Frey said. He reached out his arm, and Shari came to stand at his side, a smirk on her face. "My daughter Shari has proven herself my only worthy child."

Leresy guffawed. "Shari? She's a freak! She's a monster. Have you seen her wing, Father? I've seen better sails on slavers!"

"And I've seen slaves with more honor than you," Frey retorted. "You may blame Kaelyn, boy, but Castra Luna was your watch. And you let it fall. Shari, my daughter, will not disappoint me. The Resistance, cowards that they are, toppled the walls of Castra Luna and fled into the forests, knowing they could never defend the fort. I am giving Shari command of those ruins now. She will rebuild Castra Luna in my honor, and she will rule it well. It will never more fall under her command."

Leresy stared, his breath dying.

His lips shook.

No. Stars, no.

He let out a raw, anguished howl, reaching his hands to the ceiling.

"But Castra Luna is mine!" He shook his fists and stamped his feet. "You gave it to me, Father. To me! It was my birthday present!" He panted, frothing at the mouth, and screamed wordlessly. "You can't give it to Shari now. She's only... she's a monster! She--"

His voice morphed into nothing but a wordless, hoarse howl.

Frey watched him, eyes hard and cold. Shari stood at his side, her hands on her hips.

"Are you quite done whining, little brother?" she asked. She gave him a crooked smile and wink. "Don't feel bad. If you're a good little brother, perhaps I'll let you visit and muck out the outhouses." She smirked. "They can call you Leresy, Lord of Latrines!"

That was enough for Leresy. After all this night had brought him, that was enough. That made him snap.

He yowled. He reached for his sword a third time, again found it missing, and screamed. Then he remembered. His dagger! Of course! The dagger in his boot!

Cackling, tears and mucus and drool mingling on his face, he reached into his boot, drew the blade, and ran toward his sister. He screamed, dagger flashing in hand.

"Now you die, Shari!" he cried, laughing and crying. "Die, Blue Bitch! Die!"

He leaped and thrust his dagger.

She sidestepped, and the blade sliced the air.

He kept flying forward, tumbled, and crashed facedown onto the floor. His dagger clattered away across the mosaic.

Hands grabbed his collar. His tunic pulled back, choking him. The hands yanked him to his feet.

Frey Cadigus, Emperor of Requiem, began dragging his son toward the doors.

Leresy struggled. He mewled. He kicked. But he could not free himself. His father dragged him across the hall, between the columns and statues, over the mosaics, and under the painted ceiling. When they reached the doors, Frey tossed his son outside the palace like an innkeeper tossing out a rowdy barfly.

Leresy slammed against the stairs that led down into the night. He turned back toward his father, covered his face with his arms, and whimpered.

"Father!" he said.

Frey spat upon him, standing tall in the doorway, framed in the light of braziers. Shari stood behind him, her hands still on her hips, a sneer still on her lips.

"You have shamed me, Leresy," the emperor said. "You are henceforth banished from my court. You are henceforth banished from my city. You are no longer my son." He spat again. "Leave this city. You have one hour. If I see you again, Leresy, you will receive no such mercy. If I see you again, I will break you, hang your mangled body from this palace, and let the empire see your shame. Be gone!"

Leresy hissed and snapped his teeth.

"You will regret this, Father!" he screamed. He pointed a shaky finger. "You will regret this, Shari! I will slay you both. I will butcher you like the pigs that you are, and I will hang you here by your entrails."

With that, he stumbled down the stairs and nearly fell. He shifted into a dragon. He roared. He flew through the night. He sprayed his fire across the city; it fell in a rain of sparks.

"I am Leresy Cadigus!" he shouted as he flew, laughing and beating his wings. His fire rained and ignited roofs below. "I am Prince of Requiem. The throne will be mine--mine!"

Roaring, he dived toward his fortress, the slim tower of Castellum Tal. He slammed into the front doors in dragon form, shattering them, and rolled into the hall. He spread his wings wide and howled, and his dragon's roar echoed. All around, his drunken men fell, fled, or cheered.

"We fly out, men!" Leresy shouted. He whipped his tail, knocking over a table and shattering its mugs of ale. "We fly-- now! Follow me and you will have all the ale, women, and gold in Requiem. We fly!"

His thousand men cheered in a drunken stupor, waving mugs, jugs, and swords.

Leresy spun around in the hall, his wings and tail knocking over more tables, and lumbered outside into the night.

"Follow!" he shouted over his shoulder. "Bring the wine with you, and bring the women. We fly!"

He soared. Behind him, his cheering men emerged from the hall, shifted into dragons, and flew after him. They rose in the night, a thousand drunken dragons blowing fire. Their flames lit the darkness.

Lord of Latrines? Leresy snorted a laugh. He would make her into a latrine! When he ruled the throne, he would chain Shari beneath the sewers and let the city piss on her. He laughed, imagining it.

Nova Vita sprawled below him. He flew, howling and laughing. He streamed over the walls, and his thousand dragons flew behind him, chanting his name.

They will be my army, Leresy vowed. *I will give them ale, women, and drunken songs. And they will give me a throne.*

They flew over the forests, leaving the capital behind. The night wrapped around them, cold and black like the memory of Nairi's death.

ERRY

A lone copper dragon, she flew over the forests toward her darkest nightmare.

"Oh, griffin puke," she cursed, wings flapping. Her heart thrashed against her ribs, and she blasted nervous fire. "Damn bloody piss soup. Damn the stars and damn the Abyss and damn Frey Cadigus's hairy arse!"

She snorted smoke from her nostrils. Her wings ached. Every fiber in her body screamed at her to turn tail, to fly back north, to flee the damn south and the memories that pulsed here.

"And damn you, Tilla Roper," Erry hissed. "Damn your long bones."

She flew on, grumbling and cursing and panting.

The forest rolled beneath her for leagues, its oaks, pines, and maples turning red and yellow with autumn. The colors reminded Erry of blood and fire. Last winter, it was blood and fire that painted these trees. Today autumn's beauty only chilled her.

The old pain dug through her. The wound on her temple had healed, and even the headaches had been receding, but now it blazed with new agony. A resistor had given her that blow, slamming his tail into her head. Worse than the physical pain were the memories.

As she flew, Erry saw the battle again before her. Cannonballs slammed into dragons, tearing their magic away, scattering their human forms in a shower of blood and limbs. Soldiers lay burning upon the trees, some dead, others still screaming in the inferno. And she saw Mae Baker--her dearest friend, her silly and terrified Wobble Lips--disappearing into a rain of fire.

"Wobble Lips!" Erry had screamed and tried to find her, streaming through smoke and flame. "Mae! Mae, where are you?"

She never saw the timid baker's daughter again. Erry had fled north with the emperor, the prince and princess, and Tilla. She had fled the fire, the blood, the swarm of the Resistance.

"I left you, Mae," Erry whispered as she flew back south, back toward that old nightmare. Tears stung her eyes. "I left you to die. I'm so sorry. But I will find you again. I will find you alive, or I will find your grave, but I will find you."

She flew on, a single copper dragon in an endless sky of memory.

Finally she saw it ahead, a stain upon the forest, a pile of stone and ash like a crater.

The ruins of Castra Luna.

"Maggoty fish guts," Erry whispered, and her throat constricted. She had promised herself she wouldn't cry--she had shed enough tears during the lonely nights these past few moons-- but her eyes stung anew.

Serving in a northern fortress, Erry had heard news of her old training outpost. They said that after conquering Luna, the Resistance had ravaged and abandoned the fort, knowing they could never defend it. Erry had imagined ruins like those from the Griffin War a thousand years ago--orphaned archways, crumbling towers, walls pocked with holes, a fortress that could be patched up with good masonry and elbow grease. Yet Castra Luna... for a moment, Erry wasn't sure she even flew to the right place. Nothing remained here. Not walls, not the shells of towers, nothing but bricks and ash strewn across a clearing.

"The Resistance took apart every damn brick," she said to herself. "Nothing is left. Nothing. Oh stars, Mae."

When she flew closer, she saw that hundreds of soldiers were bustling across the ruins like ants over a smashed hive. Dragons were tugging carts full of crumbled bricks, digging foundations, and clearing rubble. Men were building scaffolding of wood and rope. Outside the ruins, a thousand troops or more drilled in a forest clearing, marching between tents.

Erry swallowed a lump in her throat.

Castra Luna. The fort where she had trained for three moons. The fort where she had met her two best--her two *only* friends: Tilla Roper and Mae Baker.

"I miss you."

Growing up in Cadport, Erry had never had friends. How could she? She was the bastard of a foreign sailor from Tiranor and a Vir Requis prostitute. Her father had never returned to Requiem. Her mother had died many years ago.

The other children of Cadport had grown up in homes, sheltered, warm, and protected. Erry had survived alone on the docks. She lived with feral cats and stray dogs. She ate whatever washed up onto the shore and whatever she could steal. She shivered at night in abandoned hovels. She begged, she stole, and sometimes--she cursed to remember it--she bedded men for a warm meal or a roof on a stormy night. Her only friends were the animals she shared the docks with. She often went moons without talking, only growling and barking and hissing among the strays.

And then... then the blessed day came.

Then she turned eighteen, and she was drafted into the Legions.

They had given her boots--real boots of leather! After years of wandering the boardwalk barefoot, the boots felt like slippers for a princess. And they gave her food--real food! The other recruits would complain about the stale wafers and dried meat, but to Erry--whose meals had often been scavenged from trash--it tasted like a feast.

And best of all... I had friends.

Flying toward the ruins, Erry blinked tears from her eyes. For three moons, she had shared a tent with Tilla, Mae, and many other girls. For the first time, Erry had felt like she belonged. In the Legions, she was no half-breed dock rat. She was a soldier, same as the others. She did not sleep among stray cats and dogs on the beach, but beside friends. Beside Tilla and Mae.

"And now you're gone, Mae," she whispered. "But I will find you, Tilla. And I will serve with you again."

She looked down, blinking her damp eyes, and a gasp fled her maw. She squinted and flew lower.

Could it be...?

Yes. Erry felt her throat tighten. Just north of the ruins, a cemetery sprawled between the trees. At first she had thought that thousands of bricks lay strewn through the forest, cast from the ruined fort. Then she realized these were craggy tombstones.

Erry pulled her wings close and dived down.

She crashed through the treetops, landed on the forest floor, and shifted into human form.

"Oh bloody stars," she whispered.

The tombstones rolled around her, carved from the old bricks of Castra Luna. Thousands spread between the trees. Those trees creaked in the wind, and their leaves rustled, a whisper of ghosts. Erry shivered and hugged herself. Even in steel armor, a sword at her side, she felt as fragile and afraid as she had upon the docks.

She began walking between the graves, her boots crunching fallen leaves. Most tombstones bore no names; they were simply engraved with a single birch leaf, an ancient symbol of Requiem.

Erry tilted her head.

"The Regime engraves the spiral upon its graves," she whispered. "The birch leaf is an older symbol. The Resistance dug these graves."

She had not imagined the Resistance would bury the dead. She had always heard that they merely burned corpses, left them to rot, or even ate them. Yet somebody had dug these graves here, raised these tombstones, and engraved each one with a symbol of Old Requiem.

As she kept wandering through the forest, Erry saw that several scattered tombstones did bear names. She recognized some; here lay the fallen youths of Cadport.

Rune must have buried them, Erry realized. *He's from Cadport too. He'd know some of those he slew.*

She sighed and lowered her head. Back at Cadport, Rune Brewer had always been kind to her. He would bring her food to the beach sometimes. Once he even let her sleep in his tavern during a storm. Yet now the boy had become a resistor. Now he had slain hundreds; burying those he slew could not atone for that.

"In only a year, so much changed," Erry whispered. "Two kids from the boardwalk, one now a soldier, one a resistor. And so many dead."

She kept wandering, reading the names of the fallen, until she saw a tall tombstone upon a knoll.

Erry froze and stared.

A ray of light fell between the trees, lighting the tombstone. Ivy crawled over its craggy white surface, and cyclamens circled its base. The trees rustled, whispering to her. This grave seemed to beckon, and Erry approached it gingerly, holding her breath.

When she saw the name upon the tombstone, she lowered her head, and a tear flowed down her cheek.

"Mae Baker," she whispered.

She looked at her friend's grave and clenched her fists.

"Oh damn it, Wobble Lips!" she blurted out. "Why did you have to go and get killed, damn you? I *told* you to fly near me." Her fists shook, and she wanted to punch the tombstone. "I told you a million times--in assault formation, look *ahead* and blow fire, not at enemies beside you." She kicked the earth, sending leaves flying onto the grave. "Now look at you. Now look at you, Wobble Lips! At least I'm spared seeing your damn lips wobble so much. At least you won't bug me again with all your wailing and tears."

She closed her burning eyes and stood for long moments, fists clenched. Finally she sighed, opened her eyes, and touched the tombstone.

"Wherever you are now, Wobble Lips, just... don't get into any more trouble, all right? Not until I see you again. And for stars' sake, don't cry so much, okay? Be strong. We all have to be strong." Her knees trembled and she knuckled her eyes. "We're going to be so damn strong, Mae, you won't believe it." She patted the tombstone. "Goodbye, Wobble Lips. Goodbye."

She turned and left.

She walked through the forest, head low.

Soon she found a gravelly road. As she walked between the trees, heading toward the ruins of Castra Luna, she unrolled the scroll she had carried all the way from her northern fort. She clutched it like a treasure.

It had taken her moons to convince her officer to write this scroll, reassigning her here. At first, Erry had agreed to do anything for reassignment. And so she had spent a moon serving her officer as a slave--scrubbing his boots, sweeping his floor, oiling his sword, polishing his armor, and begging again and again for naught. She had then changed her approach. She spent the next moon wreaking havoc in her phalanx--knocking over pots, breaking three swords, crashing into other dragons in flight, and being the worst soldier she could be. She had suffered many punisher burns during that moon, but it was worth it. Finally, after Erry had lost yet another helmet, her commander agreed to send her south.

"Remember," Erry had said, rubbing the bruises of his punisher, "I want to serve in Castra Luna, and I want to serve under Lanse Tilla. Remember that--it has to be Lanse Tilla."

Her officer had scowled, cursed... and written the scroll.

"Soon I'll see you again, Tilla," Erry whispered as she walked down the gravel road.

All my life, she thought, *I've had only two real friends. One now lies buried. The other is an officer leading her own phalanx.* Erry took a deep breath. *I might still be a lowly periva and Tilla a lofty lanse. And I might have to serve under her command, rather than fight at her side. But I can be near her again. I can be with my friend.*

She knuckled her eyes, kept walking down the road, and soon reached the ruins of Castra Luna.

The Legions had built a palisade of sharpened logs around the debris, and Erry approached an opening where two guards stood. When she reached them, they frowned down at her, two beefy men in black steel. They moved to block the palisade gateway.

"Move it!" Erry said, craning her head up to glare at them. She stood five feet tall only on tiptoes, and these brutes towered above her, but she had fought men this size before on the docks. "I'm reassigned to this fort. Let me in, mules."

The guards wore a single red star upon their armbands. They were perivas, the same lowly rank as her. They snorted.

"You got to be eighteen to join the Legions, shrimp," one said and snorted. "You look about three years old. Get lost."

Erry rolled her eyes. "And you got to have a brain to join too, and I've seen logs with bigger brains than yours." She brandished her scroll at them. "Can you even read? This is my new fort. *Move!*"

With a great shove, she pushed between them and entered the camp.

Chaos awaited her.

Dragons trundled about, snorting smoke and dragging wagons of bricks and wood. Masons cursed and yelled at one another, jabbing fingers at building plans. Workers swung hammers, erecting scaffolding. Other dragons grunted as they dug ditches. Between these workers, hundreds of troops marched in clanking armor, trained with swords, and flew overhead as dragons. A thousand legionaries must have bustled here, engineers and fighters alike.

"I'm looking for Lanse Tilla Siren," Erry said to one mason, speaking Tilla's new, noble surname. "She commands the Sea Cannons phalanx. Where do I go?"

The mason ignored her, rushed toward a worker, and began admonishing the man for using the wrong chisel.

Erry grumbled, spat, and moved on. She had to ask a dragon tugging a cart, three soldiers sorting through rubble, and another guard.

Finally the last man scratched his chin, sucked his cheek, and said, "Lanse Tilla Siren? Tall woman, sort of looks like a statue?"

Erry nodded. "That's her all right."

The legionary snorted. "You asked to serve under Lanse Siren? The Cadport Cannon?" He whistled. "You crazy or what?"

She growled at him. "You stupid or just an idiot?" She waved the scroll at him. "Yes, Tilla Bloody Siren, says so right here. Where is she?"

The soldier raised his hands in defense, and his eyebrows rose just as high.

"All right, little one, don't have a fit. It's just that, well..." He snickered. "Siren's got a bit of a reputation around here. Say she not only looks like a statue, but got a heart of stone too. Loves her punisher, that one does. But well... if you're a glutton for pain, you might like her." He gestured his chin to a gateway behind him. "Step out the palisade, down the road for two hundred yards, and look for a tent with a cannon banner. You'll find her there."

"Yeah, well, you're a glutton for... dumbness!" Erry said and marched away, fuming.

So what if people badmouthed Tilla? Erry had heard others say the same about her friend, even back in Cadport, calling her cold and haughty. But Erry had seen a different side to her. Erry had seen a kind, sensitive woman beneath the icy exterior. She had seen a friend.

I myself was always an outcast, Erry thought. *I myself was always called names. They called me a dock rat, a harlot, and a diseased stray.* She knuckled her eyes. *But I'm not. And Tilla isn't cruel. We're two outcasts, two lost souls from Cadport... and we'll get through these damn Legions together.*

She stepped through the palisade gates, walked down a dirt road, and saw a clearing between the trees. A hundred tents rose here, their black cloth emblazoned with red spirals. Troops marched between them, and several dragons flew above in patrol. If the ruins bustled with workers, here there were only fighters. These men did not wield hammers and chisels, but swords and shields.

Frey is mustering a new army here, Erry thought. *Green recruits used to train in this forest clearing. Now Castra Luna will house seasoned warriors to fight the Resistance.* She gripped her sword. *And I will fight with them.*

The tents displayed the banners of their phalanxes. Erry saw sigils of wolves, lions, dragons, swords, and many others. Each phalanx had two tents to its name: one large tent for the common soldiers, one smaller one for its commanding officer.

After walking through the camp for several moments, Erry saw two tents bearing Tilla's banners--a cannon overlooking the sea.

When she walked closer, Erry saw the phalanx training in the dirt outside. A hundred perivas and corelis--younger soldiers sporting only one or two stars--stood in black steel, swinging swords. The clashing blades rang. A hulking siragi--an older, gruffer soldier with three stars upon his armbands--was moving between the lower ranks, barking at soldiers to correct their stances and thrusts.

Behind the troops, upon a boulder, stood Lanse Tilla Siren. Erry's heart skipped a beat.

Stars, she thought and felt herself pale.

She hadn't seen Tilla in six moons, not since the battle here. But Tilla looked like she'd aged six years. Soldiers like Erry wore breastplates, vambraces, and greaves over tan leggings and tunics. Tilla now wore the full plate suit of an officer; the steel covered her from toes to shoulders, perfectly molded to her body. Her pauldrons displayed red spirals--the insignia of command. She did not bear the simple sword of a common soldier anymore, but a fine weapon with a dragonclaw pommel.

Upon her hip, she bore a punisher. Erry gulped. The wounds across her, those her former officer had given her, blazed anew. Did Tilla too punish soldiers with this weapon of lightning and pain? Erry remembered how Lanse Nairi had nearly killed Tilla with her punisher. Did Tilla herself now torture others?

But worse than the punisher was Tilla's face. Erry felt ice fill her belly. Tilla had always seemed pale and aloof, but this... this was different.

No color touched Tilla's face now; she could have been carved from marble. No emotion or life filled her eyes. As she stared upon her troops training, her eyes were dead. Cold. Hard as stone.

She looks like that statue of Frey that stands in Cadport, Erry thought and shivered. *She seems just as cold and cruel. Stars, what happened to her at Castra Academia? How, in only six moons, did they freeze her eyes?*

When Erry stepped closer to the phalanx, Tilla turned those cold eyes toward her, and their gazes locked.

Erry smiled and waved, expecting Tilla to smile too, to greet her, maybe even to rush forward and embrace her. But still no emotion filled those dark eyes. Erry didn't even see a flicker of recognition within them. Her heart sank.

Stars, doesn't she remember me?

Then Erry realized: Of course! Of course Tilla could not rush toward her, embrace her, or even acknowledge her. She was leading her own phalanx now! She had to act aloof. She had to be strong like Nairi had been. But it was all an act for her soldiers. It had to be.

Erry sucked in her breath, slammed her fist against her chest, and called out.

"Hail the red spiral! I am Periva Erry Docker. I report to duty." She raised her scroll. "I've come from Castra Lan. I'm to serve in the Sea Cannons."

Tilla's eyes narrowed the slightest bit, a movement so subtle Erry wasn't sure it even happened.

For the first time, Tilla spoke.

"Step forward, periva. Hand me that scroll."

Stars! Erry thought. Tilla's voice was even colder than her eyes. It didn't even sound human; it was the voice of a statue. Erry gulped, suddenly not sure this was an act at all. Briefly, she wondered if she had even found the right officer. Was this truly Tilla or simply somebody who looked like her?

Erry stepped forward and held out her scroll.

Everybody was watching them, she realized. The soldiers of the phalanx, a hundred men and women in steel, had stopped drilling and stared.

Tilla looked toward them, and her eyes narrowed further. "Keep drilling!" she shouted, and her voice rolled across the camp. "Do you think the Resistance is standing around gawking?"

The swords began to swing again. The men were hulking warriors, many of them standing well over six feet tall, their frames burly. Yet even they looked sheepish as Tilla commanded them.

Merciful stars, Erry thought. *She's even harder than Nairi.*

Tilla marched toward her, boots thudding, and snatched the scroll from Erry's hands. She scanned the writing quickly, then stared into Erry's eyes.

"Says here you're a troublemaker," Tilla said, scrutinizing Erry. "Says here you break swords, lose helmets, and earned the punisher every day. What makes you think you can serve here, soldier?"

Erry gasped. She wanted to shake Tilla madly, to scream at her. *Don't you remember me? You think I'm just some... some troublemaker soldier? I'm your friend! I'm Erry from Cadport!*

She glanced back at the drilling soldiers and forced herself to take a shaky breath.

It's just an act, she told herself. *It has to be. She's just acting this way for her troops.*

"Don't look at them, soldier!" Tilla barked. "I asked you a question. Look at me and answer."

Erry couldn't help it now. She gave a shaky laugh.

"Stars, Tilla," she whispered and shook her head. "Don't you remember me? It's Erry."

Tilla hissed. Her eyes blazed. She looked so much like a rabid wolf that Erry took a step back.

"Into my tent, soldier," Tilla hissed. "Go!"

With that, the young officer spun around and marched into her tent. Shakily, Erry followed her into the shadows, leaving the phalanx to drill outside.

Inside the tent, Erry saw a cot, a small table and chair, and a wooden chest. It was a small tent, maybe nine by nine feet, a retreat for an officer to find privacy from those she commanded.

Finally Tilla can drop her act, Erry thought.

"Well, this is nice, Tilla!" she said and allowed herself a hesitant smile. "Sure beats the old dirt we used to sleep on, right?" She reached for an apple on the table. "And they give you apples! Stars, I should become an officer too. I--"

"You will refer to me as *Commander*," Tilla said, eyes blazing. "Or you will refer to me as Lanse Tilla. Do you understand, soldier?"

Erry froze, the apple halfway to her mouth, and frowned.

"By the Abyss!" she said. "All right, *Commander.*" Erry laughed shakily. "You... you remember me, don't you? I--"

Tilla snarled. Erry could not believe it. The young woman--her best friend!--snarled at her. Her lips peeled back, her teeth showed, and she growled like a wolf.

"Do not test my patience," she said. "I remember you, Docker. We trained together, yes. You know it. I know it. Those days are over." Tilla took a step forward, towering over the smaller Erry. "I am your commanding officer. That's all I am to you now. Do you understand?"

Erry stood frozen, almost too shocked to breathe.

Merciful stars, she thought. *What did they do to her at the academy?*

Her eyes burned, and Erry tossed down her apple in disgust. She spat on the floor.

"Well, dog dung, *Commander*," she said, spitting out that last word like an insult. "You might remember me, but do you remember yourself? Do you remember who you are?"

Tilla clutched her punisher, and its tip crackled to life. "Be careful, periva. Be careful that--"

Erry snorted. "You think I'm scared of you, Tilla? You're just a common, seaside ropemaker's daughter from Cadport. Bloody stars, you and I pissed in the woods together. Now you act all high and mighty?" She laughed mirthlessly, and her eyes would not stop stinging. "Sweaty codpieces, Tilla! Don't you remember? I came here to serve with you again. Like in the old days. Like--"

Tilla drew her punisher. Lightning wreathed its tip.

"I will tell you this once more, periva," Tilla said. "Those days are over. You are no longer a recruit, but a soldier with insignia on your arms. I am no longer the woman you knew. I am your commander now and your officer. Salute me, hail the red spiral, and pray that I forget your words here today. Anyone else would hang for them. This is the one mercy I will show you."

Erry looked at the drawn punisher and barked a laugh.

"What are you going to do--burn me?" She snorted. "Go shove that thing up your fat arse, Roper."

Tilla moved so fast Erry barely saw it. The punisher drove forward. Lightning raced across Erry's breastplate, pain flared, and she screamed.

Her old officer had burned her before, short blasts that made her yelp and jump. Tilla was crueler. She kept her punisher against her, driving all its pain into Erry's armor, flesh, and bones. Tears ran down her cheeks. She fell to her knees. When Tilla finally pulled the punisher back, Erry doubled over, panting and spitting.

"If you will serve under my command, periva," Tilla spoke above, "you will show me respect, or you will burn."

Erry stared up, wincing. Stars floated across the tent. Tilla stood above her, her punisher still drawn, her eyes still dead.

Erry struggled to her feet.

She raised her chin, only as tall as Tilla's shoulders, but stretched to every inch of height she had. She slammed a trembling fist against her breastplate.

"I salute," she said through stiff lips. "I salute Cadport. I salute the friend I once had. And I salute the memory of Mae Baker, a memory you shame." She spat on Tilla's boots. "And you, *Commander*, can go lick horse dung."

With that, she fled the tent, shifted into a dragon, and took flight.

She soared above the clearing. She heard shouts, roars, and flapping wings behind her. Erry didn't bother looking back. She was among the slimmest, fastest dragons in the Legions. If she did not want to be caught, she wouldn't. She streamed over the forest and blazed fire skyward.

Damn you, Tilla, she thought. Her eyes dampened and she spewed her flame. *Damn you to the Abyss, and damn these Legions, and damn you, Mae, for dying, and damn you this stupid, stupid war.*

She didn't know where to go now. She didn't care. She'd had enough of forts. She'd had enough of damn commanders. She'd had enough of this whole damn world.

Erry Docker howled and flew into the horizon, tears in her eyes and fire in her throat.

RUNE

They climbed the hill, rose from the cover of trees, and beheld a canyon that halved the land.

"Cain's Canyon," Rune whispered, the wind billowing his cloak and hair. "Burn me, it's larger than I imagined. All of Lynport could fit in there."

At his side, Valien nodded and scratched his grizzled stubble. "Aye, and Lord Cain will brag to you about it, wait and see. 'All the people of Cadport could fit into my canyon!' he boasts to all who visit. The man's been hunkered down in there for years, and he never forgave Lynport for calling itself the Jewel of the South. He sees himself as a southern lord and Lynport as stealing his glory."

Rune sighed. "If he saw Lynport now, its homes rotten and its port dead, maybe he'd feel less jealous."

Valien raised an eyebrow. "Lord Devin Cain lives in a hole in the ground--literally. I think even a barren boardwalk is enough to stir his jealousy." Valien hefted his pack over his shoulders, rattling its pans and knives. "Come now, it's still a long walk there among the trees, and I dare not fly yet. The Legions patrol these skies too."

Rune stood for a moment upon the hilltop, staring down over the trees at the canyon. It stretched across the land as far as he could see. The forest plunged into it, trees tilting over its rim, roots sticking out like hair over a scar. Mist floated within its depths, and flocks of birds flew over the shadows, their cries echoing. Rune had seen wonders before: the towering Ralora Cliffs over the sea, the lost glory of Confutatis in the east, and the clock tower of Castra Luna. Yet he thought Cain's Canyon the greatest among them, certainly the largest; he could probably fit all those other wonders into its depths.

"Rune!" Valien's raspy voice rose from the trees coating the hillside below. "Come, follow. You're too visible up there."

Rune too hefted his pack, gripped the hilt of his Amber Sword, and began climbing downhill.

They walked between the trees in silence. They had been walking through this forest for three days now, leaving their camp far behind. Since abandoning Castra Luna, the Resistance had been hiding in the western forests of Old Salvandos, a lush wilderness of oaks, pines, and maples so thick no scouts could see through the treetops. Three thousand resistors still hid in their camp, living in holes, treetop nests, and hidden burrows.

Rune had found the camp a blessed change from the ruins of Confutatis, the fallen city where the Resistance had once hidden. The Legions had taken three resistors alive at Castra Luna and flown them north to the capital. That meant three bodies had been tortured, and three mouths had screamed of their old camp. And so, for several moons now, the Resistance had hidden in the wilderness. Their new forest home was humble, but green and safe. Walking here with Valien, Rune missed it. He missed his warm underground burrow with its soft bed of leaves. He missed drinking ale with his fellow resistors and whispering old stories of Requiem. And he missed Kaelyn.

You wait for me there, Kaelyn, Rune thought. *Watch over our people.* He squared his jaw. *I'll be back with aid. I promise you. I promise.*

"Rune!" rose the voice ahead, and Valien's leathery face peered from between the trees, framed with shaggy hair. "Move your arse. We have little time to spare."

Rune gave a mock salute. "I'm right on your heels, old man."

As they kept walking through the forest, Rune sighed. He had spent days now alone with Valien, whom he found far, far less pleasant company than Kaelyn. True, Valien was a great warrior, a strong leader, and a man Rune admired. But he was also gruff. He still cursed and drank too much. Whenever Rune slipped or fell behind, Valien had a sharp remark.

And the training. Stars, the training still left Rune bruised and cramped. Every evening, Valien insisted they practice their swordplay, and the man was ruthless, slamming his sword against Rune's armor again and again, denting it and bruising the flesh beneath.

"Tough in training, easy in battle," the former knight kept saying, but amusement always filled his dark eyes; Rune thought he rather enjoyed beating him black and blue.

The noon sun shone when they reached the canyon. A flock of cranes flew overhead, singing and beating their wings. The trees tilted over the crevice, clinging to the canyon's rim and nearly falling over. Rune approached gingerly, grabbed a pine, and leaned forward. The depth spun his head. The canyon plunged a mile deep, ending with a rocky floor. Mist floated in the depths like ghosts.

Valien came to stand at his side, wiped sweat off his brow, and stared down into the canyon. Burrs and mud stained his garb of leather and wool. He wheezed after the trek; the wound on his neck, suffered when saving Rune's life years ago, still pained the former knight.

"Remember," Valien said, voice a mere rasp, "Lord Cain rebelled against the Regime once. He was punished for it. His three sons were slain; Cain himself was spared, but forbidden to emerge from his canyon since. That was many years ago; you were just a babe. Cain now serves and fears the emperor. His daughter Lana is sympathetic toward the Resistance; you saw that in the capital. Lord Devin Cain himself might not hold much love for us." He stared at Rune. "We must be wary. We could find a great ally here, or we could find our deaths."

Rune squinted down into the canyon. "Where is he? You said he commands ten thousand men. I see birds and a few lizards, that's all."

Valien nodded. "I said he lives in a hole in the ground, didn't I? This is just a crack--far too exposed for the likes of Devin Cain." He squinted upward. "The sky is clear. We'll shift into dragons, fly down to the bottom, and walk from there in human forms. We're close."

With that, Valien leaped from among the trees and tumbled into the darkness of the canyon. Before he could hit the bottom, he shifted into a silver dragon, filled his wings with air, and slowed his fall.

Rune cracked his neck, hefted his pack across his shoulders, and leaped too. He dived into the canyon. The wind whipped his hair and cloak. The canyon walls rushed at his sides. With a deep breath, Rune shifted into a black dragon and stretched his wings wide. The wing caught them like sails. Rune slowed his fall and glided down.

The two dragons, silver and black, landed upon the canyon floor and shifted back into human forms.

A rain of cutlery clattered down around them. A fork nearly stabbed Rune in the shoulders.

"Stars damn it!" he said. "Damn pack never did close properly."

Valien grumbled. "Come on, we move. Quietly. This is not a safe place."

They began to walk along the canyon floor. Rune craned his neck back and gulped. The canyon walls rose a mile high; the sky was but a thin, blue strip above. Every footstep echoed.

As he looked at the craggy walls, Rune thought back to Ralora Cliffs at home. He remembered how Tilla and he used to

walk there between the cliffs and sea. They would bang wooden
swords, pretending to be old heroes. They would wrestle, whisper
quietly, or just look out across the waves.

And one night we kissed, Rune thought. *And we said goodbye.
And we vowed to see each other again.* A lump filled his throat. *And we
did. We saw each other again... and we fought with swords of steel. And I
lost her, maybe forever this time.*

He blinked furiously and banished those thoughts. Pining
for Tilla would not help now. All he could do was keep fighting.

I can still save you, Tilla, he thought. *You are good at heart. I
know it. I can still save you from the soldier they forced you to become.*

They walked for about a mile down the canyon, rounded a
bend, and Rune's breath died.

"Oh merciful stars," he whispered.

Valien came to stand beside him and nodded. "Welcome to
the Castle-in-the-Cliff, home of Lord Cain and his army."

Rune had seen castles before. He had seen the small
Castellum Acta upon the hill in Lynport. And he had seen Castra
Luna, a sprawling fort in the forest. But this was different. This
castle was not built of bricks and walls. Lord Cain's home was
carved into the cliff itself. The living stone had been chipped
away, forming a portico of columns, turrets carved with dragon
reliefs, and a balcony topped with statues of winged women. The
facade rose as tall and lavish as a palace.

Or the world's largest mausoleum, Rune thought.

A wide stairway led from the canyon floor to the castle
gates. No doors filled the archway; Rune saw only shadows
within. Two statues surrounded the entrance, carved of the same
limestone, a hundred feet tall each. Stone helmets hid their faces,
and their fists--each one large as a mule--were held to their
breasts.

"Are there no guards?" Rune said. "No doors? Do we
simply walk in?"

Valien was holding the hilt of his sword. "Careful. We don't know if we meet friend or foe here." He lowered his voice to a growl. "And remember, Lord Cain has not left this hole in years, not since losing his rebellion--and his three sons. By now, he is not what you would call sane."

"Might take one madman to help us kill another," Rune said.

He marched across the canyon toward the towering facade. He craned his neck back, admiring it from up close. The columns, balconies, and dragon reliefs soared. The two stone guardians towered thrice the height of dragons. Rune shivered. Helmets hid the statues' faces, but Rune could swear they were watching him. He raised his chin, took a deep breath, and approached the stairs that led toward the palace gateway.

Dust rained.

Stone creaked.

"Rune!" rasped Valien.

Hands grabbed Rune's shoulders and tugged. He fell several paces backward. Stone slammed down ahead of him, showering dust, and the canyon shook.

"Bloody bollocks!" Rune cursed and scrambled several paces farther back.

Before him, a great stone fist--taller than he was--had slammed onto the ground. As Rune watched, coughing and rubbing his eyes, one of the stone statues straightened and returned its fist to its chest.

"Well," Valien said, still holding Rune's shoulders, "that explains why there are no guards."

Rune nodded, legs rubbery. Looking around, he saw that cracks covered the canyon floor around the entrance. Those stone statues had slammed their fists down many times before. He wondered how many people they had crushed.

A high voice rose ahead, echoing in the canyon.

"We meet again, Relesar Aeternum!"

Rune looked up.

"Lady Lana," he whispered.

She stood upon the palace balcony, a hundred feet above them. She held one hand to her hip, the other upon her sword's pommel. Most Vir Requis bore longswords, ancient weapons of wide, straight blades; Lady Lana, however, bore a thin, curved saber like southern sailors used to wield. Lana's hair billowed in the wind, a black mane sporting a single white streak. She leaped off the balcony and shifted into a dragon, her black scales bearing a similar streak across her spine ridge. She spread out her wings, landed before Rune, and shifted back into a woman.

"The Stone Guardians were built to slay any strangers who try to enter," she said, her accent highborn and meticulous. "Thousands dwell within this hall, and the Guardians know every one. In five hundred years, none have entered here without their blessing." She reached out her hand. "It's good to finally see you in daylight, Relesar Aeternum. The sun agrees with you. Or should I call you Rune?"

Rune clasped her hand and shook it.

Back in the capital, he had seen Lady Lana masked and cloaked in shadows. Today he saw a noble face with high cheekbones, arched eyebrows, and thin, pink lips. A patch covered her left eye; the right one was gray and bright and intelligent. She looked about thirty years old, but the white stripe through her hair gave her an older, wiser look. She wore a yellow belt over a gray tunic--the colors of House Cain--and tall boots over leggings. Her cloak was dyed blue, the color of nobility, and clasped with a pin bearing the sigil of Cain: two statues guarding an archway.

"Lady Lana," Valien said in his rasp of a whisper.

She turned toward him, and a smile touched her lips.

"My lord Valien." She reached out her arms, embraced him, and kissed his cheek. "Your stubble grows rougher and whiter every time we meet."

"And you grow more beautiful," he said and kissed her hand.

Rune raised an eyebrow. "Burn me, he's a romantic," he said. "Who knew?"

Valien growled at him. "A romantic who still kicks your backside in sword sparring." He turned back to Lana. "My lady, we are here to see your father. Will he speak with us? Will you take us to him?"

Her face darkened. "My father's mood has been dark and his mind addled. He has spent too many years in the shadows. You will not find him the man he was." She clutched the hilt of her sword. "His temper flares without reason. He sees demons in every shadow. He rails against the cruelty of Frey Cadigus one day, then blesses the man the next. He is feverish with stone and stale air. In years past, I could get him to fly within this canyon and see the sky above, even if he refused to fly into the forest. Now I cannot get him to even leave his hall." She sighed. "My father has been a broken man since Frey crushed his rebellion and killed my brothers. I do not know if you can enlist him, Valien. You have my sword, always, and I've tried to soften my father to your cause. I've praised the Resistance in his ears. Whether he listened, I cannot tell; he will not speak to me of this. Maybe he will speak to you. He once greatly admired you."

Valien nodded and sighed. "He was a good man, years ago. He was a friend. I pray that I find this same man today."

"You will not," Lana said, "but I will take you to him. Follow." She turned and began walking between the Stone Guardians. "Do not fear them! They will not harm my guests. Just walk close to me."

As they followed Lady Lana, Rune glanced up nervously at the stone statues, ready to leap back should they move again. Yet they remained frozen, stone heads raised, fists still clutched to their chests. Lana led them between the statues, up a wide staircase, and toward the gates of the Castle-in-the-Cliff.

Shadows loomed before them. The gateway rose taller than dragons, carved into the living rock of the cliff. More than a gateway, this was an ornate cave. Cold air blew from within, chilling Rune, and mist swirled. As he stepped through the archway, the sound of wind and distant birds faded. He entered a realm of shadows and fog.

When he blinked, he saw a great hall, larger than any he'd ever seen. Rows of columns stretched into the shadows. Upon each burned an oil lamp, the light barely piercing the darkness. A mosaic of dragons battling griffins covered the floor. Shadows hid the ceiling. Rune had walked a hundred yards before he even realized that guards stood between the columns, cloaked in gray and armed with sabers; the shadows nearly drowned them.

"Father!" Lana called out, and her voice echoed across the chamber. "Guests are here to see you. Will you speak with them, Father?"

As they walked deeper down the hall, Rune saw a throne ahead; it too seemed carved from the raw stone of the cliff. When they walked closer, Rune saw that a man sat there.

"Stars," he whispered.

Rune had always thought Valien--with his shaggy hair, leathery face, and grizzled stubble--looked rough and weathered. Yet the man upon this throne made Valien seem as well-groomed as a prince.

Lord Cain wore shaggy gray robes lined with fur. His walrus mustache bristled beneath a bulbous, veined nose. His face was as red and wrinkled as a dried apple. His hair was even redder, wild and tangled and streaked with white. Yet despite the snow invading his hair and the grooves lining his skin, he did not seem frail. His shoulders were still wide, his body stocky beneath his robes. His hands were large and strong, clutching the armrests of his throne. A curved blade hung at his side, its pommel shaped as a roaring dragon's head. When he looked up, his eyes blazed under bushy brows--black, deep, and shrewd.

"So, Lord Valien Eleison!" he called out, voice booming; it pealed across the hall. "You've come at last to grovel and beg for my aid."

The haggard lord rose from his throne. He was a large man, as tall and wide as Valien. He drew his sword and held it aloft. His forearms were wide and crisscrossed with scars. In his youth, he must have been a great warrior; he still stood with the pride of one.

Valien kept walking forward, not slowing down. Rune and Lana walked at his sides.

"I've not come here to grovel," he rasped. "Nor to beg. I come to see a man who was once great. I come to see if greatness can still be found within him, or whether he's become but a ghost, a withered puppet for a stronger lord."

Lord Cain cackled; it sounded less like a laugh and more like a man gagging. Spittle flew from beneath his bushy mustache.

"Aye, you've still got a way with words, you bastard!" Lord Cain said. He barked a laugh. "You always were the poetic one, weren't you? Reading your books like a woman." He snorted. "True men have no use for books, Valien, nor for your fancy words. We deal with blood, blades, and dragonfire."

"You will have the glory of all three," Valien said, "if you join our cause."

They reached the throne. Lana went to stand by her father's side. Rune and Valien remained standing before him. All around, the columns rose into shadows, and the guards stood still and dark between them. The lamps burned, casting flickering light.

Lord Cain turned to stare at Rune. Those dark, shrewd eyes narrowed, scrutinizing him.

"Is this your boy, Valien?" the entombed lord asked and grunted. "Is this pup the so-called heir you've been trumpeting around? He looks more like a girl to me. Ha! This one is prettier than my daughter. My arse is hairier than his cheeks." He thrust out his chin at Rune. "Do you talk, little girl? Or do you merely drag around behind your lord as a trophy?"

Rune felt his temper flare. He grabbed his sword.

"You know Shari Cadigus, daughter of the emperor?" he said to Cain. "You know of her missing wing? My teeth tore it off."

Cain snorted. "So you fought another woman, and you couldn't even kill her. And you think you can fight men in battle? You think you can slay Frey Cadigus?" He hacked a laugh. "And you want me to help you! I wager you need help to wipe your own backside."

Rune growled. "I flew to battle. I fought Frey's men. You haven't left this cavern in years! And you call me a--"

"Rune!" Valien said, voice rough, and his eyes blazed. "We've not come here to argue with Cain, but to seek an alliance."

Cain's laughter boomed and echoed across the palace. He clutched his belly. "Ha! This boy who would be king cannot even talk without his lord lecturing him. What sort of king allows a knight to interrupt his words?" He sat back upon his throne. "Be gone, boy, before I send word to the capital that you hide in my hall."

"Me, hide in your hall!" Rune said and snorted. "You've been rotting here for too long, old man. Will you not emerge to fight? Will you leave your army here in the shadows to collect dust, or will you emerge into the sky as a dragon?"

All mirth left Cain's eyes. His face darkened, and his lips peeled back in a snarl.

"Emerge into the sky? A sky full of imperial dragons bearing Frey's sigil? Fly in a sky another man rules? No, boy. Am I not a man? Am I not a lord?" He spat on the floor. "I will not fly over another man's fields, forests, or forts. I am Lord Cain! I march and fly above earth that I own."

"You own nothing but a hole in a wall," Rune said, disgusted.

"Aye, little girl, and wouldn't you love to rule this hole in a wall? Wouldn't you love to command the army that dwells here? They are true warriors. They are true men, tested in battle, not babes fresh off the teat like you."

Rune took a step forward. "You want lands? You want skies to call your own? You want to see sunlight again, old man? I will give you land and sky if you join my cause. Fight with me, Cain, and I will give you what you desire."

Cain snorted. "Will you now, boy? You will give me lands, is that so? I will take what lands are mine, not have a whore's daughter give me a treat like a dog." He spat on Rune's boot. "If Frey should fall, I will command all the south of Requiem--from Castra Luna in the north, down to Ralora Cliffs in the south, and east across the plains of Osanna to the port of Altus Mare."

Rune's eyes widened and he guffawed. "But that's half the kingdom!"

"Aye," said Lord Cain and cackled. "Would you rather rule half a kingdom or all of nothing?"

Valien stepped forward, face red beneath his beard. "Enough, Cain! Enough of this bantering. Are you two leaders or fishwives?" He took another step forward and clutched Cain's shoulder. "Cain. We are old friends, you are I. We are both warriors. Now fight with us. Let us swing swords and blow fire together. Cadigus has you hiding in a hole like a rat. Join us, dethrone the man, and you will have the lands you crave."

Cain grumbled under his breath. He gave Valien a long look, then turned his eyes toward Rune; his tufted eyebrows turned with his stare like shutters.

"Does he know how to fight?" he said. "The boy is too soft and too young. Can he kill?"

Rune nodded, thinking back to Castra Luna, and ice filled his belly. "I've killed before. I fought at Castra Luna."

Cain barked a laugh. "Ha! Luna? You fought green recruits there, not hardened men. Can you fight a true warrior? When you fly to meet Frey and the Axehand Order, will you slay them, or will you fly away with your tail between your legs?"

Rune clutched his sword and drew a foot of steel. "I will fight. I will not run and hide."

Hide like you, he wanted to add, but bit down on the words.

"We shall see," said Cain. "Very well! I will fight with you. I will give you an army. But first, boy, you must prove your words. You must prove that you can indeed fight as you boast-- fight a true warrior." He raised his voice to a shout. "Doog! Doog, here boy. Here!"

Footsteps thudded. Grunts rose from the shadows. Rune turned toward the sound and felt the blood leave his face.

Oh bloody Abyss, he thought.

A lumbering troll of a man came lolloping from the shadows. He towered seven feet tall, his shoulders wide as an ox, his belly flabby but his arms rippling with muscles. His feet were bare, the toenails yellow, and he wore only a tattered tunic. Iron rings circled his neck and ankles, as if he'd just been unchained from a dungeon. He grunted and chortled and drooled as he approached. But worst of all was not his size. The man had no face.

A great scar rifted his head from his right ear, across where his nose should be, and down to his left jowls. The wound drove into his head, two inches thick, leaving the man one eye and just the hint of a mouth.

"Here, Doog, here!" Lord Cain said.

The huge, scarred man trundled up to his master, then stood on wobbly legs. Saliva dripped from his wound down to his shirt.

"Merciful stars, Cain," Rune said.

Cain barked his laugh, fluttering his mustache. "Meet Doog. Do you like his face? Ha! I gave him that wound myself--slammed my axe so hard into his face he leaked half his brain. He kind of looks like the canyon we live in, doesn't he?" He turned to the poor soul. "Here, boy, I have a treat for you."

Cain fished through his pocket, produced a wafer, and held it out. Doog ate it from his hand like a trained hound.

"By the Abyss, Cain," Rune muttered. "He's a man, not a dog."

Cain spat. "Ah, he's got no sense left in him. Took it with his face, I did; he's more beast than man now. I trained him myself. Want to see him do tricks? Sit, Doog, sit!"

"We have no time for this," Valien interjected. "Cain, enough of your games. Rune will fight the poor soul. And he will defeat him."

Rune bit his lip, not so sure about that. Doog was perhaps a halfwit, but he was twice Rune's size. Each of his arms could have been a person on its own.

"Valien..." he began.

The gruff knight strode toward him, grabbed his shoulders, and leaned close.

"Is there a problem, Rune?" Valien said, and a hint of a smile touched his lips. "I've trained you well. You are young and strong. You can defeat him."

Rune looked over at Doog. The brute was chortling and drooling and begging for treats from his master. An ugly sound rose from his wound, halfway between a yowl and a mewl. Rune wasn't sure whether it sounded pathetic or terrifying.

He leaned closer to Valien and whispered. "Stars, Valien, he's bigger than Beras."

Valien shrugged. "Should make a bigger sound when he falls." His face grew somber. "Rune, understand--Cain is an old sort of fighter. You're used to fighting among resistors, men of honor and hope and light. Cain is a different kind of man. He will not follow starlight or dreams of Old Requiem. He will follow *strength*. He will follow a man he believes can be king. Show him your strength today, and he will lend us his army." Valien nodded. "When you joined our fight, I never promised you safety. You knew that battles lay ahead. You fought soldiers in a great battle. This man you must fight alone." He dug his fingers into Rune's arms. "And greater enemies await you; someday you will face Frey himself in battle. First you must pass this test."

Rune looked again at Doog. He was now howling and swinging his arms; Cain was goading him with a spearhead like a man riling up a war dog before a fight.

If Kaelyn were here, she would say this is madness, Rune thought. *She would urge for calm, for peace, for another way.* He tightened his lips. *Yet Kaelyn isn't here, and Lord Devin Cain is a different sort of man; Valien is right about that. I'll have to play by his rules today.*

He nodded. "I will fight him."

They left the hall--Rune, Valien, and a hundred dwellers of the castle. They stood within the canyon. Outside the palace facade stood Lord Cain, wrapped in his ratty cloak, his wild red-and-white hair fluttering in the wind. At his side stood his daughter, the Lady Lana, clutching the hilt of her saber; her hair too billowed, its single white strand like a banner. Around them stood a crowd of canyon soldiers.

These men were Cain's personal host; they had served his family for hundreds of years, and they did not wear the black steel of the Legions. Their armor was pale, their cloaks gray like the cliffs around them. They did not bear the longswords of the Legions, but curved sabers shaped like the canyon they dwelled in. They wore the red spiral upon their armbands, as decreed for all soldiers in the empire, yet not upon their breastplates; there they sported the sigil of House Cain, two stone statues guarding a gateway.

The actual Stone Guardians towered above the men. Rune glanced up at them, then back down at the cracks at their feet. He swallowed when he remembered how close their fists had come to crushing him.

"Remember, Rune," Valien said, leaning close to whisper in his ear. "You will fight as dragons here. Fly fast. Do not hesitate to blow your fire. We have flown many times in the night. Use the sun now; let it blind your enemy."

Rune nodded and looked over at that enemy. Doog stood in the canyon, his iron collar and anklets gleaming. The beast tossed back his head and howled, a roar so loud the canyon seemed to shake and birds fled. Spittle flew from the smaller canyon rifting his face.

"I'm afraid," Rune said. Ice seemed to encase his innards.

Valien nodded. "All wise men fear battle. Only fools rush fearless into a fight. The true warrior is not he who feels no fear, but he who conquers fear."

Rune nodded, forcing himself to swallow, and clenched his fists to stop them from trembling.

I will conquer my fear, he told himself. *I will fly fast. I will use the sun. I will win this. For Kaelyn. For Requiem. For Tilla.*

"Doog!" Cain shouted and raised his fists. "Crack his bones!"

Doog repeated the gesture, raising his fists to the sky, and his howl pealed across the canyon. The scarred, collared man shifted into a dragon. Scales of motley grays, blacks, and browns rose upon him, clattering like mismatched plates of armor. His claws drove into the canyon floor, and his tattered wings raised storms of dust. Long horns grew from his head, but like his human form, the dragon Doog had no face; the same scar drove into his dragon's head. A single fang thrust out from the crevice, and fire smoldered within. His head looked like a volcano ready to erupt.

"Rune, shift!" Valien shouted.

Rune summoned his magic. Black scales flowed across him, and he beat his wings and soared.

The scarred, metallic dragon howled and flew toward him, a beast of rattling scales and smoke and spurting flame.

Rune blew his fire.

The jet blazed across the canyon, roaring and spinning. Doog howled and his flames burst, not a neat jet, but a wild fountain like exploding barrels of gunpowder. Rune's stream crashed against the inferno, and fire filled the canyon.

Rune beat his wings and rose from flame. He flew higher. The canyon walls raced at his sides. Below he saw Doog thrash in the blaze, and then the beast soared too, howling and lashing his tail. Doog blew more fire. The beast had no jaws for blowing narrow, flaming streams like other dragons; instead he spewed burning showers thick with saliva.

Rune cursed. He had trained to dodge thin jets of fire; he knew how to bank around them, then blow his own flames. Toward him rose an inescapable inferno like an overflowing smelter. He kept soaring. The fire kept rising below; Doog was still ascending, spraying his heat. The canyon walls raced at his sides, trapping Rune. The fire was rising too quickly; he'd never reach the canyon top in time.

He cursed, shut his eyes, and swooped.

He screamed as he crashed through the flames. His scales blazed; he felt the flesh beneath raise welts. He burst from the blaze, stretched out his claws, and slashed at Doog.

Rune yowled. Sparks flew. Doog's scales were thick as steel plates. Rune's claws flared in agony, not even denting the beast's scales.

He kept diving toward the canyon floor, smoke rising across him. The men howled and shouted below. Valien was shouting commands, but Rune couldn't make out the words. Doog yowled above him, and when Rune glanced up, he saw fire crashing down.

Stars damn it!

Rune swooped toward the canyon floor, then leveled off and skimmed across the cracks and stones. When he glanced over his shoulder, he saw Doog crash down onto the canyon floor, cracking the stone before rising again with a howl.

They raced through the canyon. Rune flapped his wings with all his strength, streaming over the canyon floor. The wind roared. The canyon walls blurred. Birds fled overhead. Flames crackled behind him, and when Rune glanced behind him, he saw the beast following. Doog flew at a totter. A burly dragon, his belly slammed against boulders, his tail lashed at canyon walls, and his claws tore the ground. Dust and rocks rained around him, and he screeched from his wound of a mouth, spraying fire.

Rune cursed, looked back ahead, and flew faster. His lungs and wings blazed with pain. The Castle-in-the-Cliff vanished behind.

He wanted to attack. He had trained to fight dragons. Yet this felt more like fighting an erupting volcano.

Rune snarled.

I tore off the wing of Shari Cadigus herself. I fought an army of legionaries and axehands. I can defeat this beast too.

The flames licked his tail. Rune narrowed his eyes, lowered his flight to a mere foot above the ground, and raced toward a towering boulder that rose from the canyon floor like a lighthouse. Doog squealed behind him, flames showering across the canyon and singeing Rune.

With a howl, Rune reached the boulder, curved his flight, and spun around it. Flames crashed against the stone. Rune came shooting back toward Doog and blew his fire.

The jet blazed and roared. Doog screeched. Flames crashed against him and Rune rose higher. He overshot Doog and swiped his claws, driving them across the dragon's back.

Sparks showered. Rune screamed. One of his claws tore off and clattered down. His blood spilled.

Bloody stars! he thought. Did the dragon have scales of steel?

He kept racing along the canyon, now moving back toward the Castle-in-the-Cliff. When he glanced behind him, he saw Doog following. The flames had blackened his scales, but the dragon was still howling and sputtering his fire and drool.

Rune flew with all his might, but he was too slow. Doog's claws wrapped around his tail. Rune floundered, caught in the grip. He kicked, slamming his claws into Doog's ruined race. The beast bellowed. His mouth, a mere hole with one fang, opened inside his scar. He drove his head forward and bit.

Rune roared. The fang drove into his leg, and blood spilled, and fear flooded Rune.

I can't win this. I will die here.

He kicked and beat his wings madly, unable to free himself. Doog pulled him down, and Rune slammed against the canyon floor. Rock cracked beneath him. Claws lashed him.

"Rune!" shouted a distant voice; it seemed to be calling from another world. "Rune, on your feet--burn him!"

He looked up, blinking, but saw only flames. The heat blasted his back. His scales widened in the heat and cracked. Pain drove through him like daggers, and the howls of the beast tore through him. His blood splashed across the canyon floor.

"Rune!" shouted the distant voice. "Up, damn you! On your feet."

Valien.

It was Valien shouting in the distance. In the cloud of pain, memories of his training returned to him: long nights swinging swords, flying as dragons, blasting smoke, and lashing claws tipped with wood.

Valien. Leader of the Resistance. The wisest, strongest man Rune had known. The man who raised the torch of Requiem, who gave Rune hope.

I will not die today, Valien.

He snarled, shoved against the canyon floor, and flipped onto his back.

Doog howled atop him, a demon of scale and flame, twice his size and showering fire and blood and smoke.

I maimed Shari Cadigus. I toppled the walls of Castra Luna. I can defeat him.

Doog's maw came lashing down, his fang thirsty for more blood. Lying on his back, wings splayed out, Rune blew his fire.

The jet shrieked, crashed against Doog's face, and showered back down onto Rune. He closed his eyes against the heat. The weight lifted above him. Rune leaped up, beat his wings, and flew.

He raced back toward the Castle-in-the-Cliff. Behind him, Doog howled and chased, claws banging against the floor, tail chipping the canyon walls at their sides. They raced through fire and dust and raining rocks.

I can't cut him, Rune thought. *I can't claw or bite him. I slammed my fire into his head, and still he flies.*

Rune gritted his teeth.

He's too strong. He's too big. I cannot cut or burn him.

He roared, blood in his eyes.

I will crush him.

He saw the castle facade ahead. Cain and the others still stood outside the palace, watching and howling and cheering. The Stone Guardians framed the castle gates, a hundred feet tall.

Valien's words echoed in his mind. *The true warrior is not he who feels no fear, but he who conquers fear.*

Rune roared and flew toward the palace gates. His wings beat and raised storms of dust. In mid-flight, he released his magic.

He returned to human form.

He tumbled through the air, shouted, and landed at the feet of a statue.

He looked up. He saw Doog flying toward him, belly skimming the canyon floor, claws reaching out to tear him apart.

The statue creaked above.

Rune leaped back.

The burly, scarred dragon came flying beneath the statue.

The statue's fist slammed down.

Stone drove against scales. The fist crushed Doog's head like a war hammer crushing a tin helmet. The dragon's skull caved in. Blood and gore gushed out. Doog's single fang tore free and clattered against the canyon floor. He gave a few last flaps of his wings, and his tail lashed... and he lay still.

Rune panted, still in human form, his clothes soaked with sweat and blood. Silence fell across the canyon. The hundreds of soldiers watched, not daring to breathe.

The stone statue raised its fist, straightened, and stared blankly ahead. Below, Doog's skull leaked. With a fluttering of dust, the dragon returned to human form. He lay dead, a burly man, his head caved in.

Rune stood, breath shaking, legs bleeding, and clothes smoking. He stared down at the corpse. He shook his head, clenched his fists, and looked up at Lord Cain with burning eyes.

"He was only a halfwit," Rune said, voice hoarse. "He was only a poor, scarred man with the mind of a child. And you made him fight." Rune spat. "I slew him, Cain. I slew him for you." He stepped up toward the lord, fists shaking, and hissed. "But know this--I will never more shed blood for your sport. I fly to kill Frey Cadigus next, and you will fight with me, or it will be your blood I shed once Frey's throne is mine."

Lord Cain stared back, eyes shrewd beneath his bushy brows. His lips twisted. His face was like beaten leather bristly with red and white stubble. His fists clenched too, veins rose in his neck, and Rune was sure the lord would strike him.

Then Cain snorted out a great laugh that ruffled his mustache.

"Aye, you scoundrel!" the lord boomed, grabbed Rune, and pulled him into a crushing embrace. He then shoved him back and punched Rune's shoulder. "Your cheeks might be as smooth as a virgin's teats, but you've got bollocks, boy."

He roared his laughter. It echoed across the canyon. Rune only stared, fists still tight. Sweat and blood dripped down his forehead, but he would not even blink. He kept staring at the lord.

"Fight with me, Cain," he said.

Lord Cain was still roaring his laughter, chest heaving. "Aye, I'll fight with you, lad. We two... we will shed blood together." He raised his fist and roared. "We will roast Frey's warty backside, and the south will be mine! House Cain will rise!"

His soldiers repeated the cry, raising fists and howling the name of their lord.

Rune stood still, blood dripping. Valien approached him, eyes somber, and clutched his shoulders.

"You did well, Rune," the older man said.

Rune did not turn to look at him. He only stared down at the brute's corpse.

Killing him was a mercy, Rune told himself, and his eyes stung. *Cain tortured him. Cain drove that axe into his face, then forced him to beg for treats like a dog. It was a mercy.*

And yet Rune's heart twisted, and he couldn't swallow the lump in his throat.

Lady Lana approached him too. Rune looked up at her, wondering how a woman so fair, her face pale and noble, could have been born to a monster like Cain.

"Rune," she said softly. "Stay with us tonight. Feast with us. We will tend to your wounds, then eat and drink."

Rune looked over her shoulder at Lord Cain; the man was roaring with laughter and pointing at the dead Doog.

Kaelyn's words echoed in his mind, soft and kind.

The wise work with small devils to slay the big ones.

Rune closed his eyes. She had spoken those words about Beras, and Rune clung to them now, but they could not warm the ice in his belly.

"We're leaving this place," he said and opened his eyes. He looked at Valien. "We leave now. Come, Valien. There's still an hour of daylight. We can cross a few miles before night falls." His voice sounded too dry to him, too pained. "We're going back."

Without waiting for a reply, Rune shifted into a dragon, took flight, and soared. The canyon walls blurred at his sides. When he reached the forest above, he landed among the trees, shifted back into a man, and gritted his teeth so hard they hurt. He walked through the forest, refusing to look back.

SCRAGGLES

He walked through the forest, hungry and thirsty and so weary he almost fell. His tongue lolled. His belly twisted, feeling so shrunken it could touch his back. The trees rose around him in the sunset, branches creaking and reaching out like cruel men in armor. They frightened Scraggles, but he had to keep moving. He had to find food. He had to find water. And more than anything, he had to find his master.

He had been walking for a long time now. Scraggles could barely remember the last time he lay upon a blanket, ate a true meal, or felt warm and safe. Yesterday he had caught a robin and eaten it, then retched it up later. He had not eaten since. A few miles back he had drunk from a stream, but the water had tasted foul, and his throat still blazed.

I need food, he thought. *I need real food--roast meats and stewed vegetables and anything hot and hearty.*

He thought back to the food at the Old Wheel. His master would feed him from his table, and Scraggles would feast upon roast boar, fresh bread, and cheese, and he would even drink of the tavern's ale. There had been a warm fireplace too, a rope to gnaw, and a blanket by the hearth Scraggles would rest on. There had been his master tending to him, patting him, and hugging him in the cold nights.

All that was gone now. The woman with the pale hair had snatched his master from the tavern. The dragon had swooped and its fire rained. Scraggles had barely escaped the flames. He had raced through the city, his fur smoking, seeking his master, but could not find him. He had spent moons on the boardwalk, waiting for Master to return, never losing hope. Finally he had set out into the forest, seeking him.

How far back was the town? Scraggles didn't know. How many days had he been wandering this forest? Far too many. He was so thin now. So hungry. So weak and afraid.

But I must keep going, Scraggles thought, panting as he walked over the fallen leaves. *I must find Master. I must find Rune.*

He tossed back his head and yowled. Back at the Old Wheel tavern, whenever he'd yowl, his master would come with food, with pats, with warmth and companionship. Scraggles howled again and again in the forest, as he did every day, and every time, he held his breath and expected Rune to come racing between the trees.

But he never did.

And Scraggles just had to keep walking.

Head hung low, he forced himself to move on, ignoring the pain in his paws. The sun was falling fast. If Scraggles could not find food before the darkness, the hunger would gnaw on him all night, keeping him awake. He looked around, seeking more birds, but they all stood high upon the branches. He saw a squirrel and made a halfhearted attempt to grab it, but it fled into the canopy.

Maybe I should turn back, Scraggles thought. *I could return to the town. I might find food there. I could eat dead fish on the beach or beg for scraps from passersby.*

But no. He couldn't go back. He'd come too far already. There was nothing left for him in the town. His master was no longer there. Scraggles had seen it. The pale woman had become a dragon, lifted his master, and flown off into the forest.

I will find you, Master, Scraggles thought. *I'll keep going forever, even if I die here.*

He kept walking.

The sun fell behind the trees. Long shadows stretched out, then faded into darkness. Only the stars lit the night. The wind moaned, the trees creaked, and a distant wolf howled.

Fear filled Scraggles and he mewled. Two days ago, a jackal had pounced and bitten his flank. The wound still blazed. And wolves were even larger; Scraggles had seen one howling upon a hilltop last night.

If they catch me, they will kill me, he thought and whimpered again.

He kept walking. He had to keep going. He dared not sleep, not with wolves nearby. The trees creaked in the darkness and branches snagged him. More howls rose. Scraggles walked on.

I have to rest, he thought. He was so tired. So very tired. He had to lie down. He could curl up here. He could place his head against his paws, close his eyes, and wait for death to find him. It wouldn't be long. Another day or two, and the thirst would claim him, or maybe the wolves. And his pain would end.

He blinked. He took another step. He was so weary.

I'll lie down for only a bit, he thought. *I'll close my eyes. Maybe I'll dream of Master.*

He sat upon the forest floor, the wolves howled, and Scraggles whimpered.

I miss you, Master. Do you too wander this forest? Do you too seek me?

Scraggles lay down. He placed his head on his paws and shivered in the cold. He was about to close his eyes when he glimpsed the flicker of light.

He raised his head.

He stared.

There, he saw it! Light ahead! Firelight!

Scraggles leaped to his feet. Memories of the fireplace back home filled him. He could almost feel that warmth again. A fire crackled ahead! The scent of smoke wafted, rich and intoxicating in his nostrils, overpowering. Another scent wafted beneath it; the scent of a traveler.

Master?

Scraggles ran.

He ran through the darkness. His paws banged against a root, he fell hard onto the ground, then leaped up and kept running. He followed the scent, and the light grew ahead.

He raced around an oak and saw it there.

A campfire.

A human sat there, shivering in the cold.

Master?

Scraggles froze. He stood in the shadows. He sniffed.

The human was grumbling and rubbing shivering hands before the fire. Scraggles stared, frozen in place, his tail straight like a branch. His nose twitched.

"Damn the stars and damn the Legions and damn this stupid cold!" the human said and spat.

Scraggles didn't understand those words, but the voice sounded angry.

It's not Master's voice.

Disappointment curdled in his belly like that time he'd eaten moldy cheese. Scraggles took a step forward, keeping himself hidden in the shadows, and stared more closely.

He'd have to be careful. Humans could be dangerous. Scraggles had learned that in this forest. He had come across humans here before. One had kicked him, and another had drawn his sword and scared him off. Even back home, some humans on the street would treat him cruelly, mocking him.

Some humans were friends, others were foes. Scraggles did not understand humans well, but he knew that much. He'd have to tread carefully here. If this one was a friend, there might be food and warmth here. Or there might be stones and kicks and swords.

He inched closer, crept around a tree, and stared at the traveler by the campfire.

It was a young woman. She was much smaller than his master. She was the size of a child--maybe even smaller than Scraggles--but her face seemed older, the same age as Master's face. She had short, brown hair that fell across her brow. Her face was orange in the firelight, her nose upturned, and her eyes dark.

A memory stirred in Scraggles.

He knew this one! He remembered her scent.

The memories blazed so powerfully he almost fell. In his mind, he was running along the beach again. The sand flew from beneath his paws. The salty wind filled his nostrils, rich with the scent of fish, crabs, and seawater. He ran through the waves, lapping the salty water and spitting it out, and rolling through the sand. And she was there too. This young woman with short hair would pet him, feed him scraps, and wrestle him in the sand.

She was from home!

"Good pup!" she had said on the beach, hugging him. "Good pup. You love your Aunt Erry, don't you?"

Scraggles burst into a run.

He leaped from the shadows, raced around the campfire, and stood panting before the woman.

She gasped. Her eyes widened. Scraggles froze, hesitating, not sure she would remember him. He wanted to leap onto her, but waited, a hint of fear still inside him.

Erry rubbed her eyes and blinked.

"Merciful stars!" she blurted out, squinted, and tilted her head. "I'm dreaming! Scraggles?"

It was her.

Scraggles grinned, leaped onto her, and began licking her face.

"Burn me!" she said, laughed, and fell onto the forest floor. "Scraggles, what the Abyss are you doing here? Is Rune here?"

He leaped onto her, licking her face and wrestling her and not letting her rise. She laughed, ruffled his fur, and finally pushed him off.

"Bloody stars, Scraggles, I was sure you were a wolf or outlaw or something." She looked around at the dark forest. "Cadport must be leagues from here. Are you lost? Where's Rune?"

Scraggles panted, tail wagging furiously. He didn't understand all of that. But he knew that Cadport was the name of his home. And he knew that Rune was the name of his master. She was asking about them. She wanted to find Master too, he realized.

Thinking of Master, his joy left him. Ice filled his belly, and he gave a plaintive yowl.

Erry's eyes softened. She sighed.

"You're lost too, aren't you, Scrags?" she said. She scrunched her lips, tapped her chin, and looked up at the trees. "Bollocks, old boy, but I've only been walking for three days. We must be leagues and leagues away from Cadport, *days* away." She frowned at him. "How the Abyss did you make it this far?"

He panted, leaped onto her again, and nuzzled her cheek. He wanted to tell her so much. He wanted to speak like humans, to tell her of the long days in the forest, the Old Wheel burning, and the pretty woman stealing Rune. Never before had Scraggles wished for the gift of speech so badly. He tried to talk now, giving a rumbling whine. Whenever he attempted speech back at home, Master would laugh and pat him, but Erry only sighed.

"Oh Scrags, what are you trying to tell me?"   She raised her voice and cried out. "Rune! Rune, are you out here? Stars, Rune!"

The wolves answered. Their howls surrounded the camp. Erry closed her mouth, hissed, and grabbed the hilt of her sword. Scraggles tensed, his tail shot out like an arrow, and he growled.

"I think," Erry whispered, "we better be a little more quiet." She took a step closer to the campfire, keeping her hand on her sword. "Stay close to the fire, Scraggles. Wolves fear fire. But you're brave, aren't you?"

The wolf howls continued for long moments before dying off. Erry remained standing for a while longer, staring around, then finally sat down. She rummaged through her pack and pulled out bread rolls, smoked sausages, and cheese.

"It's not much," Erry said, "and it's all the food I have left." She sighed. "I was going to save half for breakfast tomorrow, but damn it, Scraggles, you look thinner than fish bones."

Scraggles salivated and his belly rumbled. The scent of the food filled his nostrils and his head swam with hunger.

"Here, you old mutt," Erry said, sighed, and gave him a bread roll. "Eat it."

Drooling more than he ever had, Scraggles scarfed it down.

They shared the rest of the food in silence. Erry had a canteen of water too, and she let Scraggles drink half. When their meal was done, they lay down by the fire. The trees creaked, the wind moaned, and they huddled close for warmth. Scraggles sneaked under her cloak, tossed a leg across her, and licked her cheek.

"God, Scrags, your breath stinks," Erry said. "Breathe the other way!" She pushed his head away, then sighed. "Oh, Scrags, what are we even doing here? We're both lost. We both have no idea where to go."

Scraggles didn't understand that, but he knew she was sad. He could hear it in her voice. He nuzzled her with his nose, trying to comfort her, and she rubbed his neck.

"We'll figure something out," she said. Her voice cracked and her eyes dampened. "I promise you. We can't go back to Cadport. There are too many soldiers there. I bet that's why you escaped." She sniffed. "And we can't go back to the Legions anymore, not after what I did; they'd bloody hang me for that. Looks like it's just you and me in the forest from now on, pup."

Scraggles whimpered and shut his eyes. Erry sighed and held him close. The fire died to embers. They slept.

LERESY

He was drinking around the campfire with his men, singing old war songs, when his guards dragged in the kicking, muddy girl.

They had been living in the woods for many days now, never staying in one place for more than a night. A thousand gruff, loud men who loved to sing and burn bright campfires, they hid about as well as a naked prostitute among priestesses. And so Leresy had been driving them southward day by day. When the clouds offered cover, they flew. When the skies were clear, they walked under the forest canopy. When darkness fell, they drank and sang the nights away. League by league, they moved south, away from the capital, away from the emperor.

He'll come after me soon, Leresy knew. *My father will not tolerate me stealing a thousand of his soldiers. He'll send an army after me. Maybe he already has.* The thought tickled him. *Let him come! I'll slay him and his men.*

And so they sang in the dark forest, raised smoke from a hundred fires, and kept their armor on and their swords polished.

"Let Frey Cadigus fly here!" Leresy cried in the night. He drank deeply from his mug of ale. "Let him come and die in our fire."

He stumbled toward his campfire where a suckling boar was roasting. Leresy laughed to see it. The poor beast had a spit stuck up its bottom, and an apple filled its mouth. Fat and juices dripped into the embers below. Leresy imagined his father and sister roasting in his camp. They too were pigs. He would shove spits up their bottoms too and cook them alive. He gave the boar a turn, allowing the fire to roast its back.

"Tonight we drink and dine!" he shouted and waved his mug. "By the moon's turn, we will reach the sea, men. We fly south to unknown lands! We fly to Terra Incognita where no dragon has ever flown. We will claim the wild lands and live like kings!"

They cheered and waved mugs.

"My father claims he slew all other races, purifying the world," Leresy continued. "But I say he lies! I say many foreign women still live--lush, nubile women of the southern wilderness." His men cheered, and Leresy raised his voice. "We will be explorers, and we will find them! They are waiting for true men of the north to bed them. We will make them ours!"

The men howled.

One of them stood up, a gaunt and tall man named Yorne. His hair was brown and shaggy, his face weathered, and his forearms tattooed with dragons.

"To Leresy!" he announced, raised his mug, and drank.

Leresy raised his own mug in salute. "We are Leresy's Lechers!" he said. "We are an army. We will rule the wild lands overseas, and if my father flies against us, we will roast his head upon our fires."

They were carving the boar, opening another cask of ale, and singing hoarsely when the guards dragged the girl into the camp.

"Let me go, you reeking, toad-warted sons of whores!" the girl was screaming, floundering in the grip of the guards. "Let me go now, maggots, or I'll gut you like fish and piss on your graves!"

Leresy blinked, rubbed his eyes, and couldn't help but laugh. The young woman was barely larger than a child, her face still fresh with youth. Her cheeks were red, and mud caked her short hair. Her wrists were tied behind her back, and Leresy's guards manhandled her forward. The girl kicked and screamed and tried to bite, but could not free herself.

"You yeasty, sheep-bedding halfwits!" she shouted, tossing her head from side to side. "Face me like men, you puny boy-loving eunuchs! I'll crush you like the worms that you are."

The guards kept dragging her forward, moving between the campfires until they stood before Leresy. The girl kept screaming. A bruise spread beneath one of her eyes, and her lip swelled.

"Lord Leresy!" one of the guards said. "We caught this one slinking outside our camp. A common thief. Probably wanted to steal food. She had a dog too, but the mutt ran off."

"You are dogs!" the girl screamed. "Your mothers were bitches and your fathers pissed on walls!" She kicked wildly, held in midair. "Give me back my sword, and I'll slice you into rat food!"

The men of his camp gathered around and laughter roared. The young woman couldn't have weighed more than a hundred pounds in armor, and even held above the ground, her head barely reached the guards' shoulders. And yet she squirmed, shouted, and kicked like an enraged bull.

"I know this one," Leresy said. He tapped his cheek, stepped closer to the girl, and scrutinized her. "I've seen her before somewhere."

She spat at him.

The glob hit Leresy's forehead and dripped down his face.

"And I know you, Leresy Cadigus," the girl said. "You tell your thugs to untie me, or by the stars, next thing that hits your face is my boot."

Leresy cleared his throat. Stiffly, he lifted the hem of his cloak and cleaned her spit off his face.

"You know, I do love a wild woman," he said, reached out to caress her cheek, and pulled his hand back when she snapped her teeth. "I bet you're a wild one in bed."

"I thought you only bed sheep," she said and raised her chin, still held in the guards' grips.

He sighed. "Your name is Erry. I remember. Periva Erry Docker, the daughter of a whore from Cadport. You served me in Castra Luna. By the Abyss, I'm pretty sure I paid good copper for your mother a few years back." He tilted his head. "How much do you charge now? I bet you bed men for bread crusts."

"I bet you bed them for gold, Leresy," she said. "Oh yes, you're a pricey one."

He stared at her top to bottom, considering. The girl was too scrawny. She stood barely taller than a child, she had no teats to speak of--at least, none that he could see under her tunic--and her hips were narrow like a boy's. Leresy liked his women rounded enough to grab on to. This one was filthy besides, all caked in mud and sweat. And yet... she was still the only woman he'd seen in days. If he closed his eyes when bedding her and thought of Nairi instead, she would serve.

He turned his attention to the guards holding her. "Let her go. This runt used to be my soldier. She will serve me here too."

The guards hesitated. "My lord?" one said. "She bit my arm back in the forest. She kicked Joran in the shin. She might be a runt, but she's wild."

"I like them wild," Leresy said. "I will tame her. Leave her arms bound, but let her stand. She's cranky because she's hungry and thirsty. We'll let her eat and drink." He looked at her. "Share our meat and ale, Erry Docker. You were my soldier. I'll look after you." He touched her cheek. "Be a good girl now."

The guards released her. Erry landed on her feet, hissed, and whipped her head from side to side. She tugged at the ropes binding her wrists but could not free herself. Panting, she stared around the camp, letting her gaze fall upon the men, the campfires, the roasting boars, and the copious amounts of ale. Her eyes narrowed.

"Bloody shite, Leresy," she said. "You look like a pack of outlaws. Burn me!"

Leresy cleared his throat. "Well, we *are* outlaws now, in a sense." He shrugged. "I got weary of life in the court. All fancy dress and pomp and fake flattery. I told my father to go shag a dog, took my men south, and here we are. Behold!" He waved his mug around. "My new domain and my new band of merry men. Meet Leresy's Lechers!"

Erry snorted. "Leresy's Lechers? Did you invent that name?" She tossed back her head and laughed. "Merciful stars, it's not very intimidating, is it? Why not... Leresy's Lepers, or... Leresy's Bastards or something? If you're outlaws, you need to sound tough and scary, not just lustful."

"Well, the first one's disgusting," Leresy said, "and the second one don't rhyme."

"Leresy's Lechers don't rhyme either," Erry retorted, chin raised. "You're thinking of alliteration, not rhyming."

He snorted. "Big words for a dock rat." He grabbed her shoulder. "Watch your tongue, little one, lest I cut it from your mou--"

He had not finished his sentence when a shadow leaped.

Wild barking rose.

A black dog came running into the camp, a beast nearly as large as a wolf. The hound snarled and came racing toward Leresy.

"Scrags, no!" Erry shouted.

The guards cursed and one kicked, hitting the dog in the belly. The beast fell, mewled, and leaped back up.

"Scraggles, down!" Erry cried. She leaped toward the dog and leaned over it, whispering into its ear. It growled beneath her and stared at Leresy, seemingly unsure whether to huddle with Erry or resume the attack.

"Bloody stars!" Leresy cursed. "Men, kill that flea-bitten thing."

"No!" Erry shouted, and tears brimmed in her eyes. "Please, my lord! Don't hurt him. He's my dog. Well, he's a friend's dog. But I'm looking after him now." Wrists still tied behind her back, she huddled over the mutt. "Don't hurt him. I'll do anything, but don't hurt the dog."

Well well, Leresy thought. The little urchin who screamed, cursed, and kicked had a soft spot. That was good. The dog would help tame this one. He licked his lips. *And she said she'd do anything...*

"Men!" he said. "Do not harm this hound. Give him water. Feed him. Treat him as if he came from my royal kennels." He reached down and touched Erry's hair. "Stand up, child. Your dog will be safe. I'll protect him, and I'll protect you."

She stood up and glared at him. "Child? I'm nineteen years old, Leresy, same age as you."

Yet her voice had lost its fire, and her eyes were still damp.

"Very well, you're a big girl now," he said and gave her a mocking smile. "And I'll feed you too, Erry, and I'll treat you well--as well as I treat my dogs. Come with me into my tent. We'll eat and drink there, and we'll be warm." He looked at the mutt. "The dog stays here."

They stepped into his tent, leaving the songs and cheer outside.

It was a small tent, no larger than the room he'd frequent in the Bad Cats brothel. He had a cot with an old blanket, a chest of clothes, and a table laden with jugs. It was enough for Leresy. His days of pomp and grandeur seemed but a distant memory; he had lost the desire for pomp when the resistors slew his wife upon the forest.

"Stars, Leresy," Erry said softly. "I've been to your chamber at Castra Luna. You had tapestries. A stained-glass window. A bed larger than any I've ever seen. You had fine cloaks with fur and embroidery." She looked around the tent and smiled crookedly. "You live like a common soldier now."

He snorted, walked to a table, and poured a mug of wine.

"What were you doing in my chambers in Castra Luna?"

She shrugged. "Rifling through your chest of undergarments, of course. Stars, Leresy, you own more corsets than I do."

"Funny," he said. "Funny girl. That chamber, Docker... that chamber was nothing but a fisherman's hut compared to the grandeur of the capital." He stared at the tent wall, lost in memory. "Have you ever seen them? The walls and towers of Nova Vita?"

She shook her head. "I've seen the boardwalk at Cadport and I've seen forts. I've never seen grandeur, my lord."

He closed his eyes. "The walls rise so tall there, Docker. Taller than you can imagine. The towers rise above them, and ten thousand banners fly. The streets are so wide twenty soldiers march abreast. And the palace! The palace scratches the sky itself, and--" He stopped himself. He clenched his jaw. "But I will build myself a new kingdom, a better kingdom, a realm of wonder in the south, far beyond my father's reach." He turned toward her. "I will take you there with me. You are mine now, Erry Docker, and I will look after you. You are safe with me. All conquerors have concubines; you will be mine."

She gave him a crooked smile. "Will you untie me first?"

He raised an eyebrow. "Why would I do that?"

She slunk forward, pressed herself against him, and looked up into his eyes, her chin against his chest.

"Because I'm asking you nicely?"

He snorted. "I prefer you tied up."

She rolled her eyes, turned her back toward him, and bent her knees. Fast as a weasel, she reached out her tied hands, grabbed his dagger from his boot, and leaped away.

"Thief!" he shouted and gasped.

She spun back toward him, dagger clutched behind her, and flashed a grin.

"It's how I survived in Cadport." She twisted her lips, then brought her hands forward. The rope that had bound her fell severed at her feet. "How would you like your dagger back? In your neck or in your chest?"

"How about," he said, "you hand it over hilt first, and you may eat our boar, drink our wine, and share my bed. Surely those pleasures eclipse the pleasure of stabbing me."

She twisted her lips. "How fatty is the boar?"

"Very."

"We shall see. Let's eat first; I'll keep the dagger in the meanwhile."

He shouted for his men, and one brought in a plate piled high with steaming roast meat. When the man left, Leresy held out one of his two chairs.

"Sit," he said to Erry, "and we'll dine."

He had never seen a woman eat so fast.

Erry was perhaps as small as a child, but she attacked the roast boar like a starving jackal. She stuffed the meat into her mouth until her cheeks bulged, gulped noisily, and drank wine directly from the jug. After every bite, she wiped her lips with the back of her hand, then reached for more.

"Have you ever heard of chewing?" Leresy asked her, nibbling his own serving.

She glared at him over her plate. "Chewing is for fine, fancy-pants princelings like you." She stuffed more meat into her mouth. "But I'm from the docks and mgfdfffgg..."

He shook his head sadly. "You're eating your own weight in food. How do you stay so small?"

She grabbed the jug of wine, held it up with both hands, and guzzled. When she slammed it down, wine dribbled down her chin.

"I'm like a snake," she said. "I eat a lot when I can find it. It usually has to last a while."

When the plate was empty--Erry had eaten most of the meal--she licked it clean. With a sigh, she leaned back, kicked off her boots, and slammed her feet onto the table.

"I don't want to see your smelly feet," Leresy said, staring at them in distaste.

She wriggled her toes and raised an eyebrow. "They're not smelly. I'm not one of your filthy men. I'm a petite, lovely young maiden."

"I wouldn't know by the way you eat," he said. "You could eat and drink my men under the table."

She closed her eyes, and an impish smile spread across her face. After a moment, she nodded and rose to her feet.

"Very well," she said. "I'm ready now."

She walked to the bed, turned toward him, and began to undress.

Leresy stared in disbelief, one eyebrow firmly raised. Erry did not undress seductively like Dawn and Dusk and the other girls at the Bad Cats. She made it seem as casual as a girl getting ready to bathe. When all her clothes were gone, she stood before him, staring at him curiously.

"Well?" she said. "Are you just going to sit there?"

Leresy stared at her.

Bloody stars, he thought. *I was right. Barely any teats on this one.*

And yet his loins stirred, and he found himself marveling at how smooth her skin was and how lithe her limbs.

"Do you always undress in strange men's tents?" he asked, still seated at the table.

"You're not a stranger, my lord," she said. "In Castra Luna, I dreamed of this. Whenever I sneaked into your chambers--and I did several times--I dreamed of this. But I was always afraid, unsure if you wanted me. You fancied Tilla then, I knew it." Her eyes hardened. "But Tilla is gone from you now. And I'm here. You said that I'm yours now, Leresy. So make me yours."

She climbed onto his bed, lay down upon her belly, and closed her eyes.

Leresy stood up, walked toward the bed, and stared down at her. *Flaming Abyss,* he thought. He had never known a woman to give herself to him so easily--at least, not one he wasn't buying. Without her muddy clothes, and despite her boyish hair and boyish frame, she seemed oddly intoxicating to him. He sucked in his breath, and he took her.

He took her roughly. He conquered her. He had never taken a woman so roughly, not in all his days of conquering them. He hurt her. He was sure he hurt her, yet she made not a sound. She had let many men hurt her, he realized. She had let many men claim her like this, lying down with her eyes closed, offering her body to get what she needed--if not money then food or protection or shelter. Leresy did not care. From this day she would be his alone.

When he was done with her, he wanted to toss her out of his tent. He hated women sleeping in his bed; he always had. He slept alone; he always did. He going to grab her, to toss her out, but he found himself holding her desperately and stroking her hair, and tears filled his eyes.

"I love you, Nairi," he whispered. "I love you."

They lay in his bed as his candles guttered. He kept stroking her hair, short hair like a boy's, and holding her so close, and his eyes stung. He had never let a woman sleep in his bed. Tonight he slept with Erry Docker in his arms.

KAELYN

She walked through Lynport, her cloak wrapped around her and fear gripping her heart.

Soldiers lined the streets, standing vigil at every corner, their helms hiding their faces. An imperial dragon patrolled the sky, clad in black armor bearing red spirals, his flames crackling in a wake. Kaelyn tightened her cloak around her, struggling to calm her trembling fingers. She felt bare without her sword and bow, as fragile as a mouse treading among cats.

I've walked here before in disguise, she told herself. She had visited Lynport--Cadport to her father, but always Lynport to her--dressed as a priestess twice before. *I will live today too.*

She walked around a bakery where a white scarf hung at the window, a sign of mourning. This house, like many in Lynport, had lost a soldier in Castra Luna. Kaelyn swallowed an icy lump in her throat.

Today Lynport is more dangerous than ever, she knew. *Today the resistors are no heroes here, but demons. We slew the youths of this city.*

Kaelyn reached for her sword--the hundredth time today--and found it missing. She took a deep breath, steeling herself, and kept walking.

She passed by a tannery, a chandlery, a smithy, and a dozen other workshops. They were built of wattle and daub, white clay filling the space between their timber frameworks. From the ground floors wafted the sounds and smells of their trades: the ring of hammers on anvils, the tangy scent of beeswax molded into candles, the creak of looms weaving cloth, and more. At their top floors, where the tradesmen and their families lived, shadows moved behind windows and more white scarves flew.

So many scarves, Kaelyn thought, eyes stinging. *So many youths we killed.*

As she walked down the cobbled road, she looked to her left. Alleys sloped between houses down to the boardwalk. The sea churned gray there, waves spraying foam like watery phoenixes rising. She glimpsed the cannon, the oldest one in Requiem, watching the southern horizon.

The Old Wheel used to stand nearby, Kaelyn thought. As she walked by another alley, she stared south and saw an empty patch of rubble and ash. She whispered a prayer.

Yet today she had a new errand here. She raised her head and looked northwest instead. There, upon a hill, she saw the fortress rising. Kaelyn squared her shoulders and clenched her fists.

Castellum Acta rose craggy and tall, a single tower above a wide hall. Bird droppings and moss stained its tan bricks. Arrowslits lined its walls. Battlements crowned the tower, and two dragons perched there, clad in bladed helms, watching the city. Flags of the red spiral thudded around them.

Castellum Acta, Kaelyn thought with a shudder. For five hundred years, benevolent lords had ruled here, governing a prosperous port. Today a general of the Legions, a pet of the emperor, lurked behind those bricks.

The man I must kill today, Kaelyn thought.

She trudged up a narrow, cobbled road that climbed the hill. The fortress rose above her. Boulders and brambles littered the sandy hillsides, and gulls circled above, cawing in mockery. As she climbed higher, Kaelyn rose above the city roofs. When she looked behind her, she could see Lynport's boardwalk lined with rotting shops, the docks that stretched into the water like fingers, and the sea rolling into the horizon. The scent of saltwater tickled her nostrils, and the waves whispered in her ears.

"Girl!" rose a growl. "Girl, halt!"

Kaelyn spun back toward the fort, which rose a hundred yards away upon the hilltop. Two soldiers came walking down from its gates, swords drawn. Upon the tower, the sentinel dragons glared, smoke rising from their nostrils.

When the guards reached her, Kaelyn curtsied.

"Good morning, sons of Requiem," she said. "I've come to see General Gorne, lord of this fort." She handed them a scroll sealed with a snake stamp. "A birthday gift from Lord Teus of Castellum Sil. It is General Gorne's birthday, is it not?"

The soldiers frowned, and one snatched the scroll from her hand.

"What's this then?" he demanded. "This scroll is a gift?"

Kaelyn gave him a crooked smile, pulled open her cloak, and revealed the scanty silks she wore beneath.

"No, my lord," she said. "I am. Lord Teus, a friend of your commander, already paid for my services. I shall be spending the night."

Their eyes widened, and Kaelyn sighed inwardly. Men were so easy to fool. She tugged her cloak back shut and glared at them.

"Well, take me to your lord," she said. "He would not like you delaying his gift."

Soon they entered the gates of Castellum Acta. Inside the main hall, Kaelyn held her breath and her heart pounded. The whisper of waves and the salty air faded behind; she stood among stone and shadows.

Columns supported a vaulted ceiling. Doorways led to other halls; through them, Kaelyn saw a dining room, an armory, and a barracks full of cots. Dozens of soldiers moved through the chambers, and the clank of armor echoed.

At the hall's end, a trestle table stood below a banner of the red spiral. General Gorne, Lord of Cadport, sat at the head seat.

"Commander Gorne!" cried one of the guards, slamming fist against chest. "A gift for you, Commander. Lord Teus sent her."

General Gorne leaned across the table, and his eyes narrowed. Upon his breastplate, he sported an engraving of a boar, sigil of his house. The man himself bore a striking resemblance to his emblem. He was beefy and pink-skinned, and his wide nose spread across his face like a snout. His hair was such a pale blond, it was nearly white, cut to stubble too sparse to hide his scalp.

Please don't let him recognize me, stars, Kaelyn prayed, and her fingers trembled. Gorne had visited the capital eight years ago and dined with her family. Kaelyn had been only a child, but still she caught her breath. *If he recognizes me, all is lost.*

"Teus?" the porcine lord said and rose to his feet. Despite his hoggish appearance, his eyes were shrewd. "Lord Teus is an old goat's piddle stain." He glared at Kaelyn. "Who are you, girl?"

She curtsied, allowing her cloak to open seemingly by accident, revealing the silks she wore beneath. The thin cloth showed more than it hid.

"Your birthday gift," she said. "That is all, my lord. Teus has paid for me already."

Gorne stomped around the table, frowning. He moved at a waddle, nearly as wide as he was tall. When he reached her, he placed a finger under her chin--that finger was wide as a sausage-- and lifted her face toward his. He scrutinized her. His eyes were pale blue, and his nose was bulbous and veined.

"Teus must be after my son," he said, disgust dripping from his voice. "The old bastard's daughter is coming of age. The pathetic gutter lump must want to soften me before suggesting a marriage between our houses." He snorted, shoved Kaelyn back, and roared to his hall. "As if House Gorne would stain its blood with the venom of Teus!"

The soldiers across the hall cheered at this--Kaelyn guessed they'd cheer at anything their commander announced loudly enough. She cursed inwardly, and sweat trickled down her back.

He might not have recognized me, but he'll send me away, she thought with a chill. *Stars, or he'll imprison me, or he'll toss me to his men, and our plan is doomed.*

"My... my lord?" she asked. She straightened, allowing her cloak to open another inch. "Shall I return to Lord Teus? I'm already paid for, and... if your lordship would return me, I will gladly warm Lord Teus's bed instead."

He spun toward her. His lip curled back, revealing small, sharp teeth. With a hand like a paw, he grabbed her arm.

"Oh, I'll have my gift," he said, and his eyes simmered. "Teus beds only the goats he raises on that forsaken farm he calls a fort. We'll have a taste of you, girl."

He dragged her from the hall, his men howling behind, and onto a staircase. They climbed up the tower. His fingers dug into her arm, and she stumbled behind him, struggling to climb fast enough. As the stairs spiraled up, pocked with embrasures, Kaelyn glimpsed the southern boardwalk, houses stretching east and west, and the northern forests. Looking upon those misty trees, her eyes stung and her throat tightened.

You wait for me there, Valien, she thought. *I will not fail you.*

They climbed hundreds of steps, and General Gorne was wheezing when they finally reached the tower top. He yanked open a doorway and dragged her into a chamber.

Kaelyn felt herself pale. Her breath died.

"Stars," she whispered.

General Gorne snorted and dug his fingers deeper into her arm.

"Aye, you're a fine gift, child," he hissed. "A gift I won't be returning soon."

Kaelyn's eyes dampened.

Stars, oh stars, she thought.

A dozen women filled Gorne's dusty chamber. A bed rose in the back, but the women sat upon straw piles. They were naked and sallow, and chains bound them to the walls. They stared at Kaelyn with blackened eyes, and their swollen lips moved silently. One was pregnant, her belly swollen but her limbs scrawny and her eyes sunken.

"Filthy lot!" General Gorne said and spat. "Grown old and sickly, these ones have." He turned toward Kaelyn and licked his chops. "Aye, but you're fresh. You'll make a good addition to my collection."

The harem writhed upon the straw, and chains clattered. One woman, her nose bashed and bloody, reached out and whispered. Her voice was too soft to be heard, but Kaelyn could read her lips.

I'm sorry, the woman whispered. *I'm sorry.*

"You... collect them, my lord?" Kaelyn asked, heart thrashing against his ribs.

Gorne was already unbuckling his armor. His breastplate clanged to the floor, sending the women to cower against the walls.

"I bought them," he said. "They are scum, all of them. Nothing but seaside whores who polluted our docks. I gave them a home here. I cleaned up the boardwalk from its filth."

And you bedded them, Kaelyn thought. *And you beat them.* It took all her will not to snarl. *And now you will pay for your sins, Gorne.*

"They were like me," she whispered.

Gorne hissed and drooled. "You will be one of them, whore." He tugged off his tunic and boots. "I will break you in before I chain you among them."

As he began to undo his belt, Kaelyn doffed her cloak. She stood before him in her silks, legs and belly bared.

"I am yours, my lord." She climbed onto the bed, lay down, and looked up at him. "Please, my lord, be gentle with me."

He tossed off his trousers and stood naked before her, sweaty and pink. Spittle dripped down his chest.

"I will be as rough with you as I like," he said, walked toward the bed, and lowered himself atop her. "I'm going to hurt you now, and you're going to love it."

Kaelyn reached to the silks around her thigh and drew her poniard.

General Gorne's girth pressed down against her.

Her blade entered his neck.

He gasped. His eyes widened. His mouth opened and closed, struggling for words, dripping blood and saliva onto Kaelyn's chest.

She gave him a crooked smile. "I thought you liked it rough, my lord."

She twisted the blade, and he gurgled. He pawed at her, and his sausage fingers grabbed her throat.

He squeezed.

Kaelyn gasped and stars covered her vision.

She drove the blade deeper. His hand kept squeezing her throat. His blood poured down his neck, yet still he choked her. She squirmed and kicked beneath him. His body pressed against her, thrice her size and slick with sweat.

She couldn't even wheeze. Her lungs burned. She thought he'd snap her neck.

Stars damn it, die! She pulled her blade back. She thrust it again, piercing his shoulder, and more blood flowed, but he kept choking her. His eyes stared into hers, and he licked the blood on his lips.

"You..." he croaked, "will be mine..."

She felt his arousal against her. Panic flooded her and she floundered like a fish.

Oh stars, he's going to bed me here, he's going to take his prize, even as we both die.

Blackness spread across her vision, a midnight sky strewn with stars.

Her legs felt numb.

Her lungs faded into blazing embers.

Before her in the night, she saw the stars of Requiem, the stars of her fathers. The Draco constellation shone above her. She was flying toward it, a green dragon in the night. The starlit halls of her ancestors glowed above, the columns white, and Kaelyn wept for she had failed her people.

I failed you, Requiem.

She winced.

No. No, Requiem. She screamed. *Not today! Not today! Someday I will fly to you, starlit halls of spirits, but not this day. This day is for sunlight.*

With a choked cry, she thrust her poniard again.

It crashed into the general's mouth, punched through his palate, and crashed into his skull.

His fingers loosened.

Kaelyn gasped for breath.

She sucked in air, a breath she thought could swallow the chamber, the tower, and the sea outside. The blackness withdrew from her eyes like curtains lifted. Her head exploded with starlight.

She kicked, shoving the boar of a man onto the floor. She leaped over the corpse, raced to the window, and kicked it open. The sea breeze whipped her hair and stung her cheeks.

Behind her, the women whimpered. She looked over her shoulder to see them reach out to her, their chains clattering, their eyes pleading. Kaelyn sucked in her breath.

"I will return to you," she whispered... and jumped out the window.

She tumbled down from the tower, silks flapping, her bloody poniard still in her hand.

Before she could hit the ground, she shifted into a green dragon. She beat her wings, whipping the bushes and raising clouds of dust. She soared.

She rose above the tower. Upon its battlements, the two dragons shrieked. Kaelyn blasted them with fire.

They howled, blinded and burning. Before they could spray their own flames, Kaelyn swooped. She lashed her claws and swiped her tail. Blood sprayed. The tower guardians screeched, tumbled backward, and crashed to the hillside in human forms.

Kaelyn hovered above the tower, tossed back her head, and shot a pillar of flame skyward.

The fire crackled, a blazing typhoon. Kaelyn looked to the northern forest, heart thrashing.

Six thousand more flaming pillars rose from the trees. Howls shook the sky. Six thousand of her comrades--dragons of the Resistance and the canyon--rose from the forest, roared, and flew toward the city.

Below her, legionaries were streaming out of the fortress. Kaelyn blew flames, torching the Regime's banners that hung from the tower. She soared higher and cried for the city to hear.

"General Gorne is dead! Lynport is liberated! Legionaries-- lay down your arms and live!" Tears budded in her eyes, and she streamed over the city streets, roaring her cry. "Requiem! May our wings forever find your sky. Lynport is free!"

The Resistance raced over the city walls, wings blasting air. The imperial dragons swarmed from their fort, leaderless, confused, howling and sputtering flame. The forces crashed above the streets and blood rained.

TILLA

She stirred in her sleep, caught in her nightmare's claws.

"No," she whispered and kicked her blankets, struggling to wake up, but the dream pulled her deeper, and the blankets wrapped around her, and Tilla walked down dark halls while eyes burned and faces floated in mockery.

"Lowborn!" they chanted. "Lowborn scum!"

Punishers lashed out. Everywhere she turned, more faces floated, laughing, spitting at her. Lightning burned her. She ran down the hall, but more of her tormenters awaited her there. They leaped from every shadow, demon creatures with masks twisted in eternal scorn.

"I am Tilla Siren!" she shouted, eyes burning. She had chosen the name of her new, noble line; it was a strong name, the name of a mythical creature said to live in Cadport's waters. She shouted it as a charm, a spell to save her from her lowborn roots, from her shameful past upon the boardwalk, from all her dirt and misery here in the purity of the academy.

The other cadets laughed around her, beautiful youths from noble houses, their blood old and pure, their highborn accents meticulous.

"Tilla Roper!" they said, laughing. "Seaside scum. Lowborn whore. Weave us a rope, Roper!"

Again their punishers lashed out.

Tilla screamed and fell. Lightning raced across her, burning her clothes, burning her skin, crackling her bones.

"I am... Cadet Tilla... Siren!" she gasped, but tears ran down her cheeks, incurring more laughter.

They kept burning her. They hunched over her like vultures over prey, and she wept. And she begged. And still they burned her.

"Lowborn worm," one boy said and spat upon her. "Go back to Cadport, peasant."

Her screams echoed through the black halls of Castra Academia.

Her eyes rolled back, and she thought she would die.

But I did not die, her thoughts whispered in the dream, and her fists clutched her blankets. She snarled, struggling to rise from slumber, but falling back in.

I survived!

No matter how badly the highborn beat her, Tilla kept training. She did not quit. When they spat into her meals, she ate sullenly around the spit. When they dumped chamber pots on her clothes, she growled and washed them herself and trained even harder. When they beat her, she fought back, and fell, and hurt, then healed and walked again.

She fought with swords.

She flew as a dragon down dark halls.

She learned to plan battles, to break spirits, to *command*.

She was Tilla Siren, a commoner thrust into a fortress full of the children of nobles, and they tortured her, and they beat her, but she fought them and every lash made her stronger.

Every night she clutched the shield Shari had given her, the shield with her sigil--a cannon overlooking the sea, a symbol of home.

I will be like a cannon, she swore every night, lying in whatever filth her fellow cadets had soiled her mattress with. *I will be strong as iron. I will slay my enemies. I will outlast sword and fire.* She growled every night as her tears burned. *I will become an officer.*

Tilla thrashed in her bed, opened her eyes, and sat up with a pant.

Cold sweat washed her, and her chest rose and fell. Her heart thrashed. She winced and raised her arms.

"Please, don't hurt me," she whispered. "Please. No more."

But no punishers burned her. Tilla opened her eyes to slits, then let out a shaky breath. She sat in bed, shuddering. The sheets were soaked with sweat.

"Just a dream," she whispered. "Just a memory."

She had survived for six moons in Castra Academia, the great school for the Legions' officers, and she had graduated first among her class.

I am a lanse now, she reminded herself. *I wear red spirals upon my shoulders. I command. I'm south in Castra Luna now, far from the academy. I no longer have to be afraid.*

She looked down at her arms. The scars of old burns still spread there. Tilla tightened her throat.

"Scars make us strong," she whispered.

She rose from her bed, shivering; the chill of autumn filled the night. Her tent was small and barren, its black walls shuddering in the wind. A hint of light shone through the tent flap; dawn was near. With stiff fingers, Tilla approached her table, lit her tin lamp, and held her hands above it, allowing the flame to warm her.

In the flickering light, she stared down at the weapon on her table. Her punisher.

Hilt untouched, its tip was cold, but when Tilla's fingers grazed the grip, the punisher crackled to life. Lightning raced across the rod's rounded head, red and creaking like shattering bones. She pulled her fingers back and the lightning vanished.

I burned her, Tilla thought, staring down at the weapon. *I burned Erry. I burned my friend.*

"Damn it, Erry," she whispered, and her throat tightened. "Why do you still have to act like a seaside urchin? What else could I have done?"

Tilla's eyes burned, and she blinked them furiously.

No, she told herself. *Show no weakness, not even when alone. Let no pain fill you. You must be strong to survive.* She squared her shoulders.

"Only the strong will survive in the Legions," she said, staring down at her punisher. "I had to be strong, Erry. Scars make us strong."

Yet now Erry was gone, a deserter from the Legions, an enemy to be hunted and killed. Now Rune too was an outlaw, calling himself Relesar Aeternum, the heir of the fallen dynasty.

How had all this happened? Only a year ago, Rune had been a humble brewer, and she had been only a ropemaker. And now... now she was an officer in the Legions. Now Rune had a new name, proclaiming himself true king. Now he fought for Valien, the man who had slain Tilla's brother.

They all turned against me, Tilla thought and clenched her fists, and a lump filled her throat. None of them understood. None of them knew the law of this land.

"Cadigus reigns, and his law is the blade, the punisher, and the iron fist," she said, repeating the words she had learned. "The weak must be purified."

She took a deep breath, closed her eyes, and let her own weakness flow away. She let all those thoughts of home drip from her mind like poisoned blood from a wound.

I will be strong.

She dressed in her steel armor, grabbed her sword and shield, and left the tent.

The camp stretched around her, kindled with the first hints of dawn. In the eastern sky above the trees, pink tendrils stretched across blue fading to black, and the stars vanished one by one. In the west, shadows still cloaked the ruins of Castra Luna, hiding the strewn bricks and fallen walls like the midnight sea at home. Around her in the camp, the first siragis--hardened, lowborn warriors--marched between tents. Shouts rang across the clearing, and soldiers emerged for morning inspection.

As Tilla walked between the tents, whatever troops she passed--be they hulking warriors or green youths fresh out of training--stood at attention, saluted, and hailed.

She was an officer now. She bore the red spirals. She was a goddess to them.

When she reached a dirt square, she shifted into a dragon and took flight. She flew across the camp, her white scales clattering, her horns gilded like those of all officers. Below her, tents spread in rows and troops bustled. Five milanxes mustered here, moved from the western mountains, five thousand troops in all.

We will find the Resistance in these forests, Tilla vowed as she flew, *and we will crush them.*

She looked across the camp to the northern trees. The white tombstones rose there. Hundreds of youths from her home lay buried under that soil. Mae lay among them.

"I will avenge you, Mae," Tilla whispered.

She returned her eyes to the camp. A ring of dragons surrounded a dirt field. In its center rose a towering tent, large as a house and topped with the banners of Cadigus. Golden embroidery formed flying dragons across its black walls. Soldiers guarded the tent entrance, clutching halberds.

Tilla flew toward the field. She landed before the guards, shifted into human form, and raised her chin. The guards saluted her, slamming fists against chests.

I might be only a junior officer, Tilla thought. *But I'm the junior officer who saved Shari's life.*

She walked past the guards, stood at the tent entrance, and shouted her salute.

"Hail the red spiral! Tilla Siren reporting."

The princess's voice came from within. "Enter."

Tilla stepped inside. Opulence filled the tent, befitting a daughter of Cadigus. A plush bed, armchairs, and giltwood divans stood upon bearskin rugs. Golden vases of wine, platters of fruits and cheeses, and a roast goose topped a table. Racks of swords, helms, and breastplates stood everywhere, a collection worthy of an armory, all belonging to the princess of the empire.

That princess stood clad in black armor, its plates filigreed with golden dragons. Her longsword hung at her left hip, her punisher at her right. Her mane of brown curls cascaded across her pauldrons. Her back was turned to Tilla; she stood before an easel, staring at a parchment the size of a door. Upon the parchment appeared a sketch of a castle, its dozen towers lofty, its walls topped with cannons.

"Castra Sol," Shari said softly, not turning to acknowledge Tilla. "Fortress of the sun. It will rise from these ruins, thrice the strength of old Castra Luna." She caressed the parchment, fingers gloved in black leather. "It will be mine to command, a glorious castle built for one purpose--to crush the Resistance."

Tilla took a step farther into the tent.

"They toppled this fort, Commander, so we will build one larger and greater. For the glory of Requiem."

And for Mae Baker, she added silently. *For hundreds of youths from my home.*

Shari turned toward her. Her face, tanned a deep gold, had aged six years in the past six moons. Shari was only twenty-nine, but weariness filled her dark eyes, and the first lines of an eternal frown had begun to frame her lips.

She's beginning to look like her father, Tilla thought. *A face as hard, cruel, and unyielding as stone.*

"Tilla, we've received reports from the south. The news is grim." Shari reached for the table, grabbed a mug of wine, but did not drink. "We've been betrayed. House Cain has joined the Resistance. Rebellion flares in the south."

Tilla sucked in her breath. "They say Lord Devin Cain is mad! They say he's not left his canyon since we crushed his last rebellion. Does he fly against us?" She clutched her sword. "We will crush him again! Let him fly to us. We will slay him and his men upon the forest. We--"

"Tilla," Shari said, her voice softer, and ghosts filled her eyes. She winced and her left arm twitched--the side where she'd lost her wing.

"Commander?" Tilla whispered, and suddenly fear flooded her.

There is worse news, she thought and her innards trembled.

"Valien and Cain have joined their forces, and they've struck in the south. They've taken Cadport. The city has fallen."

Every weapon in this tent seemed to stab Tilla with cold, biting steel that drove the breath from her lungs.

Cadport fallen. My home. My father.

She couldn't help it. She trembled. Red flooded her eyes.

Cadport. My home. My father.

Her eyes stung and her breath shook.

"We must fly there!" she finally managed to say, speaking through stiff lips. "We will crush them, Commander. I will slay this Valien myself, and Cain, and the rest of them, and--"

Shari clutched her shoulder and glared.

"Soldier!" the princess said. "Calm yourself. Do not forget your station. I command this garrison. You command a mere phalanx. Steel yourself and stand straight." Her voice softened, her grip loosened, and she sighed. "Tilla, I know this news is difficult, but please, listen to me. Sit and drink my wine. We will not leave Cadport in their hands."

But Tilla would not sit. She would not drink. The tent swam around her.

"We have to save Cadport," she whispered. Rage flared through her, and she drew her sword. "We must slay them, Commander!"

Shari bared her teeth and grabbed Tilla's wrist. Tilla was among the tallest and strongest women in this camp, yet Shari stood even taller, and she snarled down at her like a lion staring down a wolf.

"Tilla Siren," she said, "the Resistance has given us a great boon."

"They've captured my home, Commander!" she said. Her voice shook. "They will slay the people there. They--"

"They have emerged from hiding," Shari finished for her. "They muster in a city we know, a city we can attack, a city we can trap them within. We will not let Cadport remain in their hands. Five thousand troops garrison here now, and already dragons fly to bring my father the news. When he hears of Cadport, the wrath of the Legions will muster here... and descend upon the city."

Tilla breathed heavily, chest shaking. "We will lead the charge. We will kill Valien and his men."

"But we will take Relesar alive," Shari said, and her eyes blazed; she still clutched Tilla's wrist. "You will capture him, Tilla. You will capture the heir of Aeternum, and you will carry him to the capital in your claws."

Rage pounded through Tilla. Fire pumped through her veins and spun her head.

Relesar Aeternum. She means Rune.

She thought of him again, her dearest childhood friend. The boy she would wrestle. The boy she would whisper and cry with. The boy she had kissed upon the beach and vowed to see again.

The man who led the Resistance into these ruins, she thought, *who slaughtered hundreds of our townsfolk, who now brings war to our home.*

She took a shuddering breath, squared her shoulders, and stared into Shari's blazing eyes.

"I will capture him," she whispered. "He will be ours."

RUNE

He stood upon the balcony where, only moons ago, Shari had slain a girl and severed her head. He squared his jaw, took a deep breath, and gazed down upon thousands of townsfolk who filled the square below.

Rune had faced crowds many times in the past year. He had spoken to hosts of resistors in their shadowy halls. He had fought thousands of legionaries in battle. Yet standing here, facing the people of Lynport, he felt very young and nervous, and his head spun. The crowd covered the square below--tradesmen, children, farmers, and even legionaries who had stripped off their insignia after Gorne's death. Rune wore armor now, the plates bright and the pauldrons wide, and he bore the longsword of kings, yet facing this crowd, he did not feel like a warrior or royalty.

I feel like a young brewer again, he thought.

He looked aside. Valien stood at a doorway, leaning against the doorframe, arms crossed. His hair hung wild around his leathery, scruffy face. He wore his old patches of steel over hardened tan leather. Rune wanted the man to guide him, to speak for him, but Valien didn't even step onto the balcony. He only stared at Rune from the doorway, eyes inscrutable, saying nothing.

Rune turned to look at Kaelyn. She stood beside him upon the balcony, clad in her forest garb: tall deerskin boots over gray leggings, a green tunic with a golden belt, and a blue cloak. Her sword hung at her hip, her quiver hung over her shoulder, and her golden hair billowed in the breeze. She raised her hand, two fingers pressed together in the salute of the Resistance, and spoke to the crowd.

"People of Lynport!" she said. "I've asked you to gather here today. I see skilled tradesmen, the heartbeat of this town. I see farmers, the pillars of our society. I see warriors--men who abandoned the cruelty of Cadigus, tore off their red spirals, and joined the light of old Requiem. I am Kaelyn Cadigus! I am the daughter of the tyrant. I am here to tell you: That tyrant will fall! You are free."

She stood panting and her eyes glistened. She paused as though expecting cheers or applause. The people, however, only stared at her silently. A few muttered.

Rune sighed. *Kaelyn has always seen the resistors as heroes. She will learn not all see us the same.*

With a tug on her quiver's strap and a clearing of her throat, Kaelyn collected herself. She raised her chin and kept speaking.

"People of Lynport! I present to you your new king--the true king of Requiem. Here stands Relesar Aeternum, son of Ardin, King of Requiem." She knelt, eyes damp, and stared up at Rune. "May the stars bless him."

She paused again, craned her neck up, and peeked down at the crowd. She seemed to be waiting for them to kneel too, but the crowd only muttered louder. One man grumbled, shook his head, and turned to leave the square. The rest bustled restlessly.

"Kae," Rune said softly, "I don't think they care much about old dynasties here. We're far from the capital."

She rose to her feet and glared at him. "Of course they do!" she said, turned back to the crowd, and raised her voice. "Do you not remember House Aeternum, people of Lynport? Relesar is heir to an ancient dynasty, to--"

One man below groaned. "That there's only Rune Brewer!" he shouted up at her. "Bloody Abyss, the boy sold me ale about a hundred times."

"More like a million times, Tam," said the man's wife and poked his ample gut. "Boy darn well turned you into a boat."

Nervous laughter spread through the crowd. One woman, emboldened by the chortling, pointed up at Rune and cried out.

"I used to watch him as a babe, I did! Changed his swaddling clothes more than once. Boy sure knew how to soil them!"

The laughter grew, and Rune felt his face redden. Wearing armor definitely wasn't making a difference now. Desperate, he turned to look at Valien. The gruff old knight stood in the doorway, muttering and fuming, his eyes dark. Rune wanted to plead with him for help, but Valien wouldn't even meet his gaze.

The crowd's laughter grew, and more people called out their own stories of Rune--how he'd once cried when his father wouldn't let him keep a stray kitten, how he'd walked into a cart when gaping at a pretty woman whose skirts had blown in the wind, and how his singing voice once caused flowers to wilt-- honest to goodness, half a dozen people saw it.

Rune only stood sighing upon the balcony, but Kaelyn shouted over the crowd.

"You speak of your king!" she cried, face red and eyes blazing. "Relesar is descended of a proud dynasty, of legendary Queen Lyana who founded this city, of the great King Benedictus who fought the griffins, and of the first King Aeternum himself who raised the marble halls. Relesar is a light upon Requiem, and-_"

Rune placed a hand on her shoulder. "Kae," he said, "I don't think they're listening. Let me try."

She bit down on her words and spun toward him, fuming. Pink splotches spread across her cheeks. She seemed too enraged to even breathe. Rune looked back at the crowd below. They were still laughing, and many were leaving the square.

"People of Lynport!" Rune shouted out to them. "My friends. Listen to me please. For just a moment."

Grudgingly, they turned back toward him and watched, silent. Rune felt his head spin--so many eyes stared at him!--but forced himself to plow on.

"Look," he said to the crowd. "You're right. Don't follow me because I'm so-and-so fancy king's son. Don't follow me because I'm Relesar Aeternum, an heir from some old legend. You're right, I'm just Rune Brewer."

At his side, Kaelyn gasped and began to object, but he held up his hand, hushing her.

Rune continued speaking to the crowd. "Follow me *because* I'm Rune Brewer. Follow me *because* I'm nothing but a common son of this city. Follow me because I know what it's like living here, because I felt the scourge of Cadigus, because I--like you-- saw the light of our home fade."

This got their attention. Their mirth died, and the people stared up at him, silent and listening.

Rune took a deep breath and saw Tilla's father in the crowd, a tall and wiry man with black hair. Rune pointed at him and spoke for the people to hear.

"Heri Roper, you used to sell many ropes to sailing ships. Traders from Tiranor docked here often, and your shop thrived. When the Cadigus family burned the kingdom of Tiranor, and our port rotted, you lost your livelihood." Rune turned toward another woman. "Meti Weaver, you used to sell silk to the south. You ran a shop full of seamstresses. Now you can barely sell cotton to hungry folk too poor to buy it." Rune turned to another man. "Your three sons were taken away from this very square, carted off to the Legions, and never returned."

The crowd mumbled, but this time nobody turned to leave, and no scorn filled their voices or eyes.

Rune looked upon them--his people, his townsfolk, his friends. He glanced over at Valien, and the man stared back, and now his eyes shone with approval. He gave Rune a small nod and an almost imperceptible smile. Rune turned back toward the crowd below.

"We all lost something to the Cadigus family," he said. "Some of us lost our livelihoods. Some of us lost our faith; this courthouse where I stand was once a temple to the Draco constellation, our forbidden gods. Some of us lost our loved ones. How many people did the Regime murder in this very square, beheading or whipping or breaking them upon the wheel?"

Eyes in the crowd darkened. People muttered and cursed. Anger brewed below like a sea about to erupt into a storm. But the anger was not directed at him, Rune knew. He raised his hands and spoke louder.

"Do not listen to the lies of Cadigus! They told you the Resistance is evil, that resistors hunt and kill for sport. The Resistance is not your enemy, but your ally."

Some in the crowd looked skeptical, but others were muttering their agreement, especially those old enough to remember the days before the tyrant. Voices began to rise in cheers, crying out their approval. Rune spoke louder to be heard above them.

"I am Rune Brewer!" he said. "I lived on the boardwalk. The Regime murdered my father and burned my home. I say: We are not Cadport, named after a tyrant who crushed us under his heel. We are a far older, nobler city. We are Lynport and our light will shine again." He shouted for the city to hear. "The tyrant must fall! We will fly as dragons again."

Below in the square, the crowd stared up silently. Tears filled the eyes of elders. Fire and passion filled the eyes of youths.

One young woman, a farmer holding a basket of fruit, raised her head and cried out in a clear, high voice.

"Requiem! May our wings forever find your sky."

The crowd repeated the forbidden prayer, tears fell, and Rune knew: They were his.

"Blessed be the children of Requiem," he whispered, looking upon his home.

Kaelyn reached out and held his hand, her eyes swimming with tears, her lips whispering prayers.

Rune held her hand, turned his head, and looked across the roofs of Lynport. Beyond the city walls, golden forests rolled into mist.

Frey Cadigus waited there. The Legions would be mustering.

Frey will descend upon this place with all his wrath and malice, Rune thought and shivered. *Today Lynport is free. Tomorrow blood will soak these streets.*

The people sang for stars, for Aeternum, and for Requiem, but Rune only shivered and held Kaelyn's hand tight.

LERESY

"No!" he said and slapped her hand. "Damn it, girl, I told you a million times. The griffin only moves two squares."

Erry glared at him over the board of Counter Squares, a game of the capital. Her lips twisted in a snarl; she looked to Leresy like some puppy trying to seem fierce.

"This game is bloody complicated," she said. "You said the griffin can move diagonally across the--"

"That's the *dragon*," Leresy said and rolled his eyes. "By the Abyss, woman, do you think a griffin would beat a dragon?"

The pieces were arranged across the board: griffins, dragons, phoenixes, and other creatures carved of obsidian and ivory.

Chewing her lip, Erry reached for an obsidian wyvern that stood upon a white square. Leresy slapped her hand again.

"No, Erry, if you move your wyvern, my salvana will capture your mimic. See?"

Erry fumed, her face red. "No it *won't*," she said. "Do you want to know why?" She leaped to her feet and tossed the board sideways, sending pieces flying across the tent. "Because I bloody quit this stupid dumb game you just invented!"

Leresy looked at the pieces strewn across the ground. "Counter Squares was invented hundreds of years ago."

"And it was bloody dumb then too!" Erry crossed her arms and sulked. "Who the Abyss ever heard of stinkin' griffins hopping squares, and phoenixes that can't even fly, and ivory codpieces--"

"Those are salvanae, Erry, true dragons of the west."

"Well they look like codpieces to me! Sweaty, stinking ones." She snorted. "You fancy-arse nobles with your fancy-arse games. Burn me. Give me a mug of ale, a sword to swing, and a song to sing, and I'm happier than playing any game for prissy princelings."

He reached across the table and grabbed her wrist. "I'll give you something else."

She raised her chin and shot him a haughty stare. "What is that, princeling? Another la-dee-da game a little princess taught you to play?"

He rose to his feet, pulled her from her chair, and glared down at her.

"Your big mouth is going to get you into trouble one day," he said.

She smirked. "Am I in trouble now, oh lord princeling?"

He wanted to think of some clever retort, but he was too busy tearing off her clothes; they always came off so easily in his hands. She stood naked before him, smirking, no taller than his shoulders and slim as a twig, and yet she heated his blood to a boil.

He grabbed her shoulders. He pulled her to his bed. Her eyes closed, and he took her until finally the smirk left her face.

When he was done with her, again he wanted to kick her out of his bed, out of his tent, out of his camp. Stars damn it, he was Prince of Requiem, and no woman deserved sharing his bed. Yet again, as always, he only lay on his back, and she lay in his arms, her head upon his chest, and he stroked that short, brown, boyish hair of hers. She mumbled something sleepy, and he kissed her forehead, and his heart felt more confused than all the rules to all the games in the world.

What is it about you, Erry Docker? he thought, looking down at her as she slept, her cheek against his heart.

She should be nothing to him. She *was* nothing. She was only flesh, that was all. Only a body to warm his bed and feed his hunger. She meant nothing to him, nothing! She was no better than any whore from the Bad Cats back in the capital.

Leresy took her twice a day, morning and night, and sometimes a third time at noon, thrusting into her, using her to vent all his rage, all his grief, all his pain. And she never made a sound. She did not moan, or yelp, or cry. She never wept. She never demanded love or affection or money or power--any of those things all the women in Leresy's life had demanded. She simply let him use her as he would, a doll, a toy, that was all... and then slept in his arms, her head upon his chest.

And he used her. Not for his physical needs--those had lost all flavor--but to drown the pain that forever clawed his chest. To forget the capital. To forget Nairi. And so he took her again and again, and every time he did, he could forget a little more.

"Stupid, sweaty codpiece dragons," she mumbled, and he stroked her hair, and she fell silent, her sleepy breath tickling his chest.

"Stupid, sweaty, seaside urchins," he answered softly, his arms wrapped around her.

Slowly, night by night, Leresy came to realize that more than he craved her sex, he craved to hold her. More than he wanted to enter her, to grab her, to claim her body, he craved to stroke her hair, hear her mumble, and feel her breath against him.

You came to my camp muddy and scruffy and screaming like an enraged beast, he thought, holding her close. But in his arms now, she was a frail doll, delicate and pure and so fragile she seemed made of porcelain.

And slowly, he came to feel ashamed of how he'd scorned her that first day.

"Erry Docker," he whispered. "You stupid, stupid girl."

In the morning, he walked through their forest camp. Campfires crackled around him. Men lay snoring, cursing, or squabbling over their last sausages and eggs. Some men had risen early and were banging swords together, eyes grim, still soldiers even here in the forest. Many had drawn black dogs on their shields, and some had sewn black dogs on their sleeves; Erry's mutt had become something of a mascot. As Leresy ambled through the camp, surveying his men, a smile tingled the corner of his lips.

"Good morning, you bastard prince of lechers!" one man shouted out.

Leresy gave him a mock salute. "Go shag a dog, you son of a whore."

The man roared with laughter, grabbed a skin of ale, and drank deeply. The brew dribbled down his bare chest. Few men here were better dressed. Armor lay strewn across the camp, dulled and muddy. Men roamed about shirtless, barefoot, and scruffy. Most had not shaved for days.

Leresy looked down at his own raiment. A year ago, it would have disgusted him. He wore nothing but the garb of a forester: tan breeches, a rough black tunic, and a green cloak. Yet he did not miss his fine embroidery or filigreed plates of steel.

Those were trifles of the capital, he thought, grabbed a turkey leg from a wandering drunkard, and bit into the meat. He chewed lustfully. *Here we are true men of mud, steel, and sweat. The capital can burn to the ground.*

Tears stung his eyes, but Leresy furiously blinked them away and gnawed his meat with more fervor.

"Quite a camp of disciplined soldiers you've got here," Erry said, walking at his side. Her dog trailed behind her, sniffing at campfires and catching scraps the men tossed his way.

"They are hardened men," Leresy said. "True men, not bastards like my father, and not soft boys like that so-called King Relesar. They will build me a kingdom."

As they walked through the camp, many men paused from eating, drinking, or fighting and gaped at Erry. Drool thick with crumbs dribbled down some men's chins. Erry was perhaps as scrawny and short-haired as a boy, but she was the only female in camp, and these men had seen no other woman in many days.

Sooner or later, I'll have to keep her guarded and chained in my tent, Leresy thought, *or I'll have to share her with the camp.*

The meat tasted foul in his mouth, and he tossed the turkey leg aside, grabbed a jug of wine from a man, and drank to cleanse his mouth. Thinking of Erry naked and writhing beneath these muddy, scruffy men disgusted him.

Why? he wondered. He had shared his women with these men before. He had dragged many of his whores from the Bad Cats to his barracks, allowing his troops to share in the flesh.

He looked at Erry. She was still walking beside him, one hand on her dog's back, the other clasping a bread roll. She was chewing vigorously--stars, the damn girl never closed her mouth when chewing--and mumbling something about how this camp needed some good fish to cook.

They want her too, Leresy thought as the men crawled toward her. *They will try to take her from me.*

He gripped his sword's hilt. It was the simple, unadorned weapon of a common soldier. Fleeing the capital, Leresy had left his true sword behind--a priceless artifact with a filigreed blade, a platinum hilt shaped like a dragonclaw, and a scabbard glittering with more jewels than most treasure chests. That weapon probably still lay in the Bad Cats, but his new sword, grabbed from a Lecher who'd fallen to fever, could still kill.

"Bloody bollocks, Leresy!" said one man, a drunken fool with flushed cheeks, a week-old beard, and red eyes. He tottered forward, clutching a tankard. "When are you going to share your woman with us?" He waved his drink around. "I haven't tasted me a woman since I left the capital."

Stumbling forward, he reached toward Erry's backside.

With a growl, Leresy drew his sword, swung it down, and severed the man's hand.

Erry yelped and jumped. The man screamed. Across the camp, men stumbled back and cursed.

Leresy stood shaking. *Damn him! Damn the man!* His sword wavered in his hand. Blood pounded in his ears. He could barely see through his rage.

The maimed man stumbled back, clutching his stump, and tripped over a root. He crashed to the forest floor and writhed. Leresy stepped above him and raised his sword, prepared to finish the job.

"This one is mine!" he shouted. He looked around the camp at the men who watched. His eyes burned, and spittle flew from his mouth as he shouted. "You hear that, sons of dogs? Any one of you touches my woman, I'll slice *you* into a woman and give you to the camp!"

He swung his sword down.

"Leresy, no!" Erry cried and slammed into him.

His sword drove into the dirt, missing the wounded man by an inch.

Leresy slapped her.

He slapped her so hard Erry stumbled back and clutched her cheek. Her eyes widened, and her dog barked madly, and the world spun around Leresy.

Damn it, I didn't mean to--

"I'm sorry," he whispered and reached out to her. "Erry, please, I'm only trying to protect you, I..."

She glared at him, still clutching her cheek, and shook her head wordlessly. She grabbed her dog's collar and ran back to their tent.

Leresy stood, his bloody sword still in his hand. He felt everyone staring at him. Nobody said a word.

Stars damn it, he thought. *Stars damn these men and stars damn Erry.*

He lifted the fallen tankard and drank what ale remained inside. He tossed the empty vessel down.

"I'll let this one live!" he announced. "See my mercy. Any one of you other dogs lays a hand on what's mine, I'll cut that one too."

A few of the men were grumbling. A few clutched swords. Their eyes darkened and Leresy swallowed, suddenly afraid. There were a thousand of them, and each one was older and stronger.

Without my embroidery and armor, am I still a prince here, or only a man for them to slay?

He gritted his teeth, refusing to show fear. His father had to deal with a rebellion among his people; Leresy wouldn't allow the same misfortune to strike him.

"You shall have women!" he shouted, raising his sword high. "Have I not given you women before? You will have ten thousand more! We travel south to Terra Incognita, to the great unknown grasslands east of Tiranor. There are dusky women there of legendary beauty. They run topless through fields, clad in only skirts of grass, and they crave northern men to pleasure. We will rule them!"

This assuaged the men. A few began to cheer, and soon the rest joined in.

"We will be lords of our new kingdom!" Leresy shouted. "I've given you food, drink, and gold. Stay with me, and soon we will live as kings!"

They howled their approval, waving food and drink and fists, and Leresy took a shuddering breath.

Oh stars, he thought, *please let there be women in that forsaken land we seek. If we find nothing but empty grasslands, they'll have my head... and Erry's body.*

He was about to return to his tent, speak with Erry, and try to make amends when wings thudded overhead.

The foliage rustled and bent, and Leresy cursed. His heart thudded, and for a moment, he was sure the Legions had found them. Before he could flee, a lone brown dragon crashed down through the canopy, landed in front of Leresy, and shifted into human form.

Leresy glared at the man and spat. "Damn it, Yorne. I thought you were my damn father. I told you--we don't fly in daylight, not until we leave Requiem."

Yorne spat too, expelling a great glob Leresy thought could drown a rodent. The man had served in the Legions for twenty years; he'd worn six red stars upon his armbands before Leresy had ordered the Lechers remove their old insignia. The son of a lowborn fisherman, Yorne had never gone to Castra Academia, but he had served the Legions long enough, and he'd slain enough men, to fight alongside generals and send troops to die. Tattoos of dragons coiled across his ropy arms, and his shaggy hair could not fully hide a scar that snaked across his head. He was a tall man, the tallest among the Lechers, but gaunt and weathered as a strip of dry meat.

"Your father's busy dealing with bigger problems," Yorne said. He cleaned his teeth with his tongue. "Big news stirring across the empire. The Resistance has taken Cadport."

Leresy snorted. "Cadport? It's a damn backwater. I visited once and couldn't tell their fort apart from their latrines. Who cares?"

Yorne raised his eyebrows and thrust out his bottom lip. "Aye, a backwater to us, but fifty thousand folk live there. It's the largest town on the southern coast. Lots of dragons, if the Resistance has them shifting and flying against the capital."

Leresy stomped toward a campfire, grabbed a roasting sausage, and bit into it. The skin *cracked* and juices filled Leresy's mouth.

"Let them fly," he said. "Let them burn down the damn capital. I care not. Let all of Requiem burn! We are the Lechers. The unknown lands beyond the sea will be our kingdom. Let the Legions and the Resistance kill each other until none are left."

Yorne nodded, eyebrows still firmly raised, and scratched his chin. "More like the Resistance is going to be slaughtered, seems. Your sister's mustering an army in the ruins of Castra Luna. Whole brigades gather there, and more troops arrive every day. The emperor himself will arrive with the Axehand. They'll invade Cadport by winter, they say, and stamp out the Resist--"

"I care not!" Leresy said. "Damn it, Yorne, I don't give a damn about Requiem politics. We travel overseas, and--"

He bit down on his words.

He understood.

His heart leaped.

Oh bloody shite.

His sister. His father. The two people he hated most-- traveling south into battle. There would be cannons firing, dragons flying, blood and chaos and death.

It will be my chance, he thought and clenched his fists. *My sweet vengeance.*

His thoughts returned to his last night in the capital. Shari had dragged him by the hair from his fort, tossed him at his father's feet, and seen him banished. She had stolen his fortress, leaving him nothing but a wretch.

But now, sister, now you fly to war. And when you crash against the Resistance, a host of bloodthirsty barbarians, beware... beware of the shadow at your back.

Leresy licked his lips and grinned.

"Yorne," he said, "get this camp cleaned up. I want men wearing their armor. I want guards on patrol. I want some discipline here, damn it. Whip these warriors into shape!"

With that, he spun on his heel, left the men, and stomped back toward his tent.

When he stepped inside, he found Erry sitting on the cot, hugging Scraggles and muttering curses. She raised damp eyes and glared at him. The mark of his hand still shone red upon her cheek.

He approached her. She hissed and tried to rise. He shoved her down, grabbed a fistful of her hair, and forced her to look at him.

"Dearest little urchin," he said. "Poor, pathetic little wench. What do you know of pain?"

She growled. "If you strike me again, I will slay you."

He grabbed her arms and yanked her to her feet. She stood before him, glaring up at him, her hair tousled. Leresy caressed her bruised cheek.

"I promised that you will be my southern mistress," he said. "I promised you a land of wild grass, endless summer, and lazy days of sun and starry nights. To the Abyss with that." He placed a finger under her chin, kissed her forehead, and twisted his lips into a grin. "I will make you the concubine of an emperor."

VALIEN

He stood upon the breakwater, staring out into the sea, and remembered the day he met his wife.

Boulders formed the breakwater, their lower halves green with moss, their upper halves white with gull droppings. The waves slammed against the stones, turning from gray to blue and showering foam. The breakwater ended with a cairn, and there rose Lynport's lighthouse, a tower of empty windows, craggy bricks, and memories of better days.

Valien grumbled as he walked across the slick boulders--this was easier when he was younger--and placed his hand against the lighthouse. The old bricks were clammy and mossy, but he remembered years ago when this tower was new, when he had climbed its steps to view the sea and found her above.

The lighthouse doors had rotted or burned years ago. Valien stepped through the archway and climbed the stairs again, the first time he'd climbed them in twenty years. Shattered clay jugs, an abandoned glass bottle, and an old shoe littered the steps now. A feral cat hissed at him, bristled its fur, then fled. But as Valien kept climbing, he barely saw the stairway's current state. He saw himself a young man, twenty-one years old and only knighted that summer, visiting fair Lynport to protect the sea.

He reached the lighthouse top. He stepped into a round chamber where no more fire burned. Today this chamber was empty but for a discarded mattress, a cracked pipe on a windowsill, and three kittens nestled in the corner. Outside the windows, the sea stretched into the horizon, a gray sheet splotched with patches of green and blue where the water was shallow. But when Valien closed his eyes, he saw this chamber twenty years ago. A great beacon had burned here then, the fire shimmering behind glass panes, and upon the sea a dozen southern ships had sailed, bringing their treasures into Requiem.

"And you were here, Marilion," he whispered. "You shone brighter than all the beacons in the world. You guided me home."

He could almost see her again at the window, watching the sea. She had worn a white dress that day, its hem stained with salt and sand, and her feet were bare, but Valien had never seen a more beautiful woman. Her hair cascaded down her back, the color of honey, and when she turned toward him she smiled.

"Good morning, my lord," she said. "I'm sorry. I've come to watch the sea."

She was a commoner, born and raised in the south, her only jewelry a string of seashells. She was wild and beautiful, a creature of sea and sand. Standing beside her, Valien felt stiff and awkward in his armor, a relic of ancient tradition, out of place here like some dusty grandfather clock in a fairy fort.

She laughed. "Can you speak, sir knight?"

He cleared his throat. "You have nothing to apologize for. This is your town. I've only just arrived here from the capital. I serve in Castellum Acta. I--"

"You talk too much," she said and laughed again. "Listen! Do you hear it?"

Valien listened. He heard it--the waves whispering, the seagulls calling, and the forest rustling. The girl returned her eyes to the sea, inhaled deeply, and a smile touched her lips.

"I sometimes stand here silently for hours," she whispered. "The sea speaks to me."

They spent many days that summer standing in the lighthouse, walking upon the shore, or ambling between the shops along the boardwalk. During lazy days, they caught fish and cooked them on campfires, and Marilion would play her flute and he would sing softly. At nights, they would lie upon the sand, watch the stars, and hold each other. In the autumn they wed in this very lighthouse.

Valien stood in the barren chamber, twenty years older, his hair now wild and grizzled, his armor dented and dulled, and lowered his head.

I took her with me to the capital, he thought, and agony burned his throat. *She never returned.*

Valien closed his eyes and clenched his fists. The emperor's words from last winter echoed in his mind; they hadn't stopped echoing since.

"Marilion lives!" Frey had shouted, cackling and bleeding. "She lives in my dungeon, you fool!"

Valien's fists shook. His teeth grinded. Fires burst inside him.

With a howl, he opened his eyes and pounded the wall. Blood splattered his knuckles, but Valien felt no pain. He panted and growled and shook.

"You lie!" he hissed. He stormed toward the window and stared out at the sea, as if Frey hid among the waves. "You lie, dog. She died. I saw her die! I held her as she died."

Again the blood danced before his eyes--Marilion lying upon the bed, Frey's sword in her chest, her eyes glassy and still.

"I held you," Valien whispered. Tears stung his eyes and his voice shook. "I held you as your soul rose to the starlit halls. You've been waiting for me there, Marilion."

And still Frey's voice echoed, cackling madly. "She lives!"

Valien clutched the windowsill, fingers trembling.

He was lying. He was trying to break my mind, to drive me mad. He's lied so many times before.

With a shuddering breath, Valien turned from the window and left the lighthouse.

He flew over the city, a silver dragon, slower and wider than he used to be, his left horn broken off years ago. Lynport stretched below him, a crescent moon of houses and streets embracing the coast. The cliffs of Ralora rose west of the town, while forests rolled into the north. The southern sea whispered, a deep blue patched with green, lines of foam racing across it. The smell of seawater filled Valien's nostrils even up here.

He flew toward the northern walls that separated wilderness from city. They rose a hundred feet tall, overlooking oaks, maples, and pines, the trees golden and red and filling the air with their scent. A dozen dragons hovered above the walls, wings beating, holding four cannons aloft. Below upon the battlements, men waved, cried out, and guided the cannons down into place. Dozens of cannons already topped the battlements, pointing north toward the capital.

We took a hundred guns from Castra Luna, Valien thought, gliding toward the walls. *Yet ten thousand warriors will descend upon us, maybe more. These guns will not hold them back for long.*

He spotted Kaelyn standing in a turret, a small guard tower that jutted out from the wall. Valien filled his wings with air, descended, and landed outside the structure.

Around him across the wall, men scurried to bolt cannons down, and dragons hovered above, their wings whipping Valien's hair. Valien knew he should walk among them, inspect the batteries, encourage the troops, and prepare for battle. But he only stood, staring into the guard tower, and his throat constricted.

The turret was only large enough for a single archer. Kaelyn stood inside, her back to Valien. She held an arrow nocked in her bow, and she stared out an arrowslit, watching the forest. Wind whistled through the embrasure and ruffled her golden hair.

And suddenly she was not Kaelyn, and she did not stand in a turret. She was a woman years ago, standing in a lighthouse, her hair billowing in the sea breeze. Valien stood staring and his eyes stung.

"Damn you, Kaelyn," he whispered.

Damn you. Why do you have to look like her? Why do you have to fill me with those memories, with that old sweet pain? Why do I have to fight not to hold you, not to love you, not to lose you?

She turned around and saw him, and a smile split her face, showing white teeth--*her* smile.

"Valien," she said. "How are the defenses along the boardwalk?"

He entered the turret and stood beside her. While Kaelyn was slim and barely filled the place, Valien felt burly and clunky in here, a bear trapped in a box. He peered out the arrowslit at the forest; it swayed like a sea in sunset.

"The batteries of guns are being raised, and troops are manning them," he said. "A hundred will point to the sea, should the Legions invade from the south. More guns rise upon the courthouse roof and upon Castellum Acta."

Kaelyn nodded and clasped his arm. "When the Legions arrive, we will triumph."

Valien sighed, a long sigh that clanked his armor and bones. "We will slow them down. We will slay a few. But our outfliers report ten thousand legionaries already mustered in Castra Luna; they call the place Castra Sol now. More will gather there. We have only three thousand resistors and three thousand canyon warriors." He grumbled. "Lord Cain left the bulk of his forces in the canyon. The man is mad, but we will take what help he offers."

Kaelyn's eyes shone. "Our six thousand fight for justice. One man fighting for justice is worth ten who fight under the whips of a tyrant." Her voice softened, and she held his arm.

"Valien, I am afraid. I see the same fear in your eyes. But know this: I fly with you today and always. I fought with you in our long years of hiding; I will fight with you now as we make our stand."

Valien stared at the rustling forest, imagining the assault--an entire brigade of dragons descending upon this city. Was he foolish to stay? Could they truly defend this city?

"We need more men," he whispered. "We need more guns. We need more time to train. Damn it, Kaelyn, we've never made a stand before. We've hidden in forests and ruins. We've attacked the Regime, then fled back into shadow. Never have we waved our banners, raised our heads, and invited the enemy to come."

Kaelyn nodded. "It's time to make this stand. Relesar has risen. The banner of Aeternum flies from our towers and walls. I feared battle in Castra Luna, and I cautioned you against it. Yet we flew out, we faced Cadigus in open battle, and we triumphed. I believe we will triumph here too." She touched his cheek, and her eyes softened. "Do not lose hope, Valien. We defeated the enemy at Luna. We will defeat them here."

Marilion lives! She lives in my dungeon, you fool!

The words echoed, and Valien saw that night again: His love in his arms, the sword in her chest, and the blood everywhere... so much blood.

He looked at Kaelyn--her young face, her nose strewn with freckles, her hazel eyes so large and earnest, eager for victory.

I cannot lose you too, Kaelyn. I cannot tell you how much I love you, how little I fear for my own life, how much I fear for yours.

He touched her cheek, his fingers so coarse and calloused against her pale skin. She smiled and embraced him, and her hair tickled his nostrils.

I love you, he thought, holding her close... not knowing if he meant a memory or the woman in his arms.

SHARI

Dawn rose golden over the forest, and Shari took her ward to see a man tortured.

They walked through the camp rather than flew. Shari wanted them to walk. She wanted Tilla to see the troops up close, see every spiral upon every breastplate, every eye burning with rage, every sword bright under the sun.

In battle, she will not command from above, a goddess overseeing her slaves, Shari thought. *She will fight among them in the blood and fire.*

And so they walked down the lines. Thousands of troops stood at their sides, three soldiers deep, forming palisades of metal. Their tents rose behind them, banners streaming. They stood at attention, fists against chests, men and women of the Legions. Every soldier wore a black helmet and breastplate; a longsword and dagger hung from every hip.

"We caught him lurking in the forests," Shari said as they marched down the dirt road between the troops. "He was spying on our camp and armed with a sword. I've broken him in, but I've left most of his flesh for you."

Tilla marched at her side, face blank and staring ahead. She wore the fine steel of an officer now, not merely a breastplate over a tunic like a common soldier, but full plate armor that covered her from toes to neck. She carried her helmet, a work of art shaped as a dragon's head, under her arm. She had taken well to command, Shari thought; she walked with the pride of nobility.

"I will break him," the young officer said, no emotion in her voice or eyes.

Shari smiled.

Good, she thought. *Good.*

Tilla was learning. Shari thought back to the first day she'd seen the woman in Cadport; it was nearly a year ago now. Back then, Tilla had been only a filthy commoner, but Shari had seen something in her even then. Unlike the other peasants, Tilla had not cowered before her. Tilla had not wept, fled, or broken even under the punishers of her commanders in Castra Luna, nor under the punishers of her fellow cadets at the academy.

Shari smiled. She knew, of course, of Nairi burning Tilla to near death. She knew, of course, of young nobles torturing Tilla for moons in the academy, burning her flesh and breaking her mind. She herself had ordered the punishment.

It made her strong, Shari thought, looking at the icy young officer. *It made her deadly. She will be a great commander yet. She will be like me.*

As they walked through the camp, heading toward the shack where they kept the prisoner, pain flared in Shari's shoulder. She winced and sucked in her breath. The injury still hurt most days. Even in human form, she felt the pain of her phantom wing. The wound had healed across her shoulder blade, leaving but a scar, yet the agony lingered.

Relesar tore a part of me away, she thought. *He crippled me. He made me weak.*

She had her prosthetic wing now, a creaking mechanism of wood, rope, and leather, and she had taught herself to fly with it, even to shift with it. Yet she would never fly as smoothly again. She would never swoop as fast. She would never kill with such deadliness.

Shari looked over at Tilla. The young woman, ten years her junior, walked clutching the hilt of her sword. Pauldrons covered her shoulders, and steel coated her limbs, yet Shari could see her body's strength. Her every movement spoke of a huntress. Her eyes stared ahead, narrowed the slightest, always scanning for danger, always shining with pride.

I am crippled, but she is strong, Shari thought. *She will grow stronger. She will be my killer, my sweet bringer of death.* Shari ground her teeth against the pain. *Relesar took my wing. I have taken his beloved from him... and I will make her kill him.*

That would be her greatest revenge.

They passed the last tents and troops, walked down a path, and reached the hut.

Small as a prison cell, its walls had been carved from the surrounding forest. The smell of blood, sweat, and urine flared. Flies bustled. Mewling sounded inside, a sound like a kicked dog.

Shari stood outside the door and looked at Tilla.

"You must make him talk," Shari said. "He will lie to you. He will deny all accusations. Yet you must remain strong, and you must hurt him. For the glory of the red spiral, we must shed blood."

Tilla stared at the hut. Her face remained still and pale, but Shari saw small signs of her fear: a twitch to her lips, a line on her brow, and a shadow in her eyes.

There is still softness in her, Shari thought. There was still weakness here to purify, even after a year of training. Shari allowed a thin smile to touch her lips. *I will crush that weakness. She will be my perfect killer.*

"I will make him talk," Tilla said.

Shari nodded, opened the hut door, and they stepped inside.

The man cowered there, if he could still be called a man. Blood and welts covered his flesh; he looked no better than a rotten corpse. He winced in the light, huddling deeper into the corner, clad in chains. Shari herself had given him these wounds. It was something Tilla had to see. Training was clinical. Battle was chaotic. Here before her bled the true face of war.

"Please," the man whispered through cracked lips, "no more, please. I'm only a quarryman, I--"

Shari drew her punisher and held it against him.

Lightning crackled across the man. He yowled and writhed on the floor, and still Shari held her punisher against him. She waited until his skin cracked and bled, then finally pulled the weapon back. The man lay twitching, smoke rising from him.

"You are a resistor," she said. "You serve Valien Eleison, the traitor. Why else would you lurk in the forests outside our camp?"

"I work in the quarry!" he said, blood in his mouth. "Please, ask the men who work there; they all know me. I cut bricks for this very fort! Please...."

Shari looked over at Tilla, studying her. The young woman stared down at the burnt man, face pale and lips tight.

This still frightens her, Shari thought. *Blood and burns still twist her innards. She will have to be hardened.* Shari nodded. *I will harden her soul like a smith hammering a blade.*

"Tilla," she said, "draw your punisher. Burn him."

Tilla hesitated for just an instant, the length of a breath, and her eyes gave the slightest blink, her lips the slightest twitch. But Shari saw it, and she vowed to eradicate that weakness.

"Yes, Commander," Tilla said and drew her punisher. Its tip crackled to life, racing with red energy.

And she burned him.

"Keep it there," Shari said. "More. Keep it burning."

Tilla obeyed. She held the punisher against the screaming man until welts rose, skin cracked, and blood spilled. As she worked, Shari stared at Tilla's eyes, watching, studying, smiling when she saw the weakness fade into grim intent.

"Enough," she said.

Tilla pulled back, leaving the wretch to writhe and mewl, half dead but still whimpering about his quarry.

"Now draw your blade," Shari instructed. "Slice his belly. Make him bleed out. We will not give him the mercy of a quick death."

Tilla hesitated again. Her hand closed around her sword's hilt, but she did not draw the blade.

"Commander," she said, "should we speak to the quarry? Maybe--"

Shari laughed. "You believe his lies? Resistors always lie. The punishment is death. He should be thankful for that. We could have kept him alive here for moons, even years. Cut him! Slice him open. He serves the Resistance, the rebels who slaughtered your friends, who captured your town. Even now, they slaughter innocents in Cadport."

Tilla's eyes burned with rage and pain. Her cheeks flushed and her lips twisted. With a hiss, she drew her blade.

"Cut him!" Shari commanded. "Make it hurt. He would do worse to you."

Tilla clenched her jaw. "For Cadport," she whispered... and lashed her blade.

The man screamed. Blood gushed from his stomach. He clutched at the wound uselessly. Tilla stared, and her fingers trembled, and her eyes flinched. She raised her blade again, prepared to strike the killing blow.

"No," Shari said. She caught Tilla's wrist, holding her sword back. "No."

Tilla looked at her. Sweat beaded on her pale brow.

"Commander," she said. "I can kill him. I--"

"Let him die slowly," she said. "It's good enough for him. Come with me, lanse. We'll let him die alone."

They left the hut and returned to the sunlight. When Shari looked at Tilla, she found the woman still pale, yet her eyes were dry and her lips tightened.

"Killing is hard," Shari said. "But it gets easier. Harden your soul, and you will kill many more for the Regime." She slammed her fist against her chest. "Hail the red spiral!"

Tilla returned the salute, chin raised. "Hail the red spiral."

"Return to your phalanx. We prepare for war. Soon we will fly to Cadport, and we will face the Resistance in battle... and you will face Relesar again. And you will be ready for him."

With that, Shari shifted into a dragon and took flight, her true wing thudding, her prosthetic creaking. She rose above the camp, filled her maw with fire, and blasted a flaming jet across the sky.

She grinned as she soared higher. Of course, the man *was* only a quarryman. But Tilla didn't have to know that, and Shari had enough quarrymen to spare. What mattered was not another death, but Tilla's soul--a soul Shari would break and reshape into her greatest weapon.

When she rose high enough, Shari saw the entire camp sprawled below. Across the ruins of Castra Luna, her workers were digging ditches, raising scaffolding, and building the first walls of her new castle, the glorious Castra Sol. In the forest clearing beyond the construction, her army mustered, ten thousand strong, men and women all in steel, drilling and saluting and preparing for battle.

Shari turned her head north. The forests sprawled red as blood into distant mist. Upon the horizon, she saw dragons fly, thousands of troops joining her from their northern forts.

More will muster here, Shari thought. *We will gather in strength, a great hammer ready to fall. We will fall upon the south, and Cadport will burn.*

Shari howled, roared her fire, and grinned.

ERRY

She walked through the forest until the sounds of the camp faded behind her. Scraggles walked at her side, tail slapping branches and bushes, and gave her a plaintive look. The dog could feel the sadness inside her--Erry knew that he could--and he licked her fingers.

"Come on, Scrags," she said and gave him a pat. "We have to keep moving."

Shouts rose behind her.

"Erry!" The prince was hoarse. "Damn it, Erry, come back here."

She kept walking. She was small and sneaky and silent. She had lived for years alone upon the docks, fleeing wild dogs and those who'd steal her food or break her body. If she did not want the Lechers to find her, they would not.

"We'll find a better place," she said softly to Scraggles, keeping one hand on his back as they walked. "Leresy can go eat furry bear droppings."

Scraggles wagged his tail in approval, and they kept walking through the forest. She had to move slowly--dry leaves carpeted the forest floor, crackling beneath her boots, and there were plenty branches to snap underfoot. But she was far enough now. They would never find her, not if they uprooted every tree here.

Erry reached into her pocket and fished out her medallion. She gazed at it--a silver sunburst upon a leather thong. A prayer in foreign letters gleamed upon it. It was the language of Tiranor, which she could not read.

"Tiranor," Erry whispered, caressing the medallion. "My other home."

She had never been to that southern desert kingdom. She had never met her father, the Tiran who had bought her mother upon the docks. With this medallion, the sailor had paid for his night of pleasure, then vanished back overseas the next day. When Erry was younger, a feral urchin upon the docks, she would often gaze at this sunburst and dream.

"The desert is a better place," she would whisper, shivering and cold and hungry enough to eat dead fish. "There are oases there full of dates and figs, and sandstone columns rise into the sky, and my father is a wealthy man. Wealthy enough to have paid for my mother with this silver medallion, not just copper coins. He is a great prince."

She would weep and dream of flying to that desert, but never did. The Legions had burned Tiranor years ago; everyone knew that. No more ships sailed to Requiem from that distant land. No more life filled the dunes. Her father was dead; the Legions had slain him.

And so Erry had remained in Requiem. But she had kept this medallion. She never wore it around her neck; if any caught her wearing a symbol of Tiranor, they would slay her. But she kept it always in her pocket. A prayer she could not read. A memory. A hope that a better world did exist out there.

"Maybe we should fly there, Scrags," she said, walking through the forest, her father's medallion in her hand. "Maybe he still lives out there, a prince of the desert, and we can find him."

Scraggles licked her hand, and Erry patted him, sniffed back her tears, and kept walking.

"Erry!" Leresy shouted behind; he sounded hundreds of yards away, his voice so dim, she could barely hear. "Erry, damn it, will you listen to me?"

She touched her cheek where he'd struck her. It still tingled and Erry sighed. Men had struck her before--many times and much harder. During those long years, orphaned on the docks, she had suffered many bruises and cuts. Men had tried to hurt her for sex, for theft, for pleasure, and Erry had always fought them, and she had always healed.

"He's just another one of them, Scraggles," she said, a lump in her throat. "Just like the drunkards on the boardwalk."

She had bedded such men before, so many she could not count. She had given her body for food, shelter, or warmth on a cold night. The other girls in town called her a whore, but the other girls had roofs over their heads and food on their tables.

"I never took no money," she whispered to her dog. "Never! No man ever paid for me. I am not my mother. I took food. I took a bed and a roof when it rained. But I never sold myself for money."

And then... then she had joined the Legions. Then she had met Tilla and Mae, two souls she loved dearly. Then she had a roof over her head, even if it was only a tent roof. Then she had food to eat, even if it was only scraps. Then she had protection, a sword to fight with, a *home*.

She sniffed and wiped her eyes. Yet Mae was dead and buried, and Tilla was dead inside, and here she was again. Feral and alone. Hungry. Lost.

And now... now, after all these men, it was Leresy, the prince of Requiem himself, who filled the same old role. Now another man wanted her body for food, for shelter, for promises of protection. And again--only days out of the Legions--she was selling herself.

"But no more, Scraggles," she whispered, and a tear trailed down her cheek. "I'm done with this life. I can't be that old Erry again. I can't let more men beat me, use me, toss me scraps to eat and worthless promises. I'd rather live alone in the wilderness with you, Scraggles, even if we starve to death."

The forest was thick. The fallen leaves rose above her feet. Bushes, wild grass, and ivy tangled around her legs, rising to her shoulders at some spots. The trees crowded around her--twisting oaks, craggy pines, and white birches with peeling bark. Red and golden leaves rustled above her, hiding the sky. Erry didn't even know in what direction she walked. She couldn't see more than several yards ahead. Yet she kept moving, just to get away from the Lechers, from Leresy, and from her past... from the old Erry she vowed she'd never become again.

"No more," she whispered. "Never again. I can't go back to the person I was."

His voice rose behind her. "Erry!"

He was in dragon form now; his voice was deeper and louder, ringing across the forest. Wings thudded in the distance. Erry kept moving.

"He can't see us down here," she whispered. "The trees are too thick."

She kept walking, and the wings kept beating above, and Leresy roared. The trees bent madly and leaves showered down; he was flying right above. Erry found herself gripping her sword but released it with a shaky breath.

He still can't see me, she thought. This forest rolled for leagues and leagues, and the canopy was thick as a ceiling. The dragon would have better luck finding a single fish in a murky ocean.

And then Scraggles began to bark.

"Hush!" she whispered, knelt, and grabbed the dog. "Scrags, quiet!"

Yet he kept barking madly at the sky, tail straight as an arrow. Erry tried to calm him--hugging, petting, and whispering to him--but he kept barking. Even when she tried to hold his mouth shut, he tore himself free--he was stronger than her--and barked some more.

The dragon above roared.

The canopy crashed open. Claws glinted. A red dragon swooped down into the forest, fire trailing from his maw. His tail lashed, tearing down trees, and his wings raised fallen leaves into a flurry.

Erry turned and ran.

She leaped over roots, bushes, and rocks. She didn't turn to look back. A root snagged her foot, and she crashed down into fallen leaves, filling her mouth with mud and moss. She leaped up. She kept running.

"Erry, damn it!" Leresy shouted behind her. "Stop and listen to me. I'm not going to hurt you."

"You already did, you dung-sucking gutter stain!" she shouted over her shoulder.

She could not see him, but he was near, and she cursed herself for yelling and revealing her location. She kept racing. Scraggles ran at her side. A rock twisted under her foot, and she fell again. She pushed herself up, but before she could keep running, something grabbed her tunic.

She spun around, swinging her fists, and struck Leresy hard on the jaw; he was back in human form. He grunted, his lip bleeding, but kept holding her. She struggled and screamed, but he grabbed her arms. She tried to kick, but her feet found only dry leaves, showering them onto Leresy.

"Damn it, woman," he said and spat out leaves. "Will you just listen to me? Calm down and let's talk. I just--"

Scraggles bit him.

Leresy screamed.

The black mutt clung to his leg, digging his teeth deeper. Leresy kicked, trying to shake Scraggles off, and screamed again. The dog would not release him.

"Good boy!" Erry shouted. "Bite his leg off!"

Cursing, Leresy drew his sword and raised it above the dog.

Fear flooded Erry like a bucket of ice.

She screamed, leaped, and grabbed Leresy's arm, pulling his sword down. The blade sliced her thigh, she fell to her knees, and blood dripped into the leaves.

The fight froze.

Teeth deep in Leresy's leg, Scraggles stared at the blood, released the prince, and mewled. Leresy too stared at Erry's wound. His eyes widened, and he tossed his sword into the leaves like a viper.

"Oh stars," he whispered and knelt beside Erry. "I didn't mean to... Damn it, that dog of yours, he--"

She punched him again.

She punched him so hard his head snapped sideways, and he fell onto his back.

"You drunken, flea-bitten bastard!" she said. She rose to her feet, blood dripping down her thigh, and glared down at the prince. "You gelatinous piece of chamber pot goo. You--"

Lying bleeding in the leaves, he reached up, grabbed her wrist, and pulled her down.

She fell atop him, snarled, and tried to bite his face. He held her back; her teeth missed his nose by an inch.

"Erry," he said, "listen to me, damn it. I love you, all right? And I'm sorry. I'm sorry I struck you."

She spat on his face, hitting him square in the forehead.

"Go to the Abyss," she said. "I'm not one of your whores."

"I don't want you to be one," he said, blood and spit and mud mingling on his face. "I don't want a whore. Stars, Erry, I'm too poor to afford one now anyway."

She rolled her eyes. "Your sweet talk is truly winning me over."

Yet she felt her anger ebb as her blood dripped. She rolled off him and lay at his side, staring up at the canopy.

"Erry," he said, voice choked. When she looked over, she was surprised to see his eyes dampen. "Erry, I... I haven't been right since the battle. Everything is just... my mind is all..."

"Tiny?" she suggested. "Slow as a snail? Nonexistent?"

"Muddled," he said. "Too much damn drink, and too many damn memories. Since Nairi died--since everyone died there--I just keep seeing it. The blood. The corpses. The Resistance flying against us. Stars, Erry, there were so many of them, thousands of dragons and soldiers. They knew me. They knew my name. *Death to Leresy!* they shouted." Tears joined the mess of blood, saliva, and mud on his face. "So I drank too much, and I whored too much, and I hit you. I'm sorry."

She snorted weakly and her eyes stung. "And you think you can tell me you love me now? And I'll forgive you? Did you say that to Nairi or all the girls you bought?"

"Nairi?" he said. "No. I never loved Nairi. I thought I did. She was young, beautiful, and powerful, and... a typical young man, I courted her. But loved her?" He sighed. "I loved her power. But you, Erry, you have no power."

"Again, my prince, your sweet talk is falling somewhat short of my standard."

He propped himself up onto his elbows. "Erry, damn you. You're nothing but a feral little beast. You have no money. You have no noble blood, no influence, no standing at court." He stared down at her chest. "Stars damn it, you've got barely any meat on your bones. But... you joined my camp. You wanted to be with me. And I wanted you."

"To bed me every night and dawn," she said bitterly. "To use my body, and because I'm so poor, I'd let you do it--for food, for shelter, for your promises. And I did that for a while. Because you fed me, and because you protected me." She rose to her elbows too and looked at him. "But then you struck me, so deal's off, Leresy. No more."

"The deal was off a moon ago!" he said, voice rising now. "The deal was off after the first two days." He snorted. "Use you? For sex? Erry, I don't care about that. You know what you gave me? You gave me intolerable arguments over that stupid game you just can't play. And you gave me cuss words I never even knew existed; I use some of them now. And you gave me somebody to hold at night. I never held a woman before; I never held Nairi or the others. But I hold you all night, and I stroke your hair, and I kiss you, and... when I do that, it's better than all the booze and sex. It's not just forgetting the past with you. It's seeing a future."

She was about to snort again. She was about to spit at him, punch him, and run. But she only sighed.

"Stars damn you, Leresy Cadigus," she said.

He held her hand. "Erry, I'm sorry. I'm truly deeply sorry. I... I want to show you something."

He rolled up his sleeve and she gasped. She covered her mouth and her eyes stung.

"Stars, Ler," she whispered.

He sighed and nodded. "My father gave me that scar. He burned me because I couldn't learn a sword thrust fast enough. I was only six years old." He unlaced his shirt, pulled it down, and showed her a scar across his chest. "And he gave me this scar with a hot poker. I was ten and I couldn't remember the name of some ancient fort that no longer exists." He closed his shirt. "I have about a dozen more scars across me, a dozen more stories. Erry, my siblings and I... we were raised in violence, in fear, in hate. My sister Shari turned into a heartless killer; my father broke her mind. My sister Kaelyn fled. And I, well... I'm a damn broken wreck. I drink too much and I hit you, and my past can't justify that, I know. I know it's not an excuse. I don't ask for acceptance, only for forgiveness. Will you forgive me, Erry?" His voice shook and his eyes dampened. "Because I don't want you to leave me. Please. *Please* don't leave me."

Her own eyes watered and she embraced him, laid her cheek against his chest, and felt her tears wet his shirt.

"I have scars too," she whispered. "You only have a dozen? You weakling. I have more. And I'll probably have another one on my leg from your damn sword."

He held her close, nearly crushing her. "I'll never hurt you again, Erry Docker. I promise. I promise. Just stay with me, and we'll figure things out. We'll find a home somewhere, you and I. You won't have to be my concubine or my mistress. You will just be... whatever you want to be, so long as we're together."

A weight pressed down onto Erry's shoulder; Scraggles had joined the embrace. The three lay in the forest, dry leaves falling around them, and Erry sighed.

"All right, Leresy," she whispered as he stroked her hair, not knowing if she made the right choice, but feeling too weak to run. "All right."

TILLA

On a cold rainy morning in Castra Sol, the Emperor of Requiem arrived with all his contingent and asked to speak with her alone.

Tilla was drilling that morning outside her tent, sparring with her troops and imagining swinging her blade against resistors. The forest bobbed and dripped rain beyond their tents, the wet autumn leaves turned dark as blood.

When we reach Cadport, she thought, thrusting blows against one of her troops, *they will flee into houses and holes. It will be a battle of blades then.*

The soldier before her, a young flight leader with two red stars upon his armbands, cursed as he parried. Sweat dripped down his temples. Tilla kept attacking, using every thrust she'd learned at the academy. She shuffled forward with small, quick steps, sword swinging down from side to side. It was all her opponent could do to parry. Finally Tilla slammed her sword--a dulled training blade--hard onto his pauldron.

"That's a kill!" she said.

He grunted and tossed down his own training sword.

"Commander," he said, "your sword wouldn't break through this steel. My armor is thick, and--"

"And my true blade was forged in dragonfire from northern steel," Tilla said, interrupting him. "A thrust this hard, with two hands, would cleave your armor and bone; your arm would be lying in the dust."

The young corelis--he ranked above a green periva, but below a hardened siragi--cracked his neck.

"The Resistance don't got northern steel forged in dragonfire," he argued. "Bastards fight with rusted, chipped blades."

Tilla fixed him with an icy stare. "Valien Eleison carries the sword of a knight, a blade of the old order of bellators. It would cut through your armor like parchment. Do you not dream of slaying Valien?"

The soldier stared back, then nodded and lifted his blade.

"Next man!" Tilla shouted.

Yet before another soldier could step forward to drill, roars trumpeted in the distance.

Tilla froze, sword raised.

The roars pealed across the sky, thousands of them rising from the north. The beating of wings rose like a storm. A distant voice cried out, hailing the red spiral, and countless voices answered in a chant.

"Keep training!" Tilla said. She turned to her siragi, a brawny soldier with dark eyes, her right-hand man in the phalanx. "Siragi, take command."

The man nodded and Tilla shifted. She rose from the square, white wings raising clouds of dust, her flames crackling.

She soared high above the camp. Lines of tents sprawled before her like a great city; fifty thousand now mustered here, marching and drilling. Beating her wings and rising higher, Tilla raised her head and stared into the north.

She gasped. A shiver clanked her scales like a purse of coins.

"By the Abyss," she whispered.

A great army flew ahead, as large as the army mustered below. Tilla had never seen so many dragons fly together; she could barely breathe. They flew in five great squares across the sky--five brigades, each one ten thousand dragons strong. Within each brigade, the square further divided into ten milanxes, then into ten again, forming phalanxes of a hundred.

"Fifty thousand dragons," Tilla whispered, hovering in the air, watching them fly from the north.

This was not only a force to capture a city.

This was a force to finally slaughter every last resistor.

At the head of this army, a black triangle of dragons flew like an arrowhead, and another shiver ran through Tilla.

"The emperor," she whispered, "and the Axehand Order."

They still flew a league away, but Tilla could make out Frey Cadigus, a great golden dragon, flying at their lead. Around him flew the Axehand Order, his fanatic warrior-priests. They wore black armor bristly with blades, and axeheads shone upon their stumps. They shrieked to the sky, hailing their lord, worshiping him as their god.

"Five hundred axehands fly here," Tilla whispered, "and they frighten me more than the fifty thousand legionaries behind them."

She hovered in place, watching as the northern army swallowed the forest under their shadow, roared their arrival, and descended into the camp. For the past few days, Shari had ordered troops to tear down thousands of trees north of the ruins, carving a great clearing. Now the northern host descended here in a storm of wings, an inferno of flame, and a cacophony of howls and roars and grunts. Dragons shifted into men. Legionaries took formations, tens of thousands forming lines and squares. The Axehand swept between them as ghosts, hidden within black robes and hoods. A great tent rose, its walls bedecked with spirals; the emperor strode into it.

Tilla descended, shifted into human form, and returned to her tent.

She stared into her small mirror.

A pale woman stared back, her dark eyes cold, her smooth black hair cut neatly, falling just above her chin. She knew that many called her face icy, the face of a statue. Her townsfolk had whispered this in Cadport, back when Tilla had lived as a commoner. Today her troops whispered it; she could hear them. They said her face and heart were carved of ice. They said her eyes were stone marbles, devoid of life, pity, or any feeling.

Yet they did not see her nightmares. They did not see her heart. And today... today that heart twisted with fear. That heart was not carved of ice; the ice coursed through her veins and belly.

"When I joined the Legions," she whispered to her reflection, "I vowed to banish all fear from me. Yet today I'm more afraid than ever."

She reached to the small box she kept on her table. Her fingers shook, but she took a deep breath and opened the box.

Her eyes stung.

She pulled out a seashell necklace.

"Damn it," she whispered, eyes dampening.

She caressed the seashells, listening to them chink. It was her one memento of Cadport. It was her one memory of her lowborn roots, of a ropemaker's daughter too poor to eat dinner many nights.

"It's my only memory of Rune," she whispered.

He had collected these seashells, strung them together, and given her this gift on her fourteenth birthday. Five years had passed since then, and Tilla had a sword now, fine armor, and silver in her purse, yet she kept this humble necklace.

It's the most precious thing I own, she thought.

She placed the necklace back into her box and closed her eyes.

"Oh Rune," she whispered. "Why did you do this? Why did you fall to evil? Now the Legions muster... and they will break you."

Her eyes stung. She knew what they'd do to him. Frey Cadigus would shatter Rune's bones, flay his skin, but leave him alive. The emperor would parade his trophy across the capital, letting all hear Rune scream, then finally--after days or moons or even years--he would allow Rune the mercy of death.

"Why, Rune?" Tilla whispered, clutching the box. "Why did you have to betray your kingdom? Why did you let the Resistance turn you against Requiem?" Her fingers shook. "Now I will have to hurt you, Rune. Now I will have to fight you. You could have stopped this. You forced me to do this."

Her tent flap opened behind her.

At the sound, Tilla spun around, clutching her punisher. Her troops were never to barge into her tent; she would burn anyone who did.

Her snarl died on her lips, and she released her punisher. A new gush of fear flooded her.

Two axehands stood at her tent entrance.

Their black robes draped across them, but the sleeves were short enough to reveal their deformity: axe blades strapped to their left stumps, the very blades they themselves had severed their hands with. Their hoods cast deep shadows, but Tilla caught hints of their iron masks; those masks were bolted on to the flesh, impossible to remove. Around their waists, they displayed the tools of their trade: pincers, needles, and blades for torturing their enemies.

They will use these on Rune, Tilla thought. *They'd use them on me if they knew I still cared for him.*

She slammed her fist against her chest, struggling to hide her trembling.

"Hail the red spiral!" she said.

One of the axehands spoke, his voice a hiss behind his mask, an inhuman sound.

"You are Tilla Siren. You will accompany us. His holiness, the great God of Dragons, will speak with you. Follow."

They reached out their right hands. Their fingers were scarred and wrinkled as if dipped in acid, and Tilla shuddered.

They chopped off their left hands to prove their loyalty, she thought. *What did Frey demand they do to their right hands?*

She took a deep breath, clutched her sword, and followed them outside.

They shifted into dragons. They flew over the camp; a hundred thousand troops drilled below them. As they dived toward the emperor's tent, Tilla's heart twisted, and smoke spurted from her nostrils.

Stars, he knows, she thought. *Somehow Frey knows about the seashell necklace. He knows I grew up with Rune.* Her scales clattered. *He'll have me tortured and killed.*

Yet what could she do? She could not flee; they would catch her. All she could do was fly with the axehands, speak with the emperor... and beg.

They landed outside the emperor's tent. It rose like a mansion before her, black walls thudding in the wind. A hundred axehands surrounded the tent, their black robes swaying like ghosts at midnight.

Tilla shifted back into human form, and an axehand opened the flap to Frey's tent, revealing shadows.

"Enter," the dark priest hissed, beckoning with his blade.

Tilla raised her chin, squared her shoulders, and sucked in her breath.

Strength, Tilla, she told herself. *Always be strong. Show no weakness. Weakness is death.*

She stepped into the darkness.

The tent was large and bare. Ten dragons could have stood in here, but Tilla saw only a table, two chairs, and one man.

Frey Cadigus, Emperor of Requiem, stood sharpening a dagger, rubbing stone and blade together. He stood in profile to her, staring at his blade, as if he hadn't noticed her enter. Tilla had never seen him up close before. He was a tall man, and his pauldrons flared out from wide shoulders. His armor was meticulous, the black plates lines with golden dragons, bolted together into a second skin. He wore no helm today. His face was cold and hard, the nose hooked, the brow high. Grooves framed his thin lips.

More than his blade, his armor, or his cruel mouth, his eyes frightened Tilla. When they turned to stare at her, they were cold, hard, and penetrating as swords.

Tilla saluted, slamming fist to chest.

He returned the salute, his eyes digging into her--into her mind, her heart, her oldest secrets.

"Lanse Tilla Siren," the emperor said. "Tilla of Cadport. My daughter speaks of you often." He gestured at the table. "Sit."

When Tilla stepped closer to the table and chairs, she sucked in her breath. She felt the blood leave her face.

What she'd first taken for wine jugs were actually glass jars. Inside each vessel floated a head, its mouth open in a silent scream.

Frey studied her. "Do they frighten you, child?"

Tilla tightened her lips and sat.

"No, Commander," she said and met his gaze.

A frightened child would die today, she thought. *A soldier, heart hardened, will live.*

Frey still stood. He caressed one of the jars; inside floated the head of a child, her hair long and braided, her eyes still wide with fear.

"The Aeternum Dynasty used to rule in splendor," Frey said. "They governed in halls of marble, harps, and starlight." He snorted. "They were weak. They were soft. They sang music and drank wine in their halls while our enemies mustered. They prayed to the stars as griffins, wyverns, and phoenixes slaughtered our people." He caressed a second jar; the head floating inside looked eerily like Rune. "Look at them now, lanse. Look what their weakness brought them."

Tilla stared. Bile rose in her throat. By the stars...

"The... Aeternum family," she whispered.

Rune's family.

Frey gazed at the jars as if lost in thought. "I take them with me always. I sleep by their side. I dine with them on my table. Do you know why, lanse?"

Tilla raised her chin. "To remember."

He barked a laugh. "Yes. To remember. To remember their weakness. To remember their punishment. To remember why we fight." He nodded and met her gaze. "My daughter speaks highly of you. She says you serve the red spiral well. She also says... that you knew an Aeternum."

Finally he sat too. He leaned forward in his seat and stared at her. The jars rose upon the table between them. The severed heads seemed to stare at Tilla too.

"I knew Relesar in Cadport," Tilla said, and her insides twisted. Her voice softened. "He was called Rune then."

She stared at the jars. *Rune's parents and siblings.* Tilla's throat tightened, and under the table, she twisted her fingers together. She could imagine Rune's head joining the others, staring at her with dead eyes, begging her. Tilla had to suck in her breath and grind her teeth to stop her eyes from watering.

"Tell me about him," said the emperor. "Tell me about our enemy. But do not tell me about Relesar Aeternum. I hear stories of Relesar all day from a thousand men--Relesar the brutal warrior, or Relesar the frightened pup, or Relesar the figurehead dancing to Valien's flute. I hear only stories. I hear men brag and boast, and I hear men whisper in fear." He leaned closer across the table. "Do not tell me about the heir of a fallen dynasty. Tell me about Rune. Tell me about the boy you knew."

Tilla swallowed, wanting to flee, wanting to vanish, wanting anything but this.

Stars, Rune, why did you have to join the Resistance? Why didn't you just run?

"He grew up thinking he was a mere brewer," Tilla said, and now her eyes stung. "He never spoke against the Regime. He never spoke of the lost days of Aeternum. He did not know of his heritage until the Resistance found him. He was just a commoner. He was my friend."

Those days returned to her, so powerful she could barely breathe. In her mind, she walked along the beach with him again, collecting seashells under the sun, swimming among the waves, and laughing and telling stories. And she remembered that last night. She could feel his embrace and kiss again.

"And yet," Frey said. "And yet... he rose against us. He flew against this very fortress. He slaughtered hundreds here-- hundreds of youths from his own town."

Tilla nodded. "I know," she said softly. "And I hate him for it. And I fought him that day. We locked swords in the clock tower." She looked again at the jars, then raised her eyes and met the emperor's gaze. "But Commander, I believe that he did not choose this fight. I believe that Valien Eleison poisoned his mind. I believe that the Resistance kidnapped him, forced him to hate us, forced him to fight. And I believe--I *must* believe--that he can be saved. That deep inside, he still loves Requiem."

Frey raised his eyebrows. "I should think that an officer in the Legions would crave to behead our greatest enemy."

Tilla swallowed. She had to tread carefully here. A wrong word and she herself would lose her head. She glanced again at the jars. She hated Rune. She hated all that he'd done. Yet for her memories, for her seashells, and for that kiss, she had to save him. She had to.

She returned her eyes to the emperor.

"Our greatest enemy is no single man, Commander," she said. "Our enemy is an *idea*. Our enemy is *defiance*. The Resistance is small; they cannot defeat us with strength of arms. They fight not with blades, but with foolish dreams. That's why they did not attack the capital, but plastered their words across our walls." Tilla trembled, knowing she could die any second, but kept talking. "To the Resistance, that's all Rune is. Not a warrior. Certainly not a leader. He's an *idea*. He's a memory of older days."

Frey stared at Tilla, and his eyes narrowed, and his lips tightened, and she could not breathe. She was sure he would kill her. She was sure this was her last flicker of life. When Frey opened his mouth, she expected him to call the axehands to torture and slay her.

Yet only a laugh burst from his lips, a snort of amusement.

"Ha! My daughter was right." Frey's lips twisted into a mockery of a smile. "You are a wise one, Lanse Siren. But tell me--should rebellious ideas not be crushed? A figurehead rises against us. Should we not behead him?"

Tilla shook her head, breath shaky. "Commander, it's not my role to dictate policy. You are wiser than I am. Yet if you ask me my thoughts, I will say: No." She gripped her hands under the table. "You cannot slay an idea with a blade. If you kill Relesar, you give the Resistance more power. You would turn Relesar into a martyr. The people would rally around his death; the idea would live on."

Frey nodded slowly, lips pursed. "So are we to let him live, you say? Are we to let him keep fighting, keep slaying our troops, keep spreading this *idea*?"

"No," Tilla said. "We cannot do that either. Again, Commander, you are wiser than I am. Yet since you ask me, I speak to you freely." She raised her chin and stared at him, forcing herself not to look away. "Commander, we must capture Relesar, and we must force him to abandon this idea. We must stand him upon the towers and walls of Nova Vita, and we must have him hail the red spiral. The people will see that even Relesar Aeternum, heir of the old dynasty, worships your glory." She nodded. "All fire would drain from the Resistance. Valien would be left with nothing but a few haggard fighters."

Frey nodded. "You speak wisely, child. A dead martyr is far more dangerous than a living servant. People still fight for their dead. Have their hero foreswear his fight, and their courage will abandon them. And yet, what makes you think we can sway Relesar? With torture?" He raised an eyebrow. "Would you have us torture your childhood friend?"

Tilla swallowed, remembering the man in the hut, the man she had burned and cut.

"If need be," she said softly. "Yet I believe that I can sway him more easily. Tortured lips reveal their pain; a forced vow of loyalty would sway few." She leaned across the table. "I can sway him with words, Commander. With my punisher if I must, but I believe my words will work better. Please, Commander. I know Rune. I grew up with him. He loves Requiem, yet Valien has poisoned his mind. Allow me to show him your glory! Let us capture him. Let us bring him north. I will show him your light and the errors of his ways. He will become not a tortured, sniveling slave, but a true warrior to our cause." She allowed herself a small smile. "Can you imagine a greater blow to the Resistance?"

The emperor was silent.

Tilla sat still, refusing to break their stare.

Please, Tilla prayed silently to whatever gods, new or old, might be listening. *Please let him agree. Please. I cannot see Rune beheaded, despite all his sins. I must save him.*

The emperor's stare seemed to last forever. His gaze bored into her, seeking, rifling, searching for any trace of betrayal. Tilla forced herself to stare back, chin raised and jaw squared.

Finally the emperor rose to his feet.

"You are wise, Lanse Siren," he said. "And you speak truth. My daughter is right to groom you." He placed his hand on one jar; inside floated the head that looked like Rune. "We will take Relesar alive, and it will be your task to sway him. You will use words, or you will use your punisher." His lips pulled back in a snarl. "Relesar Aeternum will stand upon the tower of Tarath Imperium, gaze upon the empire, and roar his loyalty to the red spiral. And if he will not... his head will join the others."

As Tilla flew back to her tent, her insides roiled and her wings shook.

I saved your life today, Rune, she thought as she flew over the camp. *You might never know it, but today I saved you.*

Below her, a hundred thousand troops saluted and roared. War was near.

KAELYN

My father is coming to kill me.

The words echoed through Kaelyn's mind as she crawled down the tunnel. The dirt walls closed in around her, reinforced with wooden slats. Resistors crawled behind, lamps shining, boasting of how many soldiers they'd kill. Kaelyn barely heard them.

My father is coming to kill me.

The words kept rattling in her skull. Kaelyn held a tin lamp and a parchment map of these tunnels. She knew that she crawled beneath the tannery, heading toward the butcher shop. Yet in the shadows, this seemed an older, darker place. In the shadows, she was a frightened girl again, hiding under her bed as her father raged. Again she saw his hands reaching to grab her, his rod raised to strike, his eyes blazing.

"No, Father," she whispered. "Please."

She winced. The scars flared across her body, all those scars he'd given her and Leresy. She had escaped. She had left her twin behind. She had grown into a strong woman, a warrior, a leader. Yet here in the darkness, the walls closing in around her, that strength vanished. Here she was young and afraid.

My father is coming to kill me.

"Kaelyn," Rune whispered behind her. "How far is it?"

She looked over her shoulder and saw him there, covered in grime. He crawled on his belly, holding a lamp.

"We're under Market Street," she said, checking her map. "The fur shop is above us; the butcher shop is ahead. That's where the tunnel goes."

His face was young and earnest. He still did not know enough fear. He still had not seen enough of her father's cruelty.

Kaelyn kept crawling.

Again my father reaches for me, she thought. Only now he reached toward her with an army. And if he caught her this time, if she could not scurry deep enough into the shadows, he would not just beat her. He would kill her and display her mutilated corpse to the empire.

The tunnel curved up, leading to floorboards above her head. Kaelyn pushed them aside and crawled onto the floor of the butcher shop. Rubbing dust out of her eyes, she reached down and helped Rune enter too. Ten other resistors followed, clad in leather armor and bearing swords and bows.

Kaelyn looked around her and nodded, satisfied. Large slabs of meat hung from hooks, providing many places to hide. Cleavers hung upon walls, providing extra weapons. A barrel of gunpowder stood at the door, wired to blast outward should the Legions burst into the shop.

"I want to be stationed here when the fighting starts," Rune said. He looked around, smacked his lips, and nodded. "Lots of nice, fresh slabs of ham. Perfect if you get hungry during the fighting." He nodded. "Definitely the best place to be."

Kaelyn glowered and jabbed her finger at his chest.

"You," she said, "will fight from Castellum Acta with me and Valien."

Rune rubbed his chest and moaned. "Can I fight from the bakery?"

"No!"

"How about the wine shop? I can--"

"Rune!" Kaelyn grabbed his collar. "Will you *please* stop thinking about your belly for once? The Legions fly here, and you need to stay near me and Valien in the fortress. I need to look after you."

He cleared his throat. "I am, you know, your king." He puffed out his chest. "I could just command myself to stay here with the nice food."

"You're not my king yet," she said, fixing him with her best glare. "Until we win this war, you're nothing but a silly boy with a very hungry belly and a very empty skull. Now come on, we have more tunnels to inspect."

They returned to the tunnel. They kept crawling.

They crawled for hours.

During the past two moons, they had dug a network of tunnels under every main street in Lynport. As Kaelyn crawled, she examined her map.

"In these tunnels, we can scurry between every shop in town," she whispered to herself. "We can crawl from courthouse to castle, from cobbler shop to chandlery, from forest to sea."

He is coming to kill me.

She sucked in her breath; it trembled in her lungs.

"Every doorway is booby trapped with gunpowder," she whispered. "Archers stand in every window, watching every street and alley. When the Legions swarm, we will slaughter them everywhere."

Yet her heart kept thrashing, and her fingers kept trembling, and she couldn't stop that voice from echoing.

So come, she thought and tightened her lips. *Come and let us fight. Come and let it be done.*

When evening fell, she and Rune rose from the tunnels, shifted into dragons, and flew toward the fortress on the hill. Castellum Acta now displayed the banners of Aeternum, a silver, two-headed dragon upon a green field. The Regime had been cleansed from this place. Its troops had joined the Resistance or sat chained in its dungeon.

From here we will command the battle, Kaelyn thought, flying toward the tower. *Here our fate will be decided.*

Sunset gilded the tower and the whispering sea. The scent of salt filled Kaelyn's nostrils, and the northern forest murmured and swayed. She looked toward the setting sun and felt small.

If I could fly high as the sun, she thought, *this war would seem so small to me. We would all be but specks crashing together upon the land. And still the sun would turn. And still the sea would rise and fall.*

A lump filled her throat, for this sunset, these waves, and these trees--the land itself--seemed sad to her. Kaelyn had never known peace; she'd been raised in Tarath Imperium under her father's heel. Yet here in Lynport, she caught glimpses of what peace could mean. It was a whisper of waves, a song so ancient it had no words. It was the sway of trees, an eternal dance. It was orange sunset fading into starry night.

This is what Rune always meant, Kaelyn realized. He had talked of walks along the beach, of laughter with his friends, of peace, of hope. Kaelyn had never known such things, yet she saw them in the waves, and she heard them in the wind.

And I will fight for them, she thought, the scent of water and leaves in her nostrils, tears in her eyes. *And maybe someday I will know peace too.*

"Kaelyn," Rune said, flying beside her. He nudged her with his tail. "Are you all right?"

She managed a smile. "No. I'm not all right. None of this is." She blasted smoke. "But we're going to fight nonetheless."

The two dragons reached Castellum Acta and landed upon its tower. The battlements rose around them in a henge. The town stretched below along the coast, trapped between sea and forest.

Kaelyn took a deep breath, inhaling the crisp air.

Come and fight me, Father. I'm ready.

As if in answer, a roar sounded in the north.

Kaelyn whipped her head around. Her heart thudded. For an instant, she was sure the battle had come, that Frey Cadigus flew toward them with all his wrath and might. But it was only a single dragon flying across the forest. The dragon was still distant, but when Kaelyn squinted, she saw black scales crested with a white stripe.

"Lady Lana Cain," she whispered.

At her side, Rune growled. Smoke rose from his nostrils.

"She brings news," he said. "News is never good."

The striped dragon flew closer, swallowing the miles and roaring her cry. When finally Lana reached Lynport, she flew at a wobble, smoke trailing from her nostrils. With a last flap of her wings, Lana all but crashed onto the tower top. She shifted back into human form and lay panting, a woman clad in yellow and gray, a streak of white blazing through her black hair. A pin bearing the sigil of Cain, two statues guarding an archway, fastened her cloak.

"Lana!" Kaelyn said. She too shifted into human form and knelt above her friend. "Lana, are you all right?"

Lana lay wheezing. Her skin was pale, and her fingers trembled when she adjusted her eyepatch.

"The Legions," she whispered. Fear filled her one eye. "So many... so many."

Whenever Kaelyn had seen Lana, her friend had seemed a confident warrior, a smirk on her face, her hand always clutching her saber's hilt. Yet now she trembled like a woman returned from the Abyss.

"Do they fly south?" Kaelyn whispered and clutched her friend's hand. It was ice cold. "What have you seen?"

Lana reached up. She grabbed Kaelyn's shoulder, her fingers desperate, her lips white. She seemed like a drowning woman clinging on for life.

"Kaelyn," she whispered, "we must flee."

VALIEN

He stood in the grand hall of Castellum Acta, stared into the crackling fireplace, and growled.

I need a drink.

He clenched his fists. His head spun. His throat constricted; he could feel the soldier's fingers squeezing him again, that grip from years ago that had ruined his voice. Rye would cure that pain. Rye would erase that memory. Valien grumbled.

I had to hide the boy in the nearest tavern, didn't I? Now it's burned down and my throat is parched.

"Valien," she said behind him. "Valien, please."

He turned and saw her there. As always, when his eyes first fell upon her, he saw his wife again, saw Marilion staring from beyond the years, beckoning, pleading, waiting for him to save her.

"Valien," Kaelyn repeated. "What do we do?"

He tightened his lips.

It was Kaelyn, of course. It was always Kaelyn, a new light in his life, a reminder of throbbing shadows.

Marilion lives! She lives in my dungeon, you fool!

"Valien?" she asked, voice hesitant.

She sat at the table, her quiver slung across her shoulder. Rune sat at her side, clad in black wool and brown leather, the Amber Sword fastened at his belt. Lady Lana sat there too; her face was still pale, and her fingers still trembled as she brought a mug of soup to her lips.

"We flee," Valien said. "Simple as that. We cannot fight this."

Kaelyn and Rune leaped to their feet so fast their chairs crashed down. Both began to protest at once.

"But... we've dug all these tunnels!" Rune said, face red. "We've lined the walls with cannons. We've recruited three thousand townsfolk, armed them, given them positions, trained them to fight--"

Valien glared at the boy. "Three thousand townsfolk who would die when Frey arrives."

"Valien!" Kaelyn said. She marched around the table and grabbed his arm. "We've dug in here for two moons now, and... how we can just abandon this city? After all the work we've done?"

The two kept protesting. Valien ignored them. He looked past them to Lana. She still sat at the table silently, clutching her mug of broth but not drinking. She met his gaze.

"Valien, *why*?" Rune demanded.

But it was Lana who answered.

"Because I saw a hundred thousand bloodthirsty beasts," the lady of the canyon answered. "Because I saw the cruelest army that's flown since the great wars. We've mustered fighters here, yes. We have three thousand resistors. We have three thousand townsfolk who've taken arms. We have three thousand of my own men, warriors of the canyon." She shook her head and blew out her breath. "We are outnumbered. We are outnumbered more than ten to one. We expected one brigade to fly against us, maybe two. Not this." She lowered her head. "Not this."

Rune spun toward her, glaring, and pounded the table.

"One man fighting for his home is worth ten dragons!" he said. "One resistor fighting for justice is worth ten more." He drew his sword. "I bear Amerath, the Amber Sword of Aeternum. This sword stands for light, for truth, for courage. How can I bear it and run from battle?"

Valien looked at the boy, and sadness welled up inside him.

He is like me, he thought. *Rune is like me when I was his age. Brass. More brave than wise. So often, youth speak of justice and righteousness as if they alone can win wars.*

Rune had grown in the past year; Valien had seen it. The boy had come to him green, frightened, and soft. He stood in armor now. His face was gaunt, his grip strong. Ash and stubble covered his cheeks. He was a warrior now, yet he was not wise. Not yet. Not here.

"We've been running and hiding for almost twenty years," Valien said. "We are the Resistance. We are those who strike from shadow. We are those who leap and kill in darkness. We are the demon always in the corner of the legionary's eye. This is how we've always fought."

Rune snarled at him across the tabletop. "Yet now we're here. We've chosen to take this city. We've chosen to raise our banner in the sunlight. We've chosen to defend this place. I say we stay and defend it! Yes, we expected ten thousand to fly against us. A hundred thousand? Let them come. More for us to kill."

Valien roared, a sound that echoed, hoarse and torn, in the hall.

"You crave killing, boy?" He pounded the table so hard it cracked. "Have I taught you nothing? Are you but a mindless, bloodthirsty beast? You speak of death. You speak of blood. You have seen these horrors. Would you be ready to kill your friend, the girl who saved Shari, if she meets in you battle?" When Rune paled, Valien snorted. "I thought not. You speak folly."

"I speak," Rune said, eyes burning, "like you taught me."

Valien howled again. He tossed a chair aside; it smashed against a wall.

"I taught you none of this!"

Rune stood, chest heaving and eyes still blazing. He walked around the cracked table. He clutched Valien's arm and stared at him, teeth bared.

"You taught me justice, Valien," he said. "You taught me to stand tall and fight. Before I met you, I hid in shadows, a brewer, afraid." His voice shook. "You gave me courage. Do not let that courage abandon you." He swept his arm around the hall. "Look at the sea outside the arrowslits. Look at the forest. Look at the city and its people who stand tall, ready to fight, ready to die. This is my city. This is Lynport. I will not abandon it. Not if every last legionary flies against us."

Valien's eyes narrowed. "Not even if you die? Not even if we all die?"

Kaelyn had watched the exchange silently, hands on the hilts of her sword and dagger. Finally she spoke.

"We can still win this," she said. "We will do as we planned. Nothing changes. We will fight house to house, tunnel to tunnel, alley to alley. The town is stocked with gunpowder; every door, every window, every alleyway is rigged to slay them. We have maps. We can scurry, hide, and fire arrows while they burn." She nodded and gripped his arm, her eyes large and eager. "We can *win*, Valien."

And if I lose you? he thought, gazing upon her, and his chest tightened. *If I lose you like I lost her?*

She looked up at him. Large, hazel eyes. *Her* eyes.

What would you have me do, Marilion? Valien thought, fists tight at his sides, and his eyes burned. *Would you want me to run, or would you stay here and fight?*

He turned aside. He looked out the hall's southern arrowslit. A mile away, the breakwater thrust into the sea, and the lighthouse rose. The waves crashed against it, a heartbeat, an eternal whisper of the day he'd met her.

You stood barefoot in a homespun dress, and you wore seashells around your neck. And he killed you. He thrust a sword into you, and I couldn't save you. I had to save him, Marilion. I had to. I had to save the boy.

He spun back to the hall. He stared at Rune. His wife was dead, but that babe was still here. He stood before Valien now as a man, clad in armor, Aeternum's sword in his hand, ready to fight--ready to do what Valien had saved him to do.

I saved him for Requiem, Marilion, he thought. *I saved him for this day, so we can save our kingdom. Your death will not have been in vain.*

"For Requiem," Rune whispered.

For Marilion, Valien thought.

He marched across the hall, his throat still aching. He turned toward the northern arrowslit. He pointed at the walls that guarded the forest.

"Rune, take your men and guard the northern walls. When the enemy arrives, fire all our guns into their ranks. Slay as many as you can before rushing into our tunnels."

Rune pounded the table. "Yes."

Valien turned toward Kaelyn and fixed her with a hard stare. "Kaelyn, when they fly across the city--and they will fly past the walls, even with all our cannons--you will lead our men through the tunnels. You know them best. You will emerge from every window, hole, roof, and gutter to slay them with arrows, then retreat into shadow."

She nodded, teeth bared, and drew her sword. "Yes!"

Finally Valien turned to Lady Lana.

He paused.

Iciness filled him, and he approached her slowly. She was still seated, and he knelt before her and took her hand.

"Lana, you know your task."

She nodded, face pale, and said nothing.

Valien squeezed her hand. "Lead them to safety, Lana. Tens of thousands live in this city, but they are not warriors. They are mothers, children, and elders. You must defend them. You must lead them out now--at once. Take them into your canyon. Hide them in your father's halls." He rose back to his feet. "This city will be a bloodbath."

Lana stood up too. She gave him a silent stare, then pulled him into a crushing embrace. She was a slender woman, but she gripped him with the might of a burly blacksmith.

"Be strong, warrior of Requiem," she whispered into his ear, then--surprising him--kissed his cheek. "Remember always, Lord Valien Eleison, knight of the realm--you are the light of stars."

With that she spun around. Gripping her saber, she marched toward the fortress doors, stepped outside, and shifted into a dragon. She glided across the city, roaring her call.

"People of Lynport--the time has come! We evacuate! All those who are not fighters--shift and fly. Follow me to safety!"

Valien turned from the doors, clanked up the stairs of Acta's tower, and emerged onto the battlements. He stood and watched the city. Rune and Kaelyn came to stand beside him, the wind whipping their hair.

"People of Lynport!" Lana cried, flying over the roofs. "We evacuate!"

Valien gripped a merlon, struggling to calm the tremble in his fingers. Thousands of people were emerging from their homes below. They shifted into dragons like they had drilled a dozen times; Valien himself had drilled them. They took flight.

Myriads rose into the air, a tapestry of scales of every color, shimmering and streaming across the city. Wings beat. Smoke rose in plumes.

They wobbled as they flew. Before Lynport's liberation only two moons ago, the Regime had outlawed shifting into dragons. Many elders had not flown in eighteen years. Many youngsters had never shifted at all until winning their freedom that autumn. Others had broken the laws of Cadigus, shifting at night over the sea, but most still flew as hesitantly as baby birds.

"Fly, people of Lynport!" Lana cried. "Fly with the magic of Requiem."

They flew northwest.

They flew toward the canyon, to safety underground.

Below them, the warriors--resistors, men of the canyon, and those townsfolk brave enough to raise a weapon--manned the walls.

"It is here," Valien whispered. "The great battle of our uprising. The Battle for Lynport."

He looked north. In the distance, leagues away, a shadow fell.

TILLA

They swarmed over the wilderness.

They covered the sky, a hundred thousand strong. They flew in perfect formation--ten chevrons, one after the other, ten brigades howling for blood. The beat of wings scattered the clouds and bent the forests below. Eyes blazed and scales clattered in a storm. Fire rose between fangs, shining against spiked armor. The sky burned.

War, Tilla thought, flapping her wings and staring forward with grim intent. *Blood. The great battle to end the Resistance.*

And it would be fought at her home.

She peered ahead, trying to see Cadport. She thought she glimpsed the sea, a narrow thread of blue ahead. The city was but a speck.

He's waiting there. Tilla let flames crackle in her mouth. *Rune. The man I loved. The man who turned against me. The man I must capture and convert to glory... with words or with pain.*

"You will fight well tonight, lanse," said Shari. "You will make me proud."

The blue dragon flew beside her, leading the foremost chevron of dragons. She was clad in glory. Her black armor shone with golden dragon motifs and spirals. Blades topped her helm. Her breastplate, large as a boat, shone with rubies.

"I will fight for you, Commander," Tilla answered, flying to her right, her head only several feet farther back. "We will crush them. And we will catch him."

Please, Rune, she thought as she flew. *Do not force us to hurt you. Because we will. We will.*

She looked behind her. Her phalanx, the Sea Cannons, flew there; they would lead the charge. The hundred dragons were snarling, smoke streaming from between their fangs. Tilla had been training them for two moons now, and she trusted each dragon; they were the finest warriors she knew. Behind them rolled the rest of the army. It spread into the horizon, a sea of scale, claw, and tooth.

"Does the emperor not fly with us, Commander?" Tilla asked her princess. "Nor the Axehand Order?"

Shari turned her head and stared at her, eyes shrewd, and flames sparked between her teeth.

"Emperor Frey has his own battles to fight," she said. "Do not question his wisdom. I will lead the battle today, and you will fight at my side."

Tilla nodded. She stared ahead again, squinting. The speck grew to a dot.

Cadport. Home.

As the forest rustled below, Tilla imagined the sound of waves. As dragonfire rose, she felt the warmth of the Old Wheel's hearth. As she flew to battle, she remembered flying with Rune over the sea in darkness, a dance of starlight.

Home. Her old shop. Her father. Scraggles leaping onto her. A young ropemaker with calloused, thin fingers. Weaving, dreaming, hiding.

It was her home, it was her youth, it was her family and the man she loved.

The Resistance took all that from me, Tilla thought, and flames swirled in her belly. *I will save my home. And I will save you, Rune.*

She roared a battle cry and blew fire. Behind her, a hundred thousand dragons answered her call. The might of the Legions stormed south.

KAELYN

They stood on the walls, silent.

They stared into the north.

Nine thousand men and women--resistors, warriors of the canyon, and townsfolk armed with axes and sickles. Nine thousand. Still. Watching. Awaiting the night.

The sun dipped into the west, spreading red tendrils across the sky. Clouds thickened overhead. It would be a night of no stars. A night of dragonfire.

"Whatever happens, I fly by your side," Kaelyn whispered to Valien; he stood to her right upon the wall. "Always, Valien. Always."

She reached out and held his hand, a great paw, calloused and warm and enveloping.

"Stay with me, Rune," she whispered and turned to look at him; he stood at her left. "We will roar our fire together. We will defeat them."

She grabbed his hand too and squeezed it. He stared into the northern darkness. He nodded.

"I will fly with you."

Kaelyn took a deep breath, raised her head, and stared into the shadows. She held their hands--the two men in her life, the two men she thought she'd always be torn between.

Valien--the man who'd saved her from her father, who protected her, who fought for her through blood and rain and fire. Valien--the gruff, weathered knight whose soul was torn, whose soul she had vowed to mend. She looked at him--tall, burly in his armor, his hair wild and grizzled. And she loved him. She loved him more than she'd ever loved another. Once she had thought him like a father to her, but now... now she loved him not as a daughter, but as a woman.

She looked to her left. Rune. The boy she had saved. The boy she had watched grow into a warrior. He was two decades younger than Valien, and less pain filled his eyes, and far more rage and fire. Scruff covered his cheeks now, and his body had grown hard with training. He stood clad in leather and wool, his sword upon his back. Once Kaelyn had thought him a foolish boy, then a figurehead, then a king of legend. But now, looking upon him, she did not see those things. She saw a friend. She saw a soul she loved. She saw the young man she had kissed that night, the man in whose arms she had slept.

And I love you too, Rune, she thought, looking at him. *I love you as much as I love anyone. I will fight with you to victory or death.*

She placed her hand upon a cannon and watched the northern forest. A red glow rose from the horizon like a dawn of fire. She couldn't see the Legions yet--standing upon the walls, close to the surface of the earth, the horizon only lay a dozen miles away. But she knew that glow. That was dragonfire. They flew beyond the horizon and they would soon emerge like a cruel sun.

They will be here within the hour, Kaelyn thought and sucked in her breath.

Shouts and roars rose from the east.

Alarm bells clanged.

Kaelyn's heart burst into a gallop.

The alarm. We're under attack! But how?

She shifted into a dragon. She soared and filled her maw with fire. At her sides, Valien and Rune rose as dragons too, snarling and leaking fire.

When Kaelyn looked east, she saw them there, and the breath left her lungs.

A league away from Lynport, a thousand dragons were flying along the beach, roaring and blowing fire.

"The vanguard," Kaelyn whispered, her belly twisting.

She understood at once. *Of course.* These thousand dragons, brazen legionaries, had traveled the forest as humans, hidden under the canopy, and only now emerged.

"Resistance, shift!" Kaelyn shouted, beat her wings, and rose higher. "Follow!"

She growled, narrowed her eyes, and shot eastward across the houses. The enemy hadn't reached the city yet, but they were moving fast along the shore. They flew only a moment away.

Damn my father, Kaelyn thought as she flew. *He knew we'd see his army from a distance. He knew we'd be watching the north. And his elite warriors sneaked up from the eastern trees.*

She roared and shot forward, wreathed in flame, ready for battle. She streamed over the last few houses, her fellow dragons at her sides, and dived along the shore. The horde approached.

Kaelyn was about to blow fire... when she gasped.

This is wrong.

The thousand dragons did not fly in formation, but in a confused mass. Only a handful wore armor, and even that steel was muddy and dented. They bore no red spirals.

These are not legionaries, Kaelyn realized and gasped.

The dragon at their lead, a young red beast, blasted fire and shouted out.

"Hello, sister!"

Kaelyn spat her flames onto the shore below.

"Stars damn it!" she said, turned her head around, and shouted at her warriors, hundreds of dragons who flew behind her. "Hold your dragonfire! Do not attack." She sighed. "It's my idiot of a brother."

The thousand dragons ahead halted and hovered in midair, wings whipping the sand and water below. Leresy gave her a crooked, toothy grin.

"You've got to be an idiot to fight here today," the red dragon said. "Burn me, Kae, did you know that about a million legionaries are flying your way?"

"I had an idea," she grumbled, hovering before him, her wings blasting him with air. "So... these are the famous Leresy's Lechers. I've heard of your new band of outlaws." She sniffed and wrinkled her snout. "By the stars, you lot stink."

Leresy sniffed beneath his wing and winced. "Aye, we're a salty bunch. What is the old saying? True men stink of oil, soil, and other toil. Villains smell of roses."

"What are you doing here?" Kaelyn demanded. Valien, Rune, and her other dragons hovered behind her, hissing at the beasts ahead.

Her brother twisted his scaly brow into an expression of surprise. "What do you think? I'm here to join the fun. I'm not letting you kill Father without me. I intend to roast his scaly arse myself. And looking at you lot, you could use some help."

At her side, Rune blasted flame. "I say we kill them here on the beach. Slay two villains in one day."

Leresy looked at the young black dragon. "Well well, and this must be the pup who styles himself the heir of Aeternum. Quite a temper you've got, boy. But can you back it up with fire? Fly to me; let's see."

Rune growled and made to charge, but Kaelyn darted forward, slamming him back.

"Enough!" she howled. "Leresy, we don't have an hour before Father arrives. With me--to the walls. We'll talk there. Now!" She spun toward Rune and the others. "Let him through. He won't cause trouble. If he does, I'll kill him myself."

They flew back to town.

Soon Leresy stood upon the city wall in human form, gazed north at the gathering storm, and spat.

"Burn me," he said. "Father is mad at you this time, Kae."

His Lechers stood in a courtyard below, also in human forms--a thousand sweaty, bearded men clad in motley patches of armor and leather. Their shields and sleeves bore their sigil, a black dog. Their stench wafted even to the top of the wall, where Kaelyn stood glaring at her twin.

"Leresy," she said, "this isn't one of your Counter Squares games. You don't know what you're getting into." She stared at a scar that ran down his cheek. "Is that the scar I gave you?"

He shrugged. "Father's given me worse. Now it's time to kill him. You and me. Together." He sketched a theatrical bow. "I have officially changed sides."

She grabbed and twisted his collar. "Leresy! You will die here. You don't know how to fight."

He snickered. "And you do, Kae? Look at you." He swept his arms across the walls and courtyards. "You have... what, fifteen thousand warriors here?"

She sighed. "Nine thousand," she confessed.

"Bloody shite. Well, ten thousand now with the Lechers." He pried her hands off his collar. "Sister, you need me. Let me help you."

He stared at her, his eyes earnest, and Kaelyn felt her chest deflate.

"Leresy, you are a bastard."

"That's what you need here--not righteous, noble warriors of light, but a right bastard like me and the Lechers." He winked. "We fight dirty."

She stared at the mud caking his clothes. "I'm sure you do... in more ways than one."

Rune stomped up toward them, glaring and gripping his sword.

"I've heard enough," the young heir said. "Merciful stars, Kaelyn. He's a *Cadigus*. He's a prince of the empire. We're here to kill Cadiguses, not fight alongside them."

As Rune talked, Leresy held up his hand, moving his fingers like a chattering puppet.

"In case you haven't noticed, boy," Leresy said, "you've been fighting alongside one Cadigus for a while now. Granted, she's got nicer teats than I do, but you'll find my sword just as sharp."

Rune glowered at the outcast prince. "I trust Kaelyn. She is brave and wise and loyal. I don't trust you. This is all some scheme of yours to... to take the throne for yourself! I see your ambitions, Cadigus. This is no game."

"Oh, but it is a game," Leresy said and grinned. "And you need my pieces."

"Like a pig needs more slop!"

Kaelyn watched the two argue and sighed. Though she hated to admit it, both Rune and her brother were right. She couldn't trust Leresy, and most likely, this *was* some plot of his--he would attempt to slay their father in battle and seize the throne. And yet, Leresy was right too. She did need his men.

Rune grabbed her arm and glared.

"Kaelyn!" he whispered. "You can't be considering this. We can't trust him. They say he..." His voice dropped. "They say he captures women in the capital, murders their families, and rapes them. They say he uses them for a night, then tosses their corpses into the garden."

Leresy overheard and grinned.

"Oh, they still tell those stories, do they?" he said. "Excellent! It's all rubbish, of course. Never did anything of the sort. I spread the rumors myself." He hid his mouth and whispered theatrically. "It's good for the old reputation."

Kaelyn looked at her twin--her poor, haunted, miserable brother, whose quips masked pain she could never understand. She looked at Rune who was still fuming. She looked over at Valien, who stood by a cannon, staring north and ignoring them.

She whispered to herself, "The wise work with small devils to slay the big ones."

She had spoken those words to Rune last year about Beras the Brute. They still rang true. She nodded, stepped forward, and meant to shake her brother's hand... yet she found herself embracing him.

"You poor, miserable fool," she whispered to her twin. "You know we'll both probably die here, don't you?"

He snorted a laugh. "Death's not that bad. So long as we take the old man down with us."

Tears burned in Kaelyn's eyes. The memories pounded through her: her father's hands reaching under the bed, grabbing her, pulling her out, holding her down, beating and whipping and burning her.

Please, Father! Leresy would cry. *Please. Don't hurt her. Hurt me instead. It was I who broke the toy. Please, don't hurt Kaelyn.*

She closed her eyes.

And their father had obeyed. Their father had beaten Leresy until he blacked out in a pool of blood.

All to save me... all to save his sister.

She blinked tears away and touched her twin's scarred cheek.

"Thank you, my brother," she whispered. "Welcome home."

She returned her eyes north and stared. Her brother, her companions, and all her soldiers stared with her.

In the night, the horizon burned as if the forest blazed. Distant shrieks rolled like thunder. Yet what flew toward them, just beyond the horizon, was crueler than forest fire or storm.

Death itself flew ahead.

Rain began to fall, pattering against helmets, cannons, and battlements. It soaked Kaelyn's clothes and steamed over the blazing horizon, rising as clouds.

Standing upon the wall, Kaelyn looked at her brother. She looked at Rune and Valien. She gripped her sword and sucked in her breath.

"With rain and fire," she whispered, "it begins."

RUNE

He stood upon the wall, staring north at the encroaching wave of shadow and fire.

They will be here in moments.

He swallowed and gripped his sword. He did not know if he'd live today. But if today was his death, he would die upon the walls of his home, his friends at his sides.

"That's not a bad way to die," he whispered.

I only wish I got to see you again, Tilla, he thought. *Do you fly here too? I only wish I got to hold you one last time, Scraggles. Do you run through starry meadows in the night sky?*

As if to answer his thoughts, barking rose behind him.

Rune spun around, stared down at the courtyard, and gasped.

His eyes widened.

His heart leaped.

"Scraggles?" he whispered. "You're... alive?"

The black mutt stood below, barking up at him. His tail stood out straight; he was confused, not sure if his master truly stood above.

"Scraggles!" Rune shouted.

He had a few moments. Stars damn it, he had time enough! He shifted into a dragon. He leaped off the wall, glided, shifted back into human form, and landed before his dog.

Scraggles leaped back, eyes widening. He stared, standing still, as if struggling to believe Rune truly stood before him.

"Scrags," Rune whispered, and his eyes dampened. "It's me! You remember me, right?"

He reached out to pet Scraggles, but the dog took a step back, eyes still wide, tail still straight, still unsure. His eyes seemed to say: *It looks like you, but how can this be? How can you be here?*

Rune laughed. "It's me, Scrags. I've come back."

The dog leaped.

He crashed against Rune, all one hundred furry pounds of him. His tail wagged furiously and his tongue lapped at Rune's face. Rune laughed, fell down, and the dog jumped onto him, squirming and leaping and licking him.

And then something happened that made fresh tears bud in Rune's eyes.

Scraggles began to cry.

Long, plaintive mewls rose from him, sounds of loneliness finally ended, of joy and disbelief. As he kept leaping and squirming over Rune, his cries rose across the courtyard.

Rune held the dog close.

"I'm back, my friend," he whispered, nuzzling the dog. "I'm home."

A woman's voice spoke somewhere ahead.

"Well, leaky maggot guts." A sniff sounded. "Got me all teary eyed, you two did, and I ain't cried since I stepped on a Counter Squares piece a moon ago."

Lying on the ground, his dog upon his chest, Rune looked up and his eyes widened. A scrawny young woman stood in the courtyard, barely taller than a child. She wore bits of armor over ragged wool, and mud caked her short brown hair.

"Erry?" Rune's voice rose incredulously. "Erry Docker?"

The urchin waved. "Hullo, Rune, old boy. Heard you snogged Tilla." She grinned. "Burn me, never thought you had it in you."

Rune rubbed his eyes, taking in her ragged clothes and the black dog sewn on her sleeves. "Erry! You're... one of the Lechers?"

"Of course I am! Resistance is too noble. Legions are too stiff. Both of you are mental." She shrugged. "Lechers got booze and song and you don't have to be clean. In fact, dirt is quite encouraged. I *like* that." She flashed a grin. "Rune, my dear boy, Leresy Cadigus is a right bastard, a sneaky little weasel, and a bloody pain in the arse. But he'll fight with you." She nodded. "If there's anyone he hates more than the Resistance, it's his father."

Rune rose to his feet. "Erry, I have to put Scraggles somewhere safe. We have only a few minutes. Damn!" He held the dog close. "The castle is too dangerous; there will be fighting there. There will be fighting in every damn tunnel we dug."

He looked down at the dog. Scraggles stood at his side, pressed against him, looking up with a goofy grin.

Did I find you only to lose you again, boy? Rune thought.

Erry grinned. "You resistors with your tunnels and castles. You want secret hideouts nobody can find? Ask a dock rat." She shifted into a thin, copper dragon with clattering scales. "Come on! I know a place. We have just enough time."

Rune shifted too. He was a larger dragon, his scales smooth and black, his claws long. When he flapped his wings and ascended, he lifted Scraggles in his claws.

"Hurry, Rune!" the copper dragon said, soared into the air, and winked. "We haven't got all minute."

They rose from the courtyard. They raced south over the city roofs, heading toward the boardwalk. When Rune looked over his shoulder, he could see the Legions closer now; they were rising from the horizon, a great storm cloud raining fire.

The two dragons reached the boardwalk, the place where Rune would walk so often with Tilla, the place where Erry had lived feral and orphaned.

"Here!" the copper dragon said, dived down, and landed by a crumbling windmill. Its vanes had burned years ago; an empty stone shell remained.

Rune hovered above the boardwalk, wings stirring sand and dust across the cobblestones, and placed Scaggles down. He landed and shifted back into a human.

Erry shifted too, raced into the windmill, and grinned. "Come on! Step in."

He glanced at the windmill. Rune remembered that years ago--stars, it must have been over a decade--the windmill would grind wheat into flour. An old fire had put an end to that, burning the sails, the gears inside, and the old man who had operated the place. Rune had not thought it occupied since, but when he stepped inside after Erry, he saw a tattered mattress, a few old blankets, and a colony of feral cats. The place smelled of mold and cat urine.

"Welcome!" Erry said. "Welcome to my old home. Well... one of my old homes. Well... mostly a home for my cats. Well... mostly a place my cats ate what food I found for them, then buggered off to scrounge elsewhere." She sighed and looked around the place. "It's not much, but it'll keep old Scrags safe. It kept me safe during a few storms."

Erry stood a moment, staring at the place, and to Rune's surprise, she began to weep.

"Erry," he said softly and took a step toward her.

Guilt pounded through him. He had known Erry all his life. He had often brought food to her various hideouts, played mancala with her on the beach, and once--during a heavy storm-- let her sleep in his tavern. But Erry would always run off. She'd stay one night, eat one meal, then vanish for days.

I should have done more, he thought, looking at the ruin of this place. *I should have let her stay with us forever, not just once during a storm.*

"Stars, Erry," he said and tried to embrace her. "Are you--"

She growled through her tears and shoved him back. "I don't need no hugs! I don't need no pity." She knuckled her eyes dry. "I never did. I've always fought, and I've always survived here in this damn, stupid, dirty boardwalk in this gutter of a town." She looked around the old windmill, her eyes still red. "It's dirty and it's cold and it smells like piss. But it's home." She looked up at Rune. "It's *our* home. And we're going to fight for it. Right, Rune?"

He nodded and clasped her arm. "Damn right, Err."

She nodded, sniffed, and gave Scraggles an embrace. "Stay here, boy. Stay here and be safe. Try not to wet the bed."

With that, Erry and Rune left the windmill, closing the door on Scraggles. As they shifted into dragons and took flight, Rune heard his dog crying for him and scratching the door.

I don't want to leave you, boy, he thought. *I don't want to leave you again. I'll be back soon. I promise.*

The two dragons flew back north toward the wall.

Above the forest ahead, a hundred thousand dragons screamed, blew fire, and stormed toward them.

LANA

They flew on the wind, a host of chinking scales and pluming smoke, fleeing across the forests.

"Lord Eranor!" she shouted, voice rolling across the sky. "Take your dragons and guard the northern flank. Lord Ferin! Guard the south. Fly them as fast as they'll go."

The two dragons, knights of the canyon, nodded and snorted and barked orders. The warriors they commanded, dragons clad in armor bearing the sigil of Cain, flew behind them, forming a guard around the dragons they shepherded.

We must fly fast, Lana thought, looking over her shoulder as she led the flight. *Stars, we must fly fast, or all here will perish.*

The people of Lynport flew within the ring of warriors-- women, elders, and children. Their scales were soft. Many dragons had lost their fangs to old age; others had not yet grown them. The youngest of Lynport were too young to shift; their mothers flew as dragons, holding human babes in their claws.

"Forty-seven thousand townsfolk," she whispered into the wind as she flew. "Only a handful of warriors to guard them."

A shiver ran from her horns to her tail, clattering her scales. *If the Legions catch us out here, they will slaughter us all.*

Looking upon the dragons, Lana winced, the old pain flaring. Her right eye saw refugees fleeing over autumn forests, frightened but flying fast. She had lost her left eye years ago, yet forever it kept staring, showing her a mirror image of the world. With this phantom eye, she saw the refugees dying. She saw fire wash them, cracking their scales and burning their flesh. She saw their blood rain. She saw them fall dead upon stone, emaciated, pale skin draped over their bones.

Lana grimaced, the two images overlaid before her, life and death, present and past. Always two lives flickered within her. The eye she saw with. The eye she remembered with. Which vision would prove true this day?

"Follow, dragons of Requiem!" she shouted over her shoulder. "Fly as fast as you can. Safety lies ahead."

She returned her eyes to the northwest. The forests spread into the horizon. The canyon still lay too far to see. Lana filled her maw with flame. They didn't have enough time! Damn it, they should have fled Lynport earlier. She peered east, seeking the enemy, but could not see them. Yet she knew they flew there, a hundred thousand strong.

Lana cursed.

"Fly, dragons of Requiem!" she called. "We fly to safety."

Yet they could not fly faster. These were no warriors. They were elders, youngsters, the ill and wounded.

Why didn't we flee earlier? Stars, why did we wait?

The forests streamed below them.

The sea disappeared behind.

They raced over the wilderness, alone.

Weariness tugged on Lana's bones. She spat flames and forced her wings to keep beating. Yet the people trailed behind; Lana was faster and stronger. Fear twisting her gut, she forced herself to slow down.

"Eranor, keep guarding the north flank!"

She kept flying. She forced herself to breathe, to calm her racing mind. The Legions did not care to slaughter innocents, she told herself. They wanted to crush the Resistance. They wanted Valien, Kaelyn, and Rune. It was Lynport--Cadport as they called it--that they craved, not these people.

Yet still fear pounded through her. Until she shepherded these townsfolk into the Castle-in-the-Cliff, protecting them behind strong walls and the Stone Guardians, she wouldn't feel safe.

She lowered her head as she flew, gazing down at the oaks and birches. Perhaps it was still that night she feared, that horrible night worse than any.

She had been twelve, only just leaving her childhood, the winter the Cadigus family seized the throne. How her father, huddled in his canyon, had railed against them! He had pounded the table, shouted threats, and bragged that he'd slay any man who tried to claim his dominion.

"I am lord of this canyon!" Cain had shouted, voice echoing in his hall of stone. "For too long did I serve the Aeternums. Now is our chance for glory. Now is Cain's chance to rule! I will bend the knee to no Cadigus. I will be King of the South."

And even in the northern cold, in the distant capital of Nova Vita, the Cadigus family heard word of his treason. Their spies lurked everywhere, even in those days. They descended upon the canyon that winter, tens of thousands of them, an army that covered the sky.

Cain would not fly out to meet them. He hunkered in his canyon, shouting threats in the hall, inviting the Regime to enter their tomb.

And we remained in our hole, Lana remembered. For days, for moons, for a year.

Toward the end, men were drinking their piss and eating their dogs. Thousands fell ill. The Regime tossed rotted corpses into the canyon. Stars, how it stank! The fumes seeped into the Castle-in-the-Cliff and men vomited. The old and weak perished first, then the strong began to follow. Hundreds died of starvation, thirst, or disease.

How long did it last? Lana thought. *Fifteen moons? Sixteen? More?*

Finally they could bear it no more, and Lord Cain and his household flew out to meet the Regime in battle.

They fell that day.

Thousands fell dead.

Lana fought too, young but strong enough to fly, to blow her fire, to slash her claws. She faced Frey himself in duel that day. She never forgot the heat of his fire bathing her, the agony of his claws, the sting of his tail lashing her. She never forgot her three brothers falling around her, burned with the flames of Cadigus.

And she never forgot his fangs.

She never forgot the pain of his teeth digging into her face.

"You took my eye that day, Frey," Lana whispered as she flew now, years later, a grown woman yet still so afraid, still so hurt. "When I finally woke from the sleep of wounds, I wore an eyepatch, and a trail of white filled my hair." She snarled. "You fly south again. And I will fight you again. I will fight you with every breath I have in me."

Her father had bent the knee that day long ago, and Frey had taken all their forests, fields, and hills, leaving them but a crack in the earth.

"I will not slay you, Devin Cain," the emperor had said, a great golden dragon with blood on his teeth, pinning the canyon lord beneath his claws. "Death would be too kind to you. Your punishment will be to serve me forever. But not as lord of the south. You will have no more sunlight to rule. You have holed up in your canyon for over a year now, and you will remain there for the rest of your days. In shadow. In fear. If you emerge, I will crush you. I will slay you like I slew your sons. Stay in your tomb, Lord Cain, and whenever you look upon your daughter's face, the face that I ravaged, remember my wrath... and remember my mercy."

Seventeen years had passed since. Yet still the rage pounded through her father. And still the nightmares filled her. And still her phantom eye saw that death wherever she looked.

"And still we fight," she whispered. "And I will fight you, Cadigus. Forever. For the wound you gave me. For my people. For Requiem."

They streamed over the forests, heading north, heading to safety, memory, and throbbing old pain.

RUNE

The rain fell, pattering against his helm, as fires rose ahead.

He clutched his sword with one hand, his tinderbox with another. He stared ahead. He waited.

The swarm oozed across the night, a black puddle lit with countless fires like flaming stars. The host seemed a sky of some distant, demonic nightmare spilling into the waking world. Howls and grunts rang out. Flaming pillars rose and crumbled like cathedrals of gods. They flew six miles away, then five, then only four. They covered the horizon. They drowned the land.

"Be strong, Rune," Kaelyn whispered at his side. Her face was pale, her lips tight. She clutched his hand and squeezed. "Whatever happens, be strong. I'm with you."

The Legions howled ahead. Flames roared. Their cries pealed across the sky like demon howls echoing in buried chambers.

"Crush the Resistance!"

"Slay them all!"

"Break their bones and drink their blood!"

"Burn this city!"

Rune sucked in a shaky breath and tightened his lips. He could not stop his chest from shaking. The walls themselves seemed to shake beneath his feet; he didn't know whether his legs were trembling, or whether the Legions were rattling the very earth. The rain kept falling. He kept staring, wanting to flee, wanting to shift and fly away across the sea.

He forced himself to stay still. To stare ahead. To wait.

They flew three miles away. Then two.

War. Blood. The greatest battle of our time.

"You will fight well, Rune," Valien said, standing at his left side. His voice was raspy as ever, but deep and solemn. "Your wings will find the sky. Starlight will bless you." The gruff, taller man looked at him and managed a wink. "Today we fight together as brothers."

Rune did not reply. He did not trust his voice to remain steady. All across the walls of Lynport, his fellow warriors stood, thousands of men and women in leather armor, manning cannons or holding arrows nocked in bows. They were thousands of brave fighters, and they would fight well, yet Rune had never felt more fear.

"Slay them all!" rose a shriek ahead.

"We will break them upon the wheel!"

"We will flay their skin and drink their blood!"

"Grab Relesar alive--he will suffer most!"

Rune clenched his teeth, and his sword shook. They were coming to capture him, to torture him, to break his every bone and hear him scream. They were coming to kill Valien, Kaelyn, Erry, and all those he loved. They were a hundred thousand strong. He had but ten thousand with him.

We can't win this, he thought, and his eyes burned, and his breath trembled. *We will die. We will fall. We--*

He snarled.

No, he thought. *No.*

He could not let fear claim him. Not now. Valien's words from his training returned to him.

All wise men fear battle. Only brutes rush fearless into a fight. The true warrior is not he who feels no fear, but he who conquers fear.

Rune nodded.

"I will fight," he whispered through clenched teeth. "For the Resistance. For my friends. For my home." The rain streamed down his face. "For Requiem."

The Legions swarmed ahead, closer and louder. Their roars crashed against the walls. Rune could see individual dragons now. Their eyes blazed red in the firelight. Their fangs shone. Their claws reached out. Flames blasted from them, lighting the night. They rolled into the horizon. Shari Cadigus flew at their lead, clad in black armor, spraying her flames and shrieking, her head undulating in the heat waves.

"Slay them all!"

Rune lit his tinderbox.

At his sides, Kaelyn and the other archers tugged back their bowstrings.

Beside him, Valien drew his sword and held it aloft. The blade caught the firelight.

"Archers!" he shouted. "Fire!"

A rain of arrows shot forward, shards of red in the night, and slammed into the horde ahead. The dragons shrieked. Blood splashed. They kept flying.

Valien shouter louder. "Cannons--fire!"

Rune brought tinderbox to fuse.

The smell of smoke filled his nostrils.

The dragons ahead shrieked and stormed forward, only several heartbeats away from the walls.

The fuse burned.

"No fear," Rune whispered.

An explosion rocked the city walls.

Fire exploded.

The cannons thrust backward so violently they almost fell off the wall. Light flared. A hundred cannonballs blazed into the night. The smell of gunpowder flared. Through clouds of smoke, Rune saw the volley slam into the Legions. Where the cannonballs struck scales, fire screamed and blood rained. Dragons lost their magic. Human bodies tumbled, torn apart into

limbs and torsos and severed heads. Already men were loading
new gunpowder and cannonballs, driving ramrods into muzzles.

"Archers!" Valien howled, sword raised and voice hoarse.
"Fire!"

A second volley flew. Arrows whistled and slammed into
the beasts ahead. Men shoved gunpowder into muzzles, leaped
back, and more fuses burned.

"Cannons, fire!"

The walls shook. The cannons jolted backward again.
Flames roared and exploded across the sky, deafening. The
Legions were close now, so close Rune could count their teeth.
The cannonballs ripped through them. One projectile tore into a
beast only a hundred yards away, shattering its head into red mist,
leaving a human body to tumble.

Yet still so many swarmed. Still the thousands streamed
forward, howling and raging and blowing flames.

"Archers! Fire! Keep those arrows firing!"

More arrows whistled. More blood spilled and more
dragons fell dead.

"Cannons!"

A third volley of cannonfire rocked the city. The smoke
rose thick and black and rich with the smell of gunpowder. A
hundred cannonballs ripped into the horde ahead, tearing through
armor and scales, showering blood and flame.

And then... then the Legions were upon them.

"Fall back!" Valien shouted, waving his sword. "Fall
behind, into the tunnels, go!"

Rune leaped back, ears ringing, and shifted into a dragon.
At his sides along the walls, thousands of resistors shifted too.

"Fall back!" Valien howled, a silver dragon with one horn.
"Into the tunnels!"

Rune flapped his wings, flew backward, and beheld the
wrath of Cadigus descend upon the city. The dragons covered the

sky, a burial shroud of scale and flame. Their fire shot down, blasting walls and roofs. A few resistors were too slow to shift; they were still loading cannons or nocking arrows. The Legions slammed into them, and claws ripped them apart. Other resistors managed to shift but were too slow to fly back; flames blasted them, cracking their scales and melting their eyes.

"Rune!" Kaelyn shouted. The green dragon slammed into him, pushing him lower. "Fall back!"

Hovering above the roofs, he looked around wildly.

"Where's Erry! Where's--"

"Rune!" Kaelyn shouted. "Into the tunnels!"

He nodded. They turned and dived. The rooftops and streets rushed up toward them. All around, jets of flame crashed down onto Lynport like comets, burning roofs and tearing into dragons.

"There, the smithy!" Kaelyn cried. "Fly, Rune!"

They dived over the roofs. Already many homes, those built of wood and clay, were blazing. The brick smithy, however, rose strong from the smoke. Rune and Kaelyn hissed. A stream of fire crashed down before them. They scattered, skirted the flames, and kept diving.

They all but crashed onto the cobbled road outside the smithy. When Rune glanced above, he saw the Legions covering the sky of Lynport. Thousands of flaming jets slammed down. Thousands of wooden homes blazed. Resistors were blasting flame upward and scurrying into those houses built of stone. Some resistors--or maybe they were Lechers--were brazen enough to soar, howling, into the sky of legionaries. Claws and fangs tore them apart, and they tumbled as ravaged humans. Blood filled the rain.

"Rune!" Kaelyn shouted, smoke and flame around her. "Inside!"

She shifted into human form, fired one arrow into the sky, and leaped through the smithy window. Rune blasted his flames upward into the dragon storm, shifted too, and leaped. Flames crashed down where he'd stood, missing him by inches. He scurried through the window and slammed its shuttered panels shut.

Ten other resistors filled the stone house. Their clothes were singed and sweat soaked them. A few winced; welts rose across their skin. They all held swords.

"Into the tunnels, like we trained," Rune said.

He doubted they could hear him; he could barely hear himself over the ringing in his ears. Outside the windows, scales flashed and fire blazed. The walls shook. Dragons were landing outside, claws scratching cobblestones. The legionaries' battle cries thundered as loud as the cannons.

"Find Relesar!" a voice roared outside. "Slay all others."

When he peeked between the shutters, Rune saw the imperial dragons shifting into warriors clad in black armor. Helms covered their heads and their swords blazed red in the firelight. Boots thudded across the streets.

Breathing heavily, Rune turned from the window. He stomped forward, grabbed the floorboards, and pulled them loose. A tunnel delved below.

"Follow!" he said and placed a leg into the darkness.

Before he could enter, the smithy door jolted open.

Ten legionaries stood behind it, their armor reflecting the fires, their swords raised.

A rope, attached to the door, creaked.

A barrel of bolts and gunpowder fell against the soldiers.

The explosion rocked the smithy. The door shattered, raining wood. Armor tore apart. Limbs flew across the street outside, and a severed head rolled into the smithy. Blood pooled and smoke rose. The doorway had vanished. Bodies lay strewn outside. One man still lived, screaming, his arms torn off and his entrails spilling.

One leg still in the tunnel, Rune stared.

His heart seemed to stop.

The world shook and his ears rang. He could no longer hear anything but the ringing, see anything but the ravaged bodies, the man writhing, the blood, and oh stars, he was still alive, and--

"Rune!"

Kaelyn was shouting above him. He could barely hear her beyond the ringing. He looked up and saw her face splashed with blood. She was shoving his shoulders, trying to push him into the tunnel. Outside the doorway, more legionaries were racing through the streets, and more explosions rang. Through the windows, blood and debris flew everywhere. A man ran down an alley, aflame and screaming.

"Rune!" she screamed.

He nodded, tightened his lips, and plunged into the tunnel. He fell down a shaft, hit an earthen floor, and beheld a burrow driving forward. He crawled. He had forgotten his lamp somewhere above. When he glanced behind him, he saw Kaelyn and the others crawling too; a few held flickering lanterns.

The tunnels shook, raining dirt. Blood smeared Rune's face and his arm burned. As they crawled through the darkness, he could still see the bodies and hear the screams.

TILLA

Her city burned beneath her.

The flames rose everywhere. Houses, shops, trees--they all blazed. Tilla flew, eyes stinging, the smoke swirling around her. Blood spilled. Dragons burned and fell dead. Soldiers ran, swinging swords, and explosions tore through alleyways, ripping men apart. Streets cracked. Buildings tumbled. Walls fell. Any house built of wood blazed. From the brick structures--the fort, the courthouse, the silos and shops--cannons were still firing through embrasures in the walls, tearing into dragons.

My home, Tilla thought. Her heart thrashed, her eyes stung, and the terror gripped her. *Cadport. My home. It's burning.*

"Rune!" she howled, flying above the destruction. "Rune, end this! Fly to me, Rune. Stop this warfare!"

She flew in circles above the city, seeking him. The resistors scurried below, leaping from street to street, shadows in the night. They fired arrows, then vanished into doorways and windows and holes. Cannons blazed and smoke unfurled. Imperial dragons blasted the streets with fire. Their claws tore at homes and walls crumbled. Bodies littered the streets.

"Rune!" she roared, flying above, trying to find him but seeing only shadows, only dragons drenched in fire and blood, only death and destruction.

No! No. None of this should have happened! They were supposed to capture this city, not destroy it. They were supposed to capture Rune, not topple her home above him.

"Rune, surrender yourself and this will end!" she cried, flying above the streets. A cannonball flew from a silo, and she barely dodged it. Fire rose from a rooftop, blasting her tail, and arrows shot from windows, clattering against her armor. Tilla roared, dived, and bathed the buildings with fire.

"Rune, hand yourself in!" she called. "We don't have to watch our city fall."

She looked around, seeking her old home, but could not see through the smoke. She tried to look toward the beach, that place where she'd walked with Rune so many times. Dragons flew above the boardwalk and fire rose in walls.

Cadport was crumbling below her, and she could not stop it.

"Find the boy!" Shari shrieked. The blue dragon flew at her side, howling fire. "Find Relesar. Search every building until he's found! Slay all others in your path."

Below, legionaries in human form snaked through the streets, armor clanking. They yanked open doors, only for barrels of gunpowder to burst, scattering gore across the street. They tried to climb through windows, but arrows peppered them. Every instant, resistors burst from a hole, shot arrows and thrust swords, and vanished back into hiding. The larger houses held dragons; their fire erupted from chimneys and windows, blasting any legionary who approached.

"It's like fighting gophers," Shari said in disgust. Her blue wings churned the smoke and she roared. "Tear down every house until you find him!" She whipped her head around, stared at Tilla, and snarled. "Lanse! Lead your phalanx to the courthouse; they're firing cannons from within. Stop them."

Tilla had trained for this. She had spent a year training for this. Yet now she only wanted this to end, to stop this desecration of her memories. How could she fight for the force that toppled Cadport? How could she lead dragons to burn her home? Why did Rune not emerge and end this?

"Lanse!" Shari shouted. "I gave you an order. Lead your dragons! Stop those cannons."

Fire blazed inside Tilla.

You force me to do this, Rune, she thought.

Her eyes stung and she roared.

Rune had attacked Castra Luna with his Resistance, slaughtering hundreds of soldiers from Cadport. Rune now lurked here like a coward, firing cannons from shadow rather than facing her in open battle.

"Dragons!" Tilla shouted. "Follow!"

She began to fly over the burning homes, heading toward the square. Everywhere below her, buildings burned and collapsed. Still the resistors fought from hiding, emerging from holes, windows, and tunnels to fire arrows, then scurrying back into shadow.

You did this, Rune! Tilla thought with a growl. *You hide in homes, forcing us to topple them. You lurk like a coward, forcing us to destroy our city.*

She howled, racing above the streets. Her phalanx roared behind her. Beyond roofs and alleyways, they reached the city square. The courthouse, the place where Tilla had seen Pery beheaded, rose ahead from smoke.

Its portico shook. Smoke blasted and fire blazed. Cannonballs shot from between the columns toward Tilla's phalanx.

She swerved. One cannonball roared over her head, another beneath her wing. Beside her, a projectile slammed into one of her dragons. The warrior didn't even have time to roar. The cannonball tore through his magic, leaving him to tumble to the ground in human pieces.

"Burn them!" Tilla roared. "Before they reload!"

She dived lower and skimmed over the square. The cobblestones raced beneath her. She beat her wings, racing toward the columns ahead. She could see more cannons there, their muzzles lowering to face her.

She roared her fire and soared.

The flames blasted between the columns. The cannons inside jerked violently like marionettes whose strings were tugged. Fire blasted and more cannonballs flew. Tilla rose higher, screaming. One cannonball slammed against the tip of her wing, tearing off her claw, and she howled in agony. The pain blazed through her like a fingernail ripped off a hand. Her dragons blew fire around her. Cannonballs tore through two dragons at her side, scattering human limbs across the square.

"Fill this place with fire!" Tilla screamed.

She rose above the courtyard roof. Holes had been carved into the stone; she saw them too late. Arrows fired from within, and Tilla screamed. Several arrows shattered against the breastplate that protected her belly. Two more pierced her wounded wing, tearing straight through the skin. The pain nearly blinded her, but she turned and dived.

She swooped down along the columns and sprayed her fire into the courthouse shadows.

Cannons blasted from within. A hundred cannonballs flew skyward, tearing into dragons; one skimmed along her breastplate, raising sparks. Tilla snarled. Beyond the shadows and smoke behind the columns, she saw men scurry to scoop gunpowder from barrels.

Tilla growled and blew fire.

Her flaming jet spun between two columns, raced by a cannon, and slammed against the barrels.

Tilla soared.

Arrows whistled and shattered against her armor and scales. One scraped alone her tail. Tilla kept rising.

An explosion rocked the courthouse below.

Smoke burst skyward, enveloping Tilla.

Chunks of stone flew, peppering her breastplate and slamming into her wings.

She kept soaring. The dragons of her phalanx rose along with her, howling and coughing.

"Get back down there," she shouted, "and slay them all!"

She dived back into the square. She drove through the smoke, heading toward the courthouse. She beat her wings, shoving the smoke back, and revealed three shattered columns. A chunk of roof had fallen, and blood seeped from beneath. Some columns still stood, and cannons lay overturned beside them. Resistors scurried deeper into the crumbling building.

"Warriors!" Tilla howled. "Human forms--enter after me!"

She landed by the standing columns, shifted into a human, and drew her sword. Behind her, dozens of dragons followed suit.

"Slay the Resistance!" Tilla shouted. "Slay them all."

She ran between the columns into the shadows. Her men ran behind her. Arrows flew from within, and one grazed her armor. Others slammed into men behind her; some arrows punched through steel, and the men fell.

"Slay them!" Tilla shouted. She ran, sword held above her, into a shadowy hall.

They waited there, a hundred resistors. They were ashy and bloody, yet they drew their blades, shouted, and ran toward her.

"Hail the red spiral!" Tilla cried, slammed into their ranks, and swung her blade. At her sides, her fellow warriors clashed against the enemy. Swords lashed and men fell dead.

You made me do this, Rune, Tilla thought as she swung her sword, slicing into flesh, slaying men at every turn. She screamed madly, painting the hall red. *You made me kill.*

Tears burned in her eyes, but still Lanse Tilla Siren fought and killed as her city burned around her.

RUNE

He crawled from the tunnel into the silo, covered in dirt and ash. At least, once this place had been a silo. The grain had been emptied, and the chamber now served as a pillbox, a brick outpost with embrasures along the walls for firing arrows or dragonfire.

The corpses of two archers lay here, charred black.

Fire can be blown inward too, Rune thought with a grimace, stepping over the remains.

The brick walls surrounded him, sooty and still hot. Rune sucked in his breath and shifted into a dragon, all but trapping himself between the stone walls. Through the slits, Rune glimpsed legionaries running through the city streets, shouting in the night.

He thrust his jaw against an arrowslit, sucked in his breath, and sprayed the street with fire.

Screams rose.

When his flames died, he saw soldiers falling ablaze, tearing at their red-hot armor.

"A hundred or more outside!" Rune shouted over his shoulder to the hole in the floor; more resistors hid there.

"Hold them back!" Kaelyn shouted from below.

Rune peered out the arrowslit. A dozen soldiers had fallen. A dozen more were rushing forward. He blasted them with more flames, and they fell.

A dragon shrieked.

Blasts of air pounded the street, scattering dust, discarded armor, and a severed hand. Rune glimpsed blue scales in the night--a dragon swooping toward the pillbox. A boom echoed.

The walls creaked and rained dust. The dragon slammed into the walls again, shrieking, and through the hole, Rune glimpsed a blue tail lashing.

"Damn it," he muttered. He blasted flames out the arrowslit, and the blue dragon shrieked. Rune glimpsed the beast stumbling back in the street, and his heart seemed to freeze.

The dragon had only one wing. The other was built of wood, rope, and leather.

"Shari Cadigus," he whispered.

Charred and howling, the blue dragon faced the silo again. Through the arrowslit, her eyes met Rune's.

He blasted more fire outward.

Shari shrieked.

"Resistor in the silo!" rose her howls. "Topple it down. Tear down the walls!"

More dragons slammed into the walls. Loose bricks fell and clattered.

"Get out of there, Rune!" Kaelyn shouted below.

He blasted more fire out the hole, scorching Shari, and shifted back into human form. The walls trembled and cracked around him. He leaped into the tunnel and plunged into darkness.

Kaelyn grabbed him, and they crawled as fast as they could. Above him, Rune heard the silo collapse. Bricks and dust tumbled into the tunnel, and he coughed, blinded.

"Keep crawling!" Kaelyn said and tugged his arm. They raced down the burrow. A dozen resistors crawled ahead of them, holding lamps.

Shari's voice echoed above, muffled beyond the debris.

"Clear the bricks and into the tunnel! The rats scurry there."

Rune crawled as fast as he could, burrowing forward on his elbows. Heat blazed behind him.

"Rune, they're coming after us!" Kaelyn shouted, crawling before him.

"Keep moving!" he shouted back.

Where's the rope? Damn it, where is it?

He heard the legionaries tug bricks, clearing a path to the tunnel. Rune hissed and kept crawling. Armor clanked behind him, and the cries of legionaries filled the tunnel.

There!

The rope dangled from the tunnel roof. Rune scurried by and tugged.

Hands reached out and grabbed his feet.

The tunnel collapsed behind him.

Bricks and soil crashed down, burying the legionaries who'd grabbed him. Dust blinded Rune, heat bathed him, and he coughed. When the debris cleared, he breathed raggedly.

"Another tunnel lost," he said hoarsely, tugging himself free from the dead man's grip.

They had been fighting for a night and day now. They had lost a dozen tunnels, a dozen homes, and a dozen pillboxes. The courthouse had fallen.

So many were dead.

Kaelyn coughed ahead of him, smeared with dust and dirt. She reached out and grabbed his hand.

"Come on, Rune," she said. "We have to keep moving. Keep crawling. We're almost at Castellum Acta."

He kept crawling, following her and the others. The sounds of battle faded behind. Judging by the other tunnels they had sabotaged, it would take the legionaries an hour to clear the rubble and crawl in pursuit.

But they always did follow.

They always emerged into the next hideout, swinging their swords and blowing their fire.

But he kept crawling.

He kept fighting.

It had been a night and day, and he had not eaten, drunk, or slept, but he kept going.

"How many still fight in the fort?" he asked, pulling himself through the darkness. It was almost winter, but the air was sweltering down here; he could barely breathe.

"Six hundred men last time I was there," Kaelyn replied. "But the damn Legions keep blasting fire at the walls. We're down to only ten barrels of gunpowder."

Rune felt his belly sink as he crawled.

"We will not last a day there," he said. "They are too many."

Still wriggling along the tunnel, Kaelyn snarled at him over her shoulder. "We will last a moon. We will keep slaying them. Their bodies litter the hillside, and we will slay ten of them for every one of us they kill."

They crawled for an hour, passing many forks in the tunnel where other resistors moved. Many were bloodied. Some were missing limbs. Some screamed as their comrades pulled them into safe burrows for healing. Rune could not guess how many had died already, but at every house and street where he had fought, he saw them there--the corpses of his brothers and sisters.

Finally they reached the tall, narrow shaft that rose upward into shadow. A wooden sign stood here, bearing the word: "Library". The actual library lay hundreds of yards west of here; all the signs in these tunnels were mislabeled, meant to confuse the Legions should they crawl here. Kaelyn, Rune, and the other resistors climbed the shaft, clinging to its wooden ladder. They opened a trapdoor and emerged into the hall of Castellum Acta, the fortress on the hill.

A hundred resistors stood here, surrounding a table heavy with maps, swords, and wooden pieces carved as dragons. Kegs of gunpowder rose at the back. A dozen archers stood along the walls, firing arrows from slits.

Valien stood at the table, clad in leather armor, glaring down at a parchment map of the tunnels. Other resistors stood around him, caked with dirt, and moved pieces around the map.

"Valien!" Kaelyn said, walking toward him. "The silo at Well Road has fallen. We destroyed the tunnel before fleeing."

Valien looked up, cursed, and slammed his fist against the table.

"Stars damn it." He lifted a piece of coal, and crossed out an outpost on the map. "Is the silo claimed or completely fallen?"

Rune marched forward too, wincing. Welts blazed across his body.

"Damn walls fell all around me."

Grumbling, Valien moved several small wooden dragons across the map. When Rune stood closer, he stared down at the parchment and cursed.

"Merciful stars, Valien," he said. "We've lost, what... a quarter of our tunnels already?"

The grizzled old knight nodded. "And losing more fast. I--"

Shrieks sounded outside the hall. The archers shouted and fired with more fervor.

"Another assault!" one archer cried over his shoulder. "Two phalanxes--and they're angry."

Valien was already shouting orders at his men. "Send two hundred dragons out--stop that assault!"

Resistors leaped onto a stairway and raced up, leaving the hall and climbing the tower. Wings thudded and more dragons shrieked. Through the arrowslits, Rune glimpsed hundreds of resistors flying as dragons--they had emerged from the tower top--and crashing against the enemy. Blood rained.

Rune began marching toward the tower stairs; the hall doors were bricked up, but the tower still held a trapdoor for fighters.

"I'm joining them," he said, grinding his teeth.

Before he could reach the staircase, Valien grabbed his arm.

"No, Rune," he said and glared. Weariness filled his eyes, but fire too. "You do not fly out as a dragon. You fight in the tunnels. We've discussed this. They know the color of your scales; they would mob you on sight."

Rune growled. "I want to fight in the sky!" he said. "I will not watch my comrades fly out while I cower here."

Valien tightened his grip. "Cower, Rune? No. You fight the way I need you to fight--in shadow. Striking from the dark. That is your task."

He looked out the arrowslits. The imperial dragons were crashing against the resistors. Scales flew like kicked seashells. Smoke and fire stormed across the sky. As dragons died, their magic vanished. Human bodies tumbled to the hillsides.

"We won't last much longer here," Rune said. "They fight too well in the air."

Valien nodded, released him, and returned to the table. "Which is why we must keep fighting underground. Tunnel by tunnel. House by house."

Rune walked to the table too; he had to lean against it for fear of falling. He sighed and wiped sweat off his brow.

"They are too many," he said. "They've claimed too much. How much longer can we hold out, Valien?"

He no longer asked: Can we win? He knew the answer. They could not.

"As long as we can," Valien replied. "A few days. Less than a moon. We cannot hold this city forever. But we can make them pay a heavy price here. We can make them bleed."

Rune left the table. He walked toward the back of the hall. He faced the second, smaller staircase. This one plunged down into shadow, dug into the hill. It led to a tunnel, yet not one that linked to the network.

"When do we take these stairs?" he asked softly.

Armor creaking, Valien came to stand beside him. The older man placed a hand on Rune's shoulder.

"I will not yet give the order," he said. "We cannot be seen to flee so quickly, not if we've already begun this fight."

Rune looked at him. Valien's face was haggard and leathery beneath his beard. His eyes stared grimly at the shadowy stairs. A struggle raged behind those eyes, some old memory of pain. The man's calloused fists clenched at his sides.

The tunnel leads into the sea, Rune thought, looking back at it. It led into the water where he'd swim with Tilla. The water where ships had sailed. The water this town had grown along, that had brought it life... that could now save them.

He tried to imagine crawling down this tunnel on his elbows until water roared, dark and salty and stinging his wounds. He would swim--for how long? He'd have to hold his breath for as long as he could, swimming south. He'd emerge from the sea, breathe air, sink again and swim some more.

He would flee his home... and Lynport would burn behind him.

The bodies would remain behind him.

The memories, his childhood, and Tilla... they would all remain behind.

He turned away and marched back toward the table. Kaelyn and several other resistors were frowning at the map, tracing tunnels and discussing troop movements. Rune jabbed his finger against the parchment.

"We'll strike them here in the butcher shop, the eastern gates, and the old smithy." He looked up and met Kaelyn's gaze;

she stared back, eyes haunted in her sooty face. "Are you ready to fight some more, Kaelyn?"

She managed a trembling smile, her teeth white against the mud and ash on her face. "Always."

They returned to the tunnels.

They fought on.

LERESY

He could not breathe.

The fear pounded through him. His pulse beat in his ears like war drums. The air was cold in the potter shop--he knew it was--yet sweat soaked his clothes. At his side, Yorne, that gaunt bastard, was peering out the window's shutters and saying something to Leresy, but he couldn't hear.

The damn blood in my ears is too loud! Leresy thought. He pawed at those ears, as if he could tear out the sound, but his fingers trembled. His breath shook.

He looked around him. Twenty other Lechers filled the brick shop. The shelves had fallen and the pottery lay smashed. Their tunnel gaped open in the floor. Leresy had a map of the network, and Yorne claimed to have memorized it already. But it was all a mess to Leresy. It was all a confusion of darkness and blood and everywhere his father's soldiers. How many tunnels had he crawled through? How many men had he seen torn apart, their blood splashing the city? He did not know.

I made a mistake, he thought, lips trembling. *I should never have come here. Yet how can I flee without seeming the coward?*

Yorne turned toward him. The gruff, tattooed man was still talking, but still Leresy couldn't make out the words.

I'm going to die here, he thought, staring at his men. *The enemy approaches. I'm going to die with this lot of stinking, drunken louts. Oh stars.*

"Ler!"

A small hand grabbed his arm. Leresy turned and saw Erry. The urchin was kneeling by the front door. She gave him a glower, peered out the keyhole, then turned back toward him. Soot filled her hair and coated her leather armor. A bandage wrapped around her arm.

"Erry," he whispered.

He tried to imagine the day she had first come to his camp, how they had eaten the boar, how he had taken her into his bed. He tried to imagine holding her again, stroking her hair, kissing her head, and protecting her.

When I protected her, I myself always felt so safe, he thought. *I wish I could feel safe now.* His eyes stung. *I want to be back in my tent, back with Erry in my arms, not here waiting with her to die.*

"Ler, damn it!" she said and tugged his collar. "Are you listening to me?"

She had been talking, he realized. He forced himself to swallow. He forced himself to speak through tight lips.

"Yes," he said.

She glared. "Good! They'll be here soon. They're down the block now, twenty of them, moving house by house." She grinned. "Ler, you take these ones out. It's your turn. Looks like a good batch of them too." She winked. "You'll find one of them familiar, I think."

Leresy sucked in a shaky breath.

Be strong, he told himself. *Be strong. You're a Lecher. You lead the Lechers! Show Erry you're strong.*

He moved toward the door and peered through the keyhole. A small mirror was placed across the street, hidden in a water spout. In the reflection, he could see them.

"Burn me," he whispered.

Twenty legionaries were moving down the street, bedecked in black armor. They bore loaded crossbows. They were tall, strong men, an elite group of fighters, yet their commander towered above them. The brute stood seven feet tall and wide as an ox. He did not wear the polished black armor of the Legions, but patches of rusted iron cobbled together over strips of chainmail. Scars rifted his stubbly head, and dark circles hung under his beady eyes.

"Beras the Brute," Leresy whispered. Through he still hid in the pottery shop, hidden from view, he clutched the hilt of his sword.

He kept watching, sweat trickling down his spine. The legionaries were marching down the alley; it was too narrow for a dragon. They stopped at a barbershop about fifty yards away. Beras approached the door, grunted, and kicked.

The door shattered open.

At once, the legionaries leaped forward. Crossbows thrummed. Bolts shot into the house.

"Slay all inside!" Beras howled and burst into the barbershop. His men followed, drawing their swords.

Curses rose and echoed down the alley.

"Nothing but damn dummies again!" Beras shouted. "Don't touch them, men. Damn Resistance has rigged up these bastards with Tiran fire. A spark from your sword can set them off."

The brute trundled back into the alley, and his men followed.

"Damn it," Leresy whispered. "They figured out the dummies."

He himself had almost died touching one of the straw men; Kaelyn had pulled his hand back, saving his life. The Resistance had spent days sewing these decoys together. They wore armor and helms, and they carried swords, but inside their suits, they were only straw soaked with Tiran fire. The liquid was costly--a single vial of Tiran fire cost more than ten barrels of gunpowder-- but it would ignite on a single spark. Any soldier within ten feet of a Tiran straw man would be torn apart.

As Leresy watched, Beras and his men kept moving down the street. They passed by the next house. A family had lived in the small, clay home before being evacuated. Since then, Leresy knew from his map, a family of Tiran dummies had taken residence.

"Load your crossbows," Beras ordered and kicked in this door too.

The men stepped forward. Crossbows fired.

An explosion rocked the street.

The house crumbled.

The clay walls shattered and the roof blazed. One man fell back, burning and screaming.

"More dummies," Beras said. He hawked, spat, and glared at the burning man. "Somebody put that bastard out. We keep moving. Bloody resistors are in one of these houses; dragons keep rising from this alley. Their tunnel is here somewhere."

Leresy gulped.

Stars, they're only a few doors away now, he thought. He clutched the hilt of his sword, but his hand was so sweaty the hilt kept sliding. *They will be here in moments.*

"How far are they?" Erry asked, kneeling beside him.

He pulled away from the keyhole. "Five doors down." The sounds of shattering wood and thrumming crossbows rose outside, and Leresy swallowed. "Four."

Erry sucked her teeth. "Ready?"

He nodded.

He looked up at the rope. It dangled over the pottery shop doorway. He traced it up to the rafters, where it vanished into a hole in the ceiling. Leresy tried to draw a deep breath, but it shuddered and only entered his lungs in spurts.

Another door shattered outside. More crossbows thrummed.

"Three," Erry whispered, replacing him at the keyhole.

Leresy could barely breathe. His throat was too tight. His pulse raged in his ears like galloping horses. He looked behind him at his twenty men, hardened Lechers with stubbly faces and dour eyes. They clutched the hilts of their swords, ready for battle.

Oh stars, the blood will spill. Oh stars, I'm going to die.

Leresy closed his eyes for just an instant, but it was enough. He could see the battle again, the massacre at Castra Luna. Behind his eyelids, he saw his soldiers fall screaming, so many youths torn apart.

You died there too, Nairi, he thought, and his eyes burned with tears. And now Erry was here, a new light in his life. Now Erry was in danger.

Another door shattered outside, and Erry peeked through the keyhole.

"Two," she whispered.

His throat was so dry. His breath panted. The room spun. He looked over at Erry, and his chest twisted. She was so young. She was so small. Beneath the mud caking her, she was only a frail doll, so delicate, so fair.

I can't lose her too. I can't...

A door shattered outside.

"One more door," she whispered, peering out the keyhole. "Wait for it..."

Leresy grabbed the rope. His hand shook, damp with sweat, but he clutched the rope tight like a drowning man. He could hear the soldiers creaking outside, only a few yards away. He could smell their sweat and leather.

I don't want to be here, he thought. *Stars, I want to be back home. I want to be back at the Bad Cats. Anywhere but here...*

"Wait for it...," Erry mouthed, not even daring to whisper.

Boots thudded.

Shadows fluttered under the pottery shop doorway.

"Now!" Erry screamed.

Leresy started. He stared.

"Now, damn it!" Erry cried, grabbed his hand, and yanked the rope down.

Shouts sounded outside. Leresy knelt, stared through the keyhole, and saw three barrels crash down from the pottery shop roof. They hit the alleyway and slammed into the soldiers.

"Back, damn it!" somebody cried and yanked Leresy backward.

The world seemed to explode.

Gunpowder blasted, so loud Leresy thought it would tear his eardrums. The pottery shop door crashed open. Leresy fell onto his backside and stared, eyes wide. Outside in the street, the barrels were gone. Flames roared. Soldiers lay dead, torn apart. A severed head burned. Blood spilled. A few men still lived; they clutched at their cracked armor as their innards leaked. They wept.

"Attack!" Yorne shouted, leaped over Leresy, and burst into the alley. The other Lechers ran behind him, swords swinging. Erry ran among them, howling for battle and waving her blade.

Leresy sat in the pottery shop, unable to rise, unable to breathe, just staring through the shattered door.

Five or six legionaries still stood. They swung their swords against the Lechers. Blades clanged. Yorne's sword cleaved a man's leg, then slammed down against his helm. Erry screamed as she duelled another legionary.

Leresy could only stare.

So much blood, he thought, chest rising and falling like a frightened hare. *So much death.*

"Leresy, damn it, come on!" Erry screamed outside. She gestured toward him, then cursed and raised her blade, parrying a blow.

He wanted to fight. Truly, he wanted to! He tried to rise. He could not. His legs had stopped obeying him. It was all he could do to even breathe.

"I..." he whispered and licked his lips. "I can't... I..."

He managed to rise to his feet. He gripped his sword's hilt, but his hand was too sweaty to draw it. He stumbled two steps forward, and blood flowed around his boots. He clenched his jaw and struggled not to gag.

Outside the smashed door, Beras came lolloping down the alley, boots crushing planks of wood and corpses. The brute snarled. Half his face was burnt away, yet still he raised his axe.

Erry stood with her back to him, dueling another man.

The axe rose higher above her.

Finally Leresy could move. His heart seemed to stop and his lungs to collapse, but he leaped forward. A torn howl left his lips. Screaming, he managed to draw his sword but not raise it. He flung himself into the alley and crashed into Beras, driving his shoulder into the beast.

"Erry!" he shouted.

Beras was so large he didn't fall back a single step, let alone fall; Leresy might as well shove a dragon. But his shove *was* enough to throw off the brute's aim. His axe swung down and missed Erry by an inch; it embedded itself into a corpse at her feet.

With a grunt, Beras turned toward Leresy.

The brute looked less like a man and more like a demon. The burnt half of his face twisted and leaked blood. Drool dripped between his teeth and down his chin. He towered, a foot taller than Leresy and twice as wide.

Leresy stumbled and raised his sword.

With a lurch, Beras tore his axe free from the corpse and swung it, knocking Leresy's blade aside. The man's hand--large and hairy as a paw--reached out and grabbed Leresy's throat.

Leresy sputtered. He tried to raise his sword, but Beras squeezed tighter, and the weapon fell from his hand. Stars spread across his vision.

"Well if it isn't the young princeling," Beras said. He grinned and licked his lips. "My my. Or is it princess? I never could tell with you. A pretty one, you are."

Leresy kicked. He scratched at the hand, but it was like scratching at stone. He couldn't breathe. He couldn't scream. He tried to look around for Erry, for Yorne, for the others, to plead for aid, but he could only see the burnt, drooling mask before him.

"I'm going to cut you slowly," Beras said. Blood dripped down his wound into his mouth. "I'm going to savor this, princess."

Stars floated and blackness spread.

Still clutching Leresy's throat with one hand, Beras drew his dagger and raised it.

"I'm going to start by slicing your pretty face," he said. "Then I'm going to--"

Beras howled.

His fingers opened.

Leresy gasped for breath, fell to his knees, and saw Erry behind the beast. She leaned against her sword, driving it deeper into Beras's unarmored leg.

With a thud that shook the alleyway, Beras fell to his knees and howled.

Erry. No. I can't lose you too, Erry, I can't.

Leresy grabbed his fallen sword, rose to his feet, and thrust the blade.

The steel crashed into Beras's neck and emerged bloody from the other side, missing Erry by an inch.

Leresy stood still, clutching the hilt, staring with wide eyes. His breath froze.

Blood spurted from Beras's mouth. His dagger clattered to the ground. He raised his hand, and for an instant Leresy thought he'd choke him again... and then he fell.

Beras the Brute, enforcer of Cadigus, the beastliest man Leresy had ever known, lay dead upon the ground.

I killed a man, Leresy thought, staring down at the corpse. *Stars, I killed a man.*

He had dreamed of this moment. For years, he had dreamed of making his first kill. In his fantasies, he'd always brag, walk into the Bad Cats with his victim's head, and be hailed a hero. Dawn and Dusk would welcome him with kisses, and later that day, his father would host a feast in his honor. Today Leresy doubled over and heaved; if he'd had any food in his belly, he'd have lost it.

Erry approached him, grumbling under her breath.

"Damn mule of a man," she said, staring down at the corpse. The bodies of the other legionaries lay around them, torn apart, bones rising from gore like shattered branches. The Lechers stood above the remains; Yorne was busy tugging his blade free from a breastplate it had cleaved.

Leresy took two great steps forward, climbed over the corpse, and pulled Erry into his embrace. He held her so tight he must have hurt her. Tears filled his eyes and he kissed her head, smearing his lips with mud.

"Thank the stars, Erry," he whispered.

Shrieks sounded above. Fire crackled.

"Dragons!" Yorne howled. "Into the tunnels!"

They ran. They raced back into the pottery shop. Outside, fire bathed the alley. They leaped into the hole in the floor.

They crawled in darkness, heading toward their next house.

They had been fighting for two nights and days, and Leresy hadn't slept and had barely eaten, but his body tingled with fire.

"I killed Beras the Brute," he whispered in darkness, knuckled his eyes, and snarled. "And I will kill you, Shari. And I will you, Father. I will kill every last one of you, I swear."

As they crawled, he could not stop his damn tears.

LANA

In the sunset, she saw the canyon ahead, and tears filled her good eye.

"Home," she whispered.

She beat her wings with more vigor. She glided over the forests, heading toward the chasm. The refugees of Lynport flew all around her, tens of thousands of dragons. When they saw the canyon, they wept in relief, blessed the stars, and blasted fire.

"Home," Lana repeated as she flew. "Safety."

She took a shuddering breath. Almost two decades ago, she had hidden from Cadigus for a year in this canyon. She had seen so many die around her from starvation, thirst, and disease. She herself had dwindled to only skin and bones and trembling fever.

"I lost my eye that year to his fang," she whispered. "I lost my three older brothers. Do I fly into another year of agony?" She looked behind her toward Lynport, but the city was too distant to see. "Fight well, Valien. Make this our shelter, not our tomb."

The dragons pulled their wings close and dived down, a great herd descending above the forest. The trees creaked below, the last of their autumn leaves tearing under the flap of wings. Lana sucked in the cold air, tightened her jaw, and dived into the canyon. Behind her, the refugees followed, a mass of scales and smoke and wings that blocked the sky.

The canyon walls rushed at her sides. Behind her, the myriads of dragons filled the canyon like a rushing river. She raced down this great stone corridor. The old pain pounded through her, and her missing eye blazed again, and her body shook with memory of fever. She flew.

The Castle-in-the-Cliff loomed ahead, its facade carved into the living rock of the canyon. Its limestone columns rose hundreds of feet tall. Its Stone Guardians, great statues with fists like carriages, flanked its doors.

"Home," she whispered. "Memory. Salvation."

The City of Cain delved deep into the cliff, a network of great halls, chambers, bridges, and corridors. Libraries lit with hundreds of lamps hid behind the stone. Staircases rose and fell, leading to kitchens, armories, nurseries, and barracks. All those Cain ruled lived here--the Vir Requis of the Canyon, the dwellers in stone.

We will barely squeeze Lynport into our halls, Lana thought. *They will sleep in our libraries, our armories, our corridors, and our pantries. They will hide under the stone.*

"They will survive," she whispered. "Fight well, Valien. Fight well, Rune. Defend your home. I will protect your people."

Her belly twisted with the old hunger, and her two eyes blazed, the one in her head, and the one that still screamed. One eye always seeing the present, the eye of a woman, a warrior, a leader. And one eye torn away, taken by Cadigus, the eye of a girl grown up too fast... always seeing old hunger and blood.

She landed outside the Castle-in-the-Cliff, her claws clattering against the canyon floor. She shifted into human form and gripped the hilt of her sword. She raised her eyes and stared at her home: the statues, the columns, and the wide stairs that led to a shadowy archway.

The dragons of Lynport landed around her and took human forms. Mothers clutched their children. Elders prayed to the stars, the forbidden gods of Requiem. They huddled close and gasped at the castle carved into the canyon's facade.

Lana climbed a dozen steps toward the palace doors, then turned to face the people. The Stone Guardians rose at her sides.

"I welcome you to the Castle-in-the-Cliff!" she called, her voice echoing across the canyon. With this welcome, the Stone Guardians would accept them. "Enter my home. Enter safety."

She turned, climbed the last steps, and walked through the archway.

The shadowy grand hall greeted her. Two lines of columns ran into the depths of the cliff. Braziers crackled between them, lighting a path toward her father's throne. Beyond the columns, darkness spread; Lana knew that it spread through many chambers and halls. Figures stood in those shadows, still and silent. Her father always boasted that his guards stood in darkness like vipers, ready to strike any who strayed from the path of light.

Lana turned around to face the gateway. The people of Lynport stood there, glancing into the darkness but daring not enter. They were humble townsfolk; most had never left Lynport before. They clutched their belongings: packs of clothes, bundles of firewood, pots and pans, and sacks of grain.

One eye of hope, one eye of pain. One eye saw frightened townsfolk. The other saw starving, haggard people at siege, dying upon the staircase as the Legions swarmed upon them.

"Enter my hall, people of Lynport!" she called. "Enter and find shelter, warmth, and food."

She beckoned to them. They hesitated, glancing around nervously, and Lana remembered that to outsiders, her home looked like a mausoleum to giants. Yet she kept calling to them, and they climbed the stairs. They entered the shadows.

Lana turned back toward the throne; it rose distant across the hall, so small she could hide it with her thumb. She walked across the mosaics, her boots clattering, and breathed deeply of the warm air. The shadows of soldiers fell between the columns, and the braziers crackled and tossed red light.

"Father!" she called out. "Father, I've returned."

When she drew closer, she frowned. Her father sat hunched over in his throne, wrapped in a great bear hide. A man stood beside him, clad in a red cloak lined with gold. A crimson hood hid his face. Lana gripped the hilt of her sword.

The colors of Cain were yellow and gray. The colors of the Resistance were silver and green. Who would wear red here, the color of Cadigus?

She kept walking forward. When she looked over her shoulder, she saw the townsfolk of Lynport follow, elders on canes, mothers holding babes, and children staring with wide eyes. Again her phantom eye saw them starving, naked, and begging for water. She blinked and returned her gaze ahead.

"Father!" she called.

She was close enough to see his face now. He looked up at her from under heavy eyebrows. His hair, red streaked with white, hung wildly around his leathery face. His shoulders stooped, and circles ringed his eyes.

"My daughter," he said, voice gravelly. "My daughter... He killed them. He killed your brothers." Devin Cain's fists trembled and his eyes watered. "He killed them all and he took your eye."

Lana paused. She sucked in her breath. She gripped her sword.

"That was almost twenty years ago," she whispered. "Father, we can save these people now. We can--"

Lord Cain rose to his feet. "No, daughter. I will not suffer another siege. I will not lose another child." He turned to the man robed in red. "Take your blood. Take it all and leave."

The man pulled back his crimson hood, turned toward Lana, and smiled thinly.

"Hello, Lady Lana," said emperor Frey. "It's a pleasure to meet you again." He grinned wildly and raised his voice to a shout. "Purification!"

From among the columns, the soldiers leaped. They were not men of Cain, robed in gray and wielding sabers. A thousand legionaries leaped into the hall, clad in black steel and bearing longswords, red spirals blazing upon their breastplates.

"Purification!" they cried.

The people of Lynport began to flee.

Shrieks echoed as Frey Cadigus shifted into a dragon, opened his maw, and blasted fire across the hall.

The flames roared. The people of Lynport fell and burned. Outside, the shrieks of more dragons rose, chanting for the red spiral and blasting their flames.

Lana screamed.

"Never again!" she cried. "Never again, Frey Cadigus! The Resistance will not fall."

She leaped from fire, shifted into a dragon, and flew toward him across the hall.

Crossbows thrummed. Bolts slammed into her. Before her, Frey--a golden dragon twice her size--laughed and blasted her with flame.

She fell. Her head tilted back. She stared upon carnage: people burning, people falling to the blade, people screaming as they died.

For the first time in almost twenty years, both her eyes saw the same world.

FREY

He flew back into Cadport with five hundred vermin in his claws.

His wrath spread behind him. His thousands of claws tightened, crushing the traitors. Their blood fell like drool. He laughed and blew fire from a forest of maws and lit the heavens that he ruled. He spread across the land, a beast with two hundred thousand wings, a hive of scale and steel and everywhere the red spiral that snaked through his mind.

"We have your pets, Relesar!" he shrieked from his golden head, letting the cry roll across the city of ruin and death.

Behind him, his lesser heads howled with laughter, this sea of might, this writhing cloud that cloaked the city, and Frey laughed and blasted flame and his claws dug into flesh.

It burned inside him, twisting, always aflame, always bleeding.

Hail the red spiral!

It coiled around his spines, pulsing with his blood, a parasite sucking on his marrow and organs and essence.

Hail the worm!

"Relesar!" his jaws cried. "Relesar, emerge from your hiding, or they will die."

He cackled, staring at the fortress that rose upon the hill. The boy still hid there, cowering. The fallen knight still lurked there, broken and trembling. His daughter still huddled behind those bricks, spreading her legs for the men he would kill.

"Relesar!" he howled.

Behind him, the many heads of the beast roared flame and chanted his cry.

"Relesar! Relesar!"

"Purification!" the golden head cried.

"Purification!" the minions answered.

Frey howled, spraying drool and flame. "Hail the red spiral!"

His heads answered the cry, and Frey cackled. He remembered a day long ago when he was just one body. He remembered a thin, pale youth, the son of a logger. He remembered walking through the forests at night, desperate for firewood, desperate to appease the father who'd beat him.

The boy hated the darkness. He boy hated the woods and the shadows that lurked there. Things crawled in the dark, insects and rodents and worms that broke under his bare feet. How they stained his feet! How the crushed, coiled things bled upon his soles, red spirals that stained him, that he could never wash off, that tainted him anew every night.

The curse of the woods. The worms left it on him. A curse he could never shake, that invaded through his feet into his bones, into his heart, into his skull, that wrapped around his spine and drove him to greatness.

It made him strong.

"Hail the red spiral!" he cried.

Now he was many. Now he was Legions. Now he no longer feared monsters, for he himself was a beast, a hive of flame and steel and worship and purity.

He flew down above the roofs of the seaside city. The ragged men all hid in their tunnels, fearing his might. The cannons had fallen silent. The boy still had not emerged.

"I will slay one of your precious vermin every minute until you face me!" Frey shouted and laughed. "I snatched them from your canyon, boy. I killed most but not all. I will kill the rest here until you emerge."

In his lead claws, the claws of the emperor, he held two of
the townsfolk, a brother and sister. He clutched them so tightly
they could not shift into dragons, only writhe as frail humans. He
flew with them near the tower upon the hill. They no longer shot
arrows. They no longer fired guns.

Frey grinned.

"You fear to slay the people I hold!" he shouted. "You
fools. You should slay me on sight. Now they shall die!"

Frey tossed the brother and sister from his claws. They
tumbled through the sky, bleeding and nearly dead. Before they
could shift into dragons, Frey blasted them with flames.

They screamed.

They died.

They fell and crashed, burning, onto the roofs below.

Now howls rose from the tower. Now arrows whistled and
cannons blasted. Frey laughed and flew backward, dodging the
fire.

"Emerge and fight me, Relesar!" he shrieked. "Emerge or I
will kill two more. Face me in battle, coward, or they all shall die!"

The beast laughed with a hundred thousand jaws, and its
wings and scales spread into the distance. The city below lay in
shadow and desolation.

Frey smiled.

"It is pure."

TILLA

He was killing them.

Oh stars, he was killing them.

Tilla wanted to howl. She wanted to weep. She wanted to blow fire against the emperor. She wanted to fly between cannonballs and arrows, to capture Rune or die upon the roofs of their city.

He was killing them. Oh stars, he was killing them all.

Flying a hundred yards away from the emperor, Tilla stared, barely able to breathe, not even able to cry. Among the five hundred prisoners, she saw her own father. The old ropemaker was bleeding, his face pale, struggling in the grip of a drooling dragon.

He will kill him. Tilla panted. *My emperor will kill my father.*

"Relesar!" the emperor cried, laughing in the sky. His great wings beat. Flame wreathed him. He grabbed two more townsfolk from the claws of his minions, gripped the bodies so tight their ribs snapped, and raised them.

"Relesar!" Frey called. "I will slay two more. Emerge and fight me, or all will die."

Tilla knew those two in Frey's claws, an old man and a woman. She had grown up with them. She had bought pottery from their shop. They had looked after her when she'd been a girl, she remembered. They had always been so kind. She could not let them die.

She whipped her head around and stared at Castellum Acta. The fort rose upon the hill. Cannons lined its battlements and windows. Archers stood firing from its arrowslits. Behind iron, steel, and stone, Rune hid.

And they were dying.

Tilla knew the price of disobedience. Soldiers were to fly in silence, to laugh only when the emperor laughed, to cheer only when he cheered. They were nothing but reflections of his glory. Yet today Tilla had to risk her life. She had to save what she still could of Cadport, her home which lay in ruins below.

"Rune!" she called out. "Rune, please! Come out to us. He will kill them!"

More arrows flew from the fort. More cannons fired, tearing into imperial dragons who flew too close.

Yet he did not emerge.

"Hear them scream, Relesar!" Frey cried, laughed, and tightened his claws.

The two potters tore apart.

They fell to the city below, lacerated, and crashed into the rooftops.

"No..." Tilla whispered, and tears budded in her eyes.

I can't do this, she thought and panted. *I can't fly here anymore. I can't take part in this massacre. I can't let my father die.*

She looked at Frey; he was grabbing two more prisoners in his claws. She looked down at her hometown which lay in ruin, bodies and blood and debris everywhere.

"How can I fight for this?" she whispered, her voice too soft in the battle for any to hear. "How can I serve this Regime that crushes my home?"

Tilla raged.

She raged against the Regime.

She raged against the emperor.

She wanted to fly at Frey, to burn him, to slay the beast and tear out his heart.

I served you, Frey, she thought, and fire crackled in her maw. *I served the glory of the red spiral, and now you crush my home. Now you kill all those I've ever known.*

She looked at the fortress where the last resistors hid, bloodied and dying. She looked down at the city where thousands lay rotting.

She lowered her head.

There was no fighting the Cadigus family, she knew. Even with thousands of warriors, the Resistance only crashed against the might of the Legions and died. And the city died. And all its refugees died.

"You cannot fight him, Rune," Tilla whispered. "He is too great. You can only serve the red spiral. To fight him brings death to us all." She raised her voice to a howl. "Rune, please! Emerge! I will protect you, I promise."

Yet still he hid, and Tilla roared, wept, and raged.

Why would he not come to her?

Did he not care that Frey was butchering his people?

Tilla trembled, her wings roiling smoke and fire around her.

I serve Requiem, she thought. *I serve life. I serve my city.*

"And you're letting it fall, Rune. Your rebellion killed them all." Again she cried out. "Rune!"

The Legions howled and jeered around her. The emperor cackled and grabbed two more prisoners, mere children.

"Relesar, two more!" the emperor cried.

Two more bodies fell.

Two more lights went dim.

Tilla wept and roared her fire and called his name, but he would not come.

RUNE

"Let me go," he said, eyes burning, and tried to wrench himself free. His throat tightened. His legs shook. He twisted and tugged, but Valien would not release him.

"You cannot," said the older man. His teeth were bared. His eyes blazed. He clutched Rune's arms, holding him back. "Rune! Do not give him what he wants."

Yet Rune kept struggling. He kept staring through the hall's arrowslits. The scaly mass covered the sky outside. Frey Cadigus cackled, claws still stained with blood and bits of flesh. Behind the emperor, his dragons held hundreds of other townsfolk.

"They're going to die, Valien!" Rune called, struggling madly. He wanted to break free, to rush up the tower, to leap from the battlements and shift into a dragon, to fly at Frey and slay the man with all his fire and rage.

"If you fly out there, *you* will die," Valien said, refusing to release Rune; the man's grip was iron. "Rune. Look at me. Listen to me."

Rune spun away from the arrowslit. His eyes were damp and burning, but he stared at Valien. The leader of the Resistance stared back, eyes hard as his grasping fingers. Behind him, the other resistors stood gazing at Rune too. Their eyes were haunted. Their faces were somber. Even Kaelyn stared silently, her eyes large and cold like frozen dreams of winter.

"They will all die," Rune whispered.

Valien would not release him. "Rune, if you fly out, he will kill you." Valien ground his teeth. "But not at once, Rune. He will take you alive to the capital. He will torture you. He will display your mangled body to the masses and have you wail for their amusement. Years down the line, when your mind is broken like your body, then, Rune... then he will finally give you the mercy of death. If you fly out to meet Frey now, that is your fate."

Rune swallowed and trembled. Sweat drenched him. He panted, barely able to suck breath down his throat.

"I cannot simply let them die," he whispered. "Valien... stars. He has hundreds out there. Did he already kill the others?"

He did not want to weep. Yet his voice cracked, and a lump filled his throat, and he could barely see through his burning eyes.

Tilla, he thought. *Stars, do you fly there too? How can you serve him? Tilla, what do we do?*

Valien's eyes softened just the slightest. His grip loosened by just a thread.

"I don't know," he said, his voice raspier than ever. "He might have killed them all, yes. If he met the people of Lynport on their way to the canyon, he might have slain all those he didn't bring here to torture. Rune--do not let their deaths be in vain."

Rune peered back outside. Frey grabbed two more prisoners in his claws. He rose higher, disappearing from the arrowslit's range of view, but his voice still rolled across the city.

"I have two more, Relesar!" the emperor shrieked, his voice demonic, the sound of storm and lightning. "Emerge to fight me, or they too will perish."

Rune looked back at Valien and the others.

"I can't let them die," he whispered. He turned to face Kaelyn; she stared back with haunted eyes. "Kaelyn, tell him. Tell him we can't let them die."

She stepped closer, her lips trembled, and she touched Rune's arm. A tear streamed down her cheek.

"They must die," she whispered.

Behind Rune, two screams pierced the sky.

Kaelyn lowered her head and her tears fell. Rune started, gasped, and tried to turn around, but Valien still held his arms, refusing to release him.

"Come, Rune," the man said. "Into the tunnel. You do not need to hear this. It's time to leave."

Outside the tower, the emperor's voice roared across the sky.

"Two more dead, Relesar! Hundreds more remain. Emerge from your hole, coward!"

Rune shook. He let Valien guide him away from the arrowslit. They walked toward the narrow staircase that plunged into the hill. The stairs led to a tunnel, Rune knew. The tunnel led to the sea.

"Rune," Kaelyn said softly, holding his arm, "you must do this for their memory. The people of Lynport will die. But if you are captured, all hope is lost. Millions across Requiem will suffer." Her tears fell. "For those millions, you must live."

Rune let them walk him across the hall.

So here is how it ends, he thought, eyes stinging. *Lynport is fallen; all we tried to save here will die. And we will flee. And we will fight on. To dream of another battle, I must let all my memories, all my soul, all my past perish.*

Yet how could he fight again with such pain inside him?

Rune looked up at Valien, looked at this broken man with hard eyes, with old pain, with creases of endless nightmares across his face.

This is what I would become, Rune realized. A broken man. He would grow old in hiding. He would grow old in pain, the past always clutching, always pulling him deeper into darkness.

No. He could not do this.

Valien held his arm, guiding him forward, and for the first time since Rune had met him--for the first time in a year of blood, fire, and death--Valien's eyes dampened, and his voice tore with pain.

"We will not forget them, Rune," he said. "We will enter this tunnel. We will crawl through darkness to the sea. We will swim. We will flee this battle." His voice shook and his jaw twisted. "We will fight another day."

They walked toward the tunnel.

Valien looked around the hall at the resistors who gathered, several hundred in all.

"We've been fighting for seven nights and seven days," he said, looking at his men. "We've killed thousands of the enemy. We've shown that we could bleed them." He raised his hand, two fingers pressed together. "The Resistance will live on! Relesar Aeternum will reign. Today we flee into the sea. Today we lose a battle. Tomorrow we will rally, and we will grow in strength, and we will give the Regime no rest. Into the sea! Into darkness and water. Requiem! May our wings forever find your sky."

The men returned the salute. They chanted the prayer together. They began to enter the darkness.

Into the sea, Rune thought, watching them leave. *Into hiding. Into war and pain and endless memory.*

More men stepped down the staircase, one by one, their eyes hard and their faces ashy, warriors of Requiem. Rune watched them leave.

Valien released his grip on Rune and placed a hand on his shoulder.

"It's time," the gruff man said.

Kaelyn held his hand. "We will still fight together, Rune," she whispered. "I promise you. Always. I will always fly by your side."

Rune stared at the men stepping into the darkness. He could imagine them crawling underground, emerging into the sea, swimming through darkness, leaving this ruin behind, and rallying in some distant land for another battle in another town.

"They will fight on," Rune whispered. "And they will still have courage in their hearts." He looked at Valien and Kaelyn, his guiding stars, two people he had followed through fire and blood, two people he loved. "But my heart will not mend after this day. My heart is forever in Lynport. This is my home, and here I must fall." His voice tore and his eyes swam. "Goodbye."

He broke free.

Before they could grab him again, Rune ran.

"Rune!" Kaelyn shouted behind him, voice torn.

He did not turn back. He raced across the hall. He leaped onto the tower staircase.

"Rune, do not do this!" Valien roared behind. "Rune, listen to me!"

But he would not listen.

I can't, he thought, eyes burning. *I can't let them die. If torture and death await me, so be it. I cannot let the last of my townsfolk perish here.*

He ran up the tower stairs.

"Rune!" Kaelyn cried; he heard her running upstairs a few steps behind. "Rune, please!"

"Go to the sea, Kaelyn!" he said. "Go with Valien. Fight on. Fight for my memory. Go!"

He ran.

He reached the tower top.

He raced between guards, crashed through a trapdoor, and emerged onto the battlements. He shifted into a dragon.

The sky writhed, a canopy of scales and flames and claws. The Legions stormed above him in a whirlpool, wings roiling smoke and fire and drool. Rune soared toward them, a single black dragon entering the storm. The emperor himself cackled above, the epicenter of terror, a shard of gold like a cruel sun, death and blood in his claws.

"I fly to you, Frey!" Rune cried. "I fly to you. Release them. Let them live."

Below him upon the tower, Kaelyn's voice rose, torn and pleading.

"Rune!"

He looked back at her. Kaelyn stood upon the tower, still in human form, reaching up to him, pleading, tears on her cheeks. The wind from countless wings billowed her hair. Tears filled her eyes. Ash and soot coated her cheeks.

"Rune," she said, lips trembling. "Please. I love you. Please."

The Legions cackled and roared above. Claws reached down to lash Rune. Pain drove through him. The swarm engulfed him.

"Goodbye, Kaelyn," he whispered as the beasts tightened around him, a great serpent of the skies, hiding all from view.

Scales and flame rolled across him.

He saw nothing else.

Goodbye.

Flapping his wings within the storm, caught in the whirlpool of fangs and steel and fire, he looked above him, seeking the emperor, seeking the man who'd destroyed his town, his soul, his life.

Yet when he looked above, the golden dragon was gone.

A white dragon hovered there, her scales glimmering, her eyes soft with tears.

Rune breathed shakily.

"Tilla," he whispered.

Her tears fell. She glided down toward him, a moonlit angel of celestial halls, and her claws shook.

"Rune," she said. "Rune."

And he was flying with her again, side by side over the sea at night. They danced around the moon. They stood upon the beach, held each other, and shared a kiss of farewell.

"Rune," she had said to him that day, a barefooted youth with seashells around her neck. "Fly with me. One last flight.

They had flown together then, two youths entering a war too big for them, leaving their home and flying into a battle they could not win.

They flew together now too, gliding in darkness and fire.

Tilla. Pillar of my memory. Anchor of my soul.

She reached out toward him, the Legions at her back, a hundred thousand demons cackling and howling for his death.

"Tilla," he whispered again, too tired to fight, too torn to shout.

Her claws wrapped around his shoulders, and her tears fell upon him.

"It's over now," she whispered. "We're together again."

The emperor laughed in the distance, and the Legions tightened around Rune. Claws cut him. Tails lashed him. His blood spilled. His breath died.

His magic left him.

He floated among the Legions in human form, cut and bleeding, Tilla's claws wrapped around him. The last things he saw was her eyes, dark and whispering of home.

KAELYN

She stood among the ruins, staring north across the sea.

The wind caressed her hair like his fingers had that night long ago, hiding in different ruins so far away. That had been in the cold north, in Requiem, in the land they had fought and killed and bled and cried for. That had been home.

That land had fallen.

"Relesar Aeternum," she whispered into the waves that rolled below the hill, and her voice shook. "Rune."

This southern island was small, smaller than the town she had fled. Standing here upon the hilltop, she could see the shore encircling her, forming a sanctuary in the Tiran Sea. The hillsides rolled below her, thick with boulders and cedars and pines. Where hills ended, wild grass and mint bushes faded into golden sand and azure, glimmering waves.

Where Kaelyn stood, high upon the island's peak, old ruins rose. An orphaned archway stretched above her, green with creeping ivy. The wall that had once held it lay fallen; grass and weeds overgrew its bricks. An ancient stairway plunged down the hillside, most of its steps now buried under dirt and grass. Three columns stood below upon the beach, the remnants of some old port or temple. A dozen more columns lay fallen among palm trees and brambles. Gulls, cranes, and small birds she could not name flew above.

"You would have liked it here, Rune," she whispered to the trees, the wind, and the sea that spread deep blue into the horizon. "You would have stood here with me, hand in hand, and told me about the old ships that would sail here, and you would name the birds that fly."

It was an island too small for maps. An island too small for the Legions to find.

An island you will never know. Tears filled her eyes and her throat tightened. *I miss you Rune.*

"Kaelyn."

The voice rose behind her, raspy like wind over gravel. She turned to see Valien.

He wore his old furs and wool, but his armor was gone. His hair hung around his face, streaked with more white than she'd ever seen in it. His face had always seemed so hard to Kaelyn, a face like tough leather, like a craggy cliff, a face with the strength of ancient stone. His eyes had always seemed so wise, eyes that hid all the secrets in the world, eyes she would follow into the Abyss itself.

Yet now... now she saw the sadness in him. Now the sunlight fell upon that face she loved. Now those eyes gazed north across the sea, and she saw the pain of her heart reflected in them.

He misses him too. And he misses her. His Marilion.

Kaelyn stepped toward him. She took his hands--great, calloused paws twice the size of her small, white palms. He towered over her, and she looked up at him, a deer before a bear.

He lost her, but he has me. He has me always.

Valien embraced her, and she laid her head upon his scarred chest, and she felt warm, and though fear trickled through her, there was still some safety here in his arms. He stroked her hair.

"Will we ever see him again?" she whispered.

Valien held her close. He was silent for a long time.

"I don't know," he finally said, voice soft. "But we will not abandon him to torture and death. And we will not abandon Requiem." He held her cheek and looked into her eyes. "I don't know what strength I still have, Kaelyn. I don't know what battles I can still win. But so long as breath rattles through me, and so long as my sword can swing, I will fight. I will fight for our home... and for him. For Relesar Aeternum."

She shook her head. "Don't fight for a king. Fight for Rune."

They turned back toward the north. They stood under the stone archway. Ivy dangled around them and mottles of sunlight danced like fairies. The wind from the sea played with their hair and filled their nostrils, scented of water, salt, and cedar. The waves whispered below across the sand and ruins.

"Lynport too now lies in ruins upon a beach," Kaelyn whispered. "I will not forget you, Requiem. I will not forget you, Rune."

They stood for a long time, silent, watching the sea.

LERESY

They lay on the beach at night, watching the moon and stars. The waves whispered, the trees rustled, and the sea glistened in the moonlight, but Leresy could not see this beauty.

He saw men torn apart with gunpowder, screaming in the dirt, their severed limbs littering the street.

He saw Beras clutching his throat and raising his dagger.

He saw his father flying above, tearing bodies apart, cackling like he would years ago when beating Leresy and his twin.

He closed his eyes.

How can you forget? he thought. *How can you forget old pain? When night falls and all sound and light of the day fade, how do you stop the memories from rising?*

Food had lost its flavor. The world had lost its beauty. This was all the remained to him now. Memories. Visions of blood. A chill in his belly he could not shake.

"Ler?"

She lay beside him in the sand, her dog curled up and sleeping on her feet. Leresy turned his head and looked at her.

"Erry," he whispered, and his eyes watered.

Erry Docker.

She lay naked in the sand, her slim body caked with the stuff. He had once mocked her skinny limbs and boyish frame, her short hair that always lay tangled across her brow, and her lowborn blood. Today Leresy could not see the light of stars, nor hear the music of the waves, yet Erry was beautiful to him. She was a precious doll. She was his to protect, to cherish. She was the only thing good he had left.

No, he thought. *The only thing good I ever had.*

He placed a hand on her waist and stroked her. He leaned forward in the sand and kissed her lips.

"I'm sorry, Erry," he whispered.

He expected her to snort, to laugh, or to launch into some creative string of cusses. This was Erry Docker, after all; she was a snort and a curse wrapped in skin. Yet her eyes only softened, and she touched his cheek.

"For what?" she said.

It was he who ended up snorting, though it sounded almost like a sob.

"Do you need to ask?" he said. "Do I really need to list everything?"

This made her grin, her huge grin that showed so many teeth. She stuck her tongue out and poked him in the ribs.

"Not forgiven," she said. "Damn it, Leresy, you are a bloody piece of work, you are." She sighed. "I don't know why I lie here with you."

"Because I'm devilishly handsome?" he suggested and blinked to clear his eyes. "Because I saved your life? Because I'm your knight in shining armor?"

She sighed. She rolled onto her back and looked up at the night sky. Her dog stirred and fell back into sleep.

"You're not," she said softly, and her eyes grew somber. "You're not, Leresy. You're not heroic. You're not noble. You're not a knight." She looked at him. "You're a damn bastard, but... so am I. And we have each other. And we're learning. And we're getting a little better. That counts for something, doesn't it?"

He nodded, throat tight. He could speak no louder than a whisper, not without chancing his voice cracking.

"It counts for a lot."

She lay still for a moment, watching the stars, then propped herself up on her elbows. She placed a hand on his chest, leaned over him, and dusted sand from his hair.

"Valien and the others want to keep fighting," she said. "They counted over a thousand surviving resistors on this island. They think more might have fled into the forests of Requiem." She bit her lip. "They will go back, and they will find new allies, and they will fight on. What do we do, Ler? Do we join them?"

He touched her cheek, marveling at how her features were so soft and small; she seemed made of porcelain.

"I gave Valien the rest of the Lechers," he said. "Three hundred battle-hardened brutes. That's my gift to his Resistance. May they fight well. The bloody lot stank anyway; I couldn't stand the stench." He sighed and looked up past Erry at the stars. The Draco constellation shone, the old gods. "But I won't join him. You're right, Erry. I'm not a hero. I'm not a knight or a warrior at all." His throat tightened. "I thought I was. When I ruled Castra Luna, I thought I was a great fighter, but... I was a boy. A foolish boy."

She nodded. "A very foolish one. I remember."

It was his turn to stick his tongue out. "You fancied me even then. I knew it." He smiled weakly. "You were bad at hiding it. So what will you do, Erry Docker of Lynport? Will you fly off with the warriors and fight and maybe die another day? Or will you stay here with me?"

She raised her eyebrows, still playing with his hair. "With you and what--sand?"

"Sand," he said. "Palm trees heavy with dates and pines heavy with nuts. Mint bushes for tea. A spring of fresh water. All the fish that we can catch." He grinned. "I'd rather like seeing you wear a skirt of leaves and clam shells on your breasts, a wild islander."

"I should think," she said and straddled him, "that you should prefer me like this--naked as the day I was born."

He chewed his lip and looked up at her, examining her body in the moonlight. "You are damn right."

He made love to her, the sand beneath them, the stars of his fathers above. So many times he had taken her to his bed, had used her, had clung to her to forget his pain. Yet now he made love to her, and now he loved her, and for a moment under the stars, Erry Docker in his arms, Leresy Cadigus could forget. He could no longer see the memories.

They will always be with me, he thought, holding Erry as she slept against his chest. *But so will Erry. So will this woman that I love. And that's not too bad.*

He closed his eyes, kissed her cheek, and slept.

RUNE

They flew in darkness for a long time.

She held him in her claws like a mother bird clutching her young. Sometimes he heard her say his name. Sometimes he felt the rain and the wind, and sometimes he could see her, a white dragon under the sky. Sometimes he thought he could hear the sea below.

He dreamed.

He had lost so much blood. The chains bound him so tightly. A sack covered his head, leaving him always in night, always in sleep and memory and nightmares. They flew. They flew in darkness. They flew for a long time.

"Rune," she said softly. "Rune, I'm here."

It was her voice. Tilla. She stood before him on the beach, and he embraced her, and they kissed. The waves raced over the sand and wet their feet, and she scurried away like always, and he laughed.

The sky cackled and creaked and clattered. Heat blasted him and he heard dragonfire storm all around. He floated through the sea at home. He floated through a sea of dragons in the sky. But she was here. His love. His Tilla.

"Rune," she whispered, her claws gentle around him. "We're almost home."

He tried to open his eyes. He saw nothing but the sack. He tried to call to her, but his throat was too parched, and he was too weak. So many wounds. So much blood lost.

They flew.

They flew in darkness for a long time.

After dreamscapes and eras of memory, trumpets sounded ahead.

"Silver trumpets will call you home," a knight had said in eras long forgotten.

And now they called. And Rune knew them. He saw only darkness, but he heard their song. They were calling him to his new home. To Nova Vita. To the capital of Requiem.

To the place where they would break him.

"Rune," she whispered. "Do not be afraid. I'll be with you."

Rain pattered him. Clouds grumbled above. And the dragons roared. Thousands of throats bellowed their rage. Dragonfire crackled and heat blasted Rune. Air from countless wings pummeled him, and the emperor howled ahead, a shriek like wind through canyons.

"We have captured the heir! Relesar Aeternum is ours!" The emperor's voice rose like steam from a kettle, a voice of demons. "Purification! The Resistance is fallen. Requiem is pure!"

And they cheered.

Rune heard them cheer below.

A million people lived in the capital, they said. Rune could not see them. He could see nothing but the sack around his head and blurs of red where firelight flared. But he heard them. He heard the million. And they howled for his death.

"Hail the red spiral!" the emperor shrieked, and they answered. The cry rolled across the Legions. It rolled across the city below. It tore through Rune and it tore through the kingdom he loved.

"Hail the red spiral! Purification!"

The rain fell, and Tilla's claws tightened around him, but her grip did not hurt.

She did not mean to hurt him.

She was protecting him.

"Rune," she whispered. "You will worship him. You will join us. And the pain will end."

The roaring swelled like an ocean below.

Wind shrieked and his ears popped as they descended.

He did not know where they landed. They left the sack over his head. They left the chains wrapped around him, binding his arms to his sides.

And they shouted.

And they shoved him.

Rough hands grabbed and tugged him. Something sharp jabbed his side. Something hard--perhaps a steel-tipped boot-- drove into his spine, and he fell to his knees and cried.

"Move him forward!" rumbled a deep voice.

"Get him into the darkness!"

Tilla's voice rose too. "Leave him! He is mine. He is my catch. He is mine to break!"

Steel hissed--blades being drawn from sheathes. Swords clashed. Hands grabbed him and tugged him to his feet.

"You will have your chance, Siren," spoke another voice, and Rune recognized it; it was Princess Shari speaking. "He tore off my wing. He will be yours, but first I will have vengeance."

Boots kicked him. He fell again. Fists landed upon him. Something heavy clashed against his head, and his cheek hit the ground, and laughter rose, and voices screamed. He screamed too. He screamed louder than them all.

He fell into darkness.

He floated on the sea.

He flew under the stars with her at his side.

They stood again on the beach, and he embraced her, and she kissed him, and her fingers touched his hair.

"Rune," she whispered. "Rune, I'm here."

Her lips were soft. Her hands caressed his cheek. The waves rolled around them, the stars shone above, and the cliffs of Ralora rose behind them. He was home.

"Rune," she whispered again. "Rune, they're gone. Open your eyes. Look at me."

I can see you, he thought. *We stand on the beach again. Your face is pale like moonlight, and your black hair is waving in the wind, and you are mine. You are the woman I love.*

"Rune... Stars, Rune, can you hear me?"

He opened his eyes.

And he saw her.

Dream melted into pain.

She knelt above him, no longer the pale youth he'd known, but a woman with haunted eyes, her face smeared with ash, her cheek scarred with war. Brick walls topped with battlements rose behind her.

"Tilla?" he whispered.

He could not rise. He could barely keep his eyes open. They had broken his body. They had shed too much blood. She squeezed his hand, but he could not squeeze back.

"Rune," she whispered, and a trembling smile found her lips, and her tears fell upon his face. They stung.

She was here. This was real. She was with him again, and he wept.

"It's over now." She kissed his lips. "You saved our people. It's over. They will no longer hurt you. You only have to do what we say. You only have to join us, to hail the red spiral, to serve the emperor." Her tears ran along her lips. "And we'll be together again."

"I..."

I can't do that, Tilla, he wanted to say. *I can't. Let me die. Let me die here in your arms.*

But his throat felt too tight.

"Come, Rune, you must stand now," she said. She placed her arms around him and tugged. "We have to go. Quick, before they return."

He rose to shaky feet and leaned against her. Chains still wrapped around him, slick with blood. He wore nothing but rags beneath. Tilla stood clad in fine armor, holding him up.

"You'll be with me now, Rune," she said. "You'll be safe if you obey."

They limped across a courtyard. All around them, the brick walls rose in the night, topped with battlements. Clouds hid the stars. They stood in the courtyard, alone.

"Tilla," he whispered hoarsely. "Tilla, fly. Take me in your claws and we'll fly from here."

She helped him walk, her arms around him.

"There is no fleeing him," she said. "There is no fighting him. You must join us. That is all you can do. You must serve him like I do."

He looked ahead. A barred door stood open in a wall, leading to a cell. Inside he saw a pile of straw, a hole in the floor, and chains dangling from the ceiling. Old blood encrusted the walls.

"Tilla," he said, nearly too parched to speak, "what is this place?"

"You won't have to stay here long," she whispered, guiding him toward the cell. "Only until he thinks you're broken. Only until he hears you worship him. Rune... it doesn't have to hurt. Your pain can end."

The courtyard swam around him. He would have fallen were Tilla not holding him. He tried to break free from her, but he was too weak. He tried to shift into a dragon, but couldn't muster the magic.

"Tilla," he whispered, and his voice cracked, and his eyes stung. "Please. They're gone now. The legionaries. The dragons.

The emperor. They're gone. Shift into a dragon, Tilla! Shift and hold me in your claws and fly from here."

She shook her head, and her tears fell, and she kept moving forward, pulling him with her.

"I cannot," she whispered.

"We can escape," he said, looking above. The sky cleared. He could see the stars. "I can fly myself, maybe. Let's fly from here. Let's fly home."

They reached the cell. She paused. She released him, and he stood on shaky feet before her, the world spinning.

"Rune," she whispered, and she was beautiful in the starlight, a statue of marble. "Do you remember that night on the beach? Our last night?"

He nodded, a lump in his throat. "I never forgot."

She embraced him. She touched his cheek, and she kissed him. They shared a long, deep kiss, a kiss like that last night, a kiss of goodbye. It tasted of tears and of memory.

She pulled back, and her lips shook.

"That was our home," she whispered. "But it's gone now. The city burned. There is nowhere left to fly to." She gripped his arms. "Rune... you *are* home."

She shoved him into the cell.

He fell to the floor, landing on old blood.

"Tilla!" he shouted. "Tilla!"

He rose to his feet and stumbled toward her.

She gave him a last look, her eyes large and haunted, eyes that reflected the sea, the stars, and the city that was no more.

She slammed the door shut, leaving him alone in darkness, hurt and cold and mourning the burning of his home... and the breaking of her soul.

THE END

NOVELS BY DANIEL ARENSON

Standalones:
Firefly Island (2007)
The Gods of Dream (2010)
Flaming Dove (2010)

Misfit Heroes:
Eye of the Wizard (2011)
Wand of the Witch (2012)

Song of Dragons:
Blood of Requiem (2011)
Tears of Requiem (2011)
Light of Requiem (2011)

Dragonlore:
A Dawn of Dragonfire (2012)
A Day of Dragon Blood (2012)
A Night of Dragon Wings (2013)

The Dragon War
A Legacy of Light (2013)
A Birthright of Blood (2013)
A Memory of Fire (2013)

KEEP IN TOUCH

www.DanielArenson.com
Daniel@DanielArenson.com
Facebook.com/DanielArenson
Twitter.com/DanielArenson

www.ingramcontent.com/pod-product-compliance
Lightning Source LLC
Chambersburg PA
CBHW031711170626
46808CB00005B/1704